He Went With
Vasco Da Gama

Publisher's Note

He Went With *Vasco Da Gama* was written over 80 years ago and tells the story of a young man accompanying Vasco Da Gama on his adventures around the world.

An excellent storyteller, Louise Andrews Kent provides the reader with the opportunity to experience a different time and place through the eyes of the main character, including the social customs, religious beliefs, and racial relations. Taking place over 500 years ago, many parts of life are foreign and sometimes offensive to us now, including specific customs, practices, beliefs, and words. To maintain and provide historical accuracy and to allow a true representation of this time period the words used and the customs and attitudes described have not been removed or edited.

This edition published 2022
by Living Book Press

ISBN: 978-1-922919-01-4 (hardcover)
        978-1-922919-00-7 (softcover)

He Went With Vasco Da Gama

Louise Andrews Kent

ILLUSTRATED BY
Paul Quinn

Living Book Press

Dear Prent:

Either I don't write fast enough or you grow up too fast. I thought I'd get this book written for you before you were taller than I am, but what can we do about it? Not much at this point, except hope that you will still like to read about the red-headed boy who went with Vasco da Gama.

I remember your asking me once how I began work on a book. This time I began by reading all the books I could find about Portugal. The one I liked best was Philip Marden's *A Wayfarer in Portugal*. For the main facts about Vasco da Gama I used two books published by the Hakluyt Society: Ravenstein's translation of *A Journal of Vasco da Gama's First Voyage* and Gaspar Correa's *Land of India*. Both books have been translated from the original Portuguese, so I was able to get along knowing only a few words.

One thing I did find out was a little about Portuguese pronunciation. When you see an *h* after an *n*, or an *l*, you pronounce the *h* as though it were a *y*. That is: *Senhor* is *Senyor*; *Coelho* is *Co-el-yo*, and so on. Words that in English we'd say in one piece are spoken in two pieces. For instance, the name of Captain Coelho's brother looks like a girl's name, Joãn, but it is *Jo-an*. The Portuguese really write it this way: João, and expect us to know that we must put in an *n* after the *a* and drop off the second *o*. Someone said you ought to pronounce the *n* as if your mouth were full of chewing gum, and you chewed a few times after you had said the *n*. This seems like a lot of work to me, and I don't like gum anyway. I think it will be all right if you call him 'Jo-an.' After all it's only Portuguese for 'John,' a useful name that sounds much the same whether it's French 'Jean,' Spanish 'Juan,' Dutch 'Jan,' or Irish 'Shane.' The two boys, Joãn Coelho and Shane O'Connor, really had the same first name, though I doubt if they knew it.

Then there is that disagreeable old party, Judge Calves, whose name has nothing at all to do with young cattle—the kind I saw you roping at the Rodeo! Better pronounce it 'Cal-ves'—that will be a little more like it.

Both Shane and Dennis O'Connor remind me a little of you. They both had your habit of drawing pictures. You might have liked them, but you may be glad you didn't have to make the voyage with them when I tell you that the Berrio was somewhere near the size of a fifty-ton schooner. Get your brother to show you one in Bar Harbor some day.

When you come to Kents' Corner we will sing you Shane's songs. We know the tunes because we made them up. Of course, they have to be played on the accordion instead of the harp. We got the ideas for the words mostly from Camoens, who was a great poet in Portugal not long after Vasco da Gama's time. Camoens wrote a long poem about Vasco's voyage to India: interesting, but I like his short ones better.

I never supposed Portuguese people in 1497 would be much like Vermonters in 1937, but I discovered that they liked to make up little tunes and fit words to them, adding new verses whenever they felt like it. So as that's a favorite sport at Kents' Corner, these Portuguese explorers might fit in there better than we'd think offhand.

I don't really expect Vasco to turn up there, but don't think *you* aren't expected, Prent. Here is your invitation, printed, you observe. When you get an invitation like that, you answer it *in person*. I know that must be etiquette because it was invented by

Your cousin who sends you this book

Louise Andrews Kent

Brookline, *December,* 1937

CONTENTS

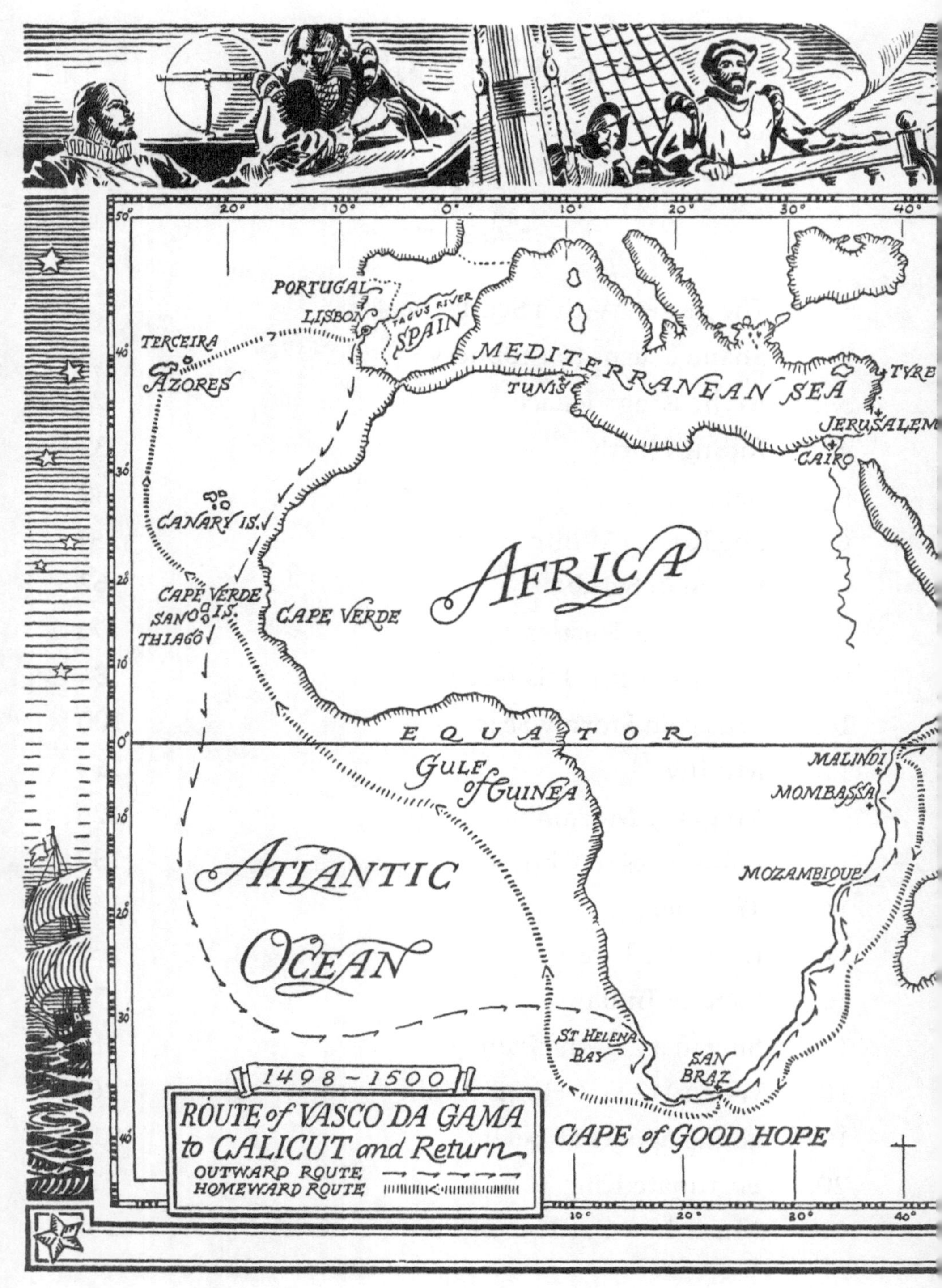
20°
10°
0°
10°
20°
30°
40°
50°
40°
36°
28°
16°
0°
16°
20°
30°
40°
PORTUGAL
LISBON
TAGUS RIVER
SPAIN
TERCEIRA
AZORES
MEDITERRANEAN SEA
TUNIS
TYRE
JERUSALEM
CAIRO
CANARY IS.
CAPE VERDE
SAN
THIAGO
IS.
CAPE VERDE
AFRICA
EQUATOR
GULF of GUINEA
MALINDI
MOMBASSA
MOZAMBIQUE
ATLANTIC
OCEAN
ST HELENA
BAY
SAN
BRAZ
1498 ~ 1500
ROUTE of VASCO DA GAMA
to CALICUT and Return
OUTWARD ROUTE
HOMEWARD ROUTE
CAPE of GOOD HOPE
10°
20°
30°
40°

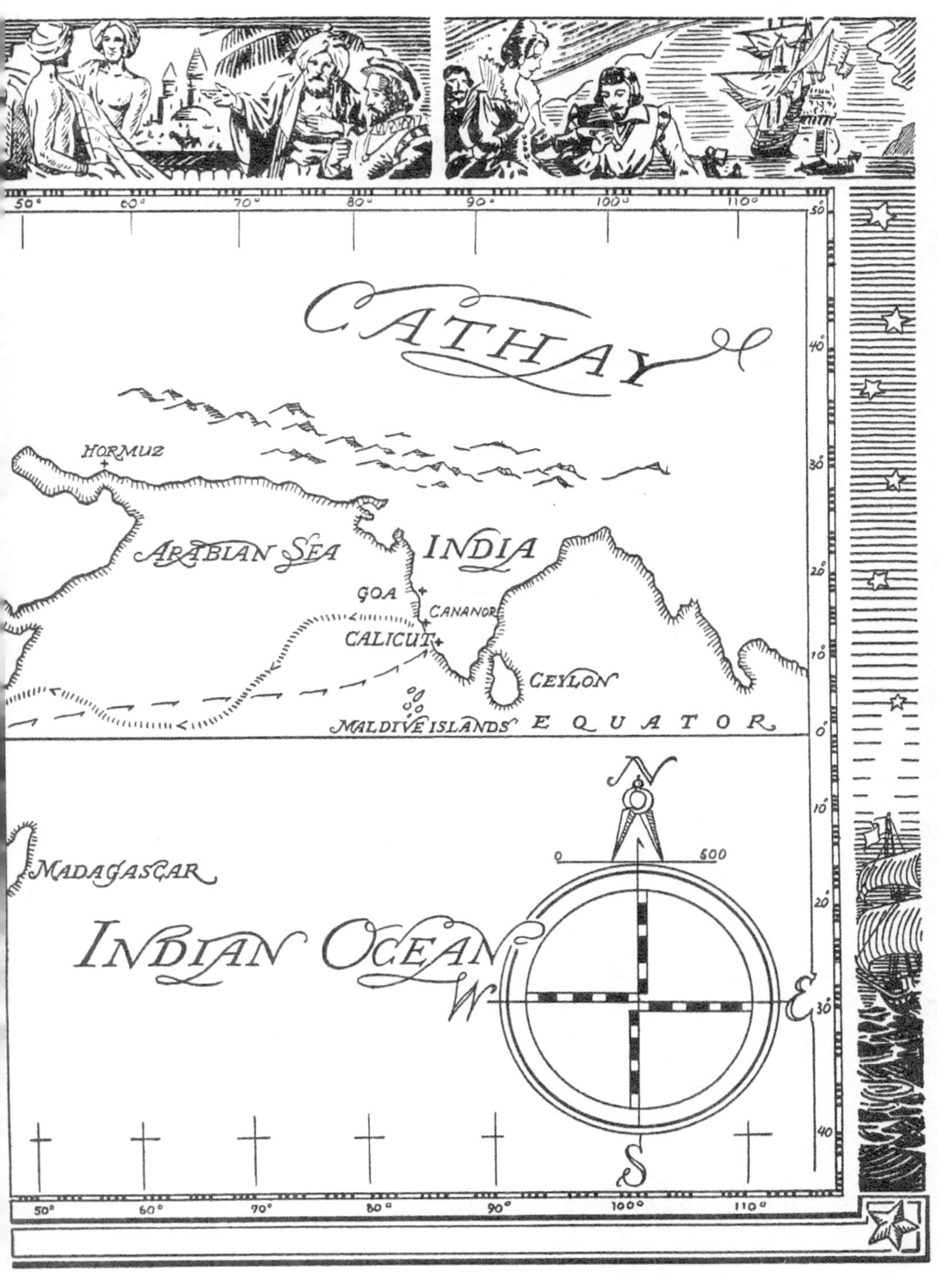

50° 60° 70° 80° 90° 100° 110°
CATHAY
HORMUZ
ARABIAN SEA
INDIA
GOA
CANANOR
CALICUT
CEYLON
MALDIVE ISLANDS
EQUATOR
N
0 500
MADAGASCAR
INDIAN OCEAN
W E
S
50° 60° 70° 80° 90° 100° 110°
50° 40° 30° 20° 10° 0° 10° 20° 30° 40°

THE LETTER WITH A SCARLET SEAL

IT WAS growing dark in the Street of the Rat. Far to the west of Lisbon the sun was dipping into the Atlantic, but only a little of its red glow reached into the narrow street that twisted uphill among the old brown houses. They were already old in the year 1497. Columbus had made his famous voyage only five years before.

The tall boy in the black velvet coat hurried up the street after a fish-seller. As he watched the sun he had been thinking about Columbus. He forgot the explorer as the shallow baskets of sardines swaying from the end of a long pole caught his eye. The fishman's crimson sash and cap and baskets swung around a corner.

The boy ran, caught up with the man, panted out his question:

'Can you tell me, please, where the Jew, Abraham Zacuto, lives?'

The fish-seller waved toward a house at the top of the hill. It was taller than those below it. It seemed, Joän Coelho thought

as he looked at it, like a dark tower against the pink of the western sky.

He took a letter fastened with scarlet wax out of his belt and went up the steps towards an oak door banded with iron and bristling with iron spikes. Joãn was just going to knock on it when he heard voices inside and stumbling footsteps.

The door swung open suddenly, almost hitting Joãn in the face. He sprang aside. A boy about his own age, a redheaded boy with a big red dog at his heels, plunged through the door. The boy landed sitting down on the stone steps. The dog stopped with a scratching of toe-nails and began licking his master's cheek. He whined softly and waved a silky red tail.

From inside an angry voice called: 'This is the last time. The very last. Go back to the bogs you came from. The dog would make a better astrologer...'

The boy on the steps looked up at Joãn Coelho and smiled, showing very white teeth in a freckled face.

'Sure the little man's right!' he said, getting up and shaking himself. 'The dog knows more than most men, don't you, Connemara boy?'

He brushed the dust off his dingy green and brown kilt.

'We'll be going, Con,' he said, and started down the hill.

'Oh, but wait!' Joãn said. 'I have a letter. An important letter for Zacuto the astrologer.'

'It's not for me, then,' said the red-headed boy cheerfully. 'Shane O'Connor's my name. No one writes me letters with grand scarlet seals stuck all over them.'

He spoke in Portuguese, but slowly, with a rise and fall to his voice that made the words sound strange although he said them clearly.

'Nothing's to stop you giving it to him,' Shane O'Connor went on. 'The door's open wide enough. He can't do much more than kick you downstairs, which I must say he's good at. It's not often he does that. He's a good little man if you don't anger him.'

Shane smiled again and spoke once more to the dog.

'Time we left this distressful country, Con. Let's shake the dust of it from our feet.'

'You know a better country, do you?' Joãn said, drawing his eyebrows together.

'You never heard of Ireland, I suppose,' Shane said softly.

'Yes, I have. It's over there.' Joãn waved his hand towards the fading sky. 'I'm no dunce. Portuguese boys know about all countries. The sea's our road.'

Shane said mockingly: 'You've sailed around the Cape of Storms, I suppose.'

'No, but my brother's friend Bartolomeo Diaz did. And we don't call it the Cape of Storms now. It's named the Cape of Good Hope.'

'You were too busy to go on that trip, I suppose. Perhaps you went with Columbus?'

'No, I'm waiting for a better man. Columbus just found the back door to India—if he's found it at all. We Portuguese will find the front door,' Joãn said proudly.

'Columbus made one mistake,' Shane admitted. 'He took no Irishmen with him. He couldn't expect to do much without someone from our green land along.'

'Why did you go away from your green land if it's so wonderful?' Joãn asked.

He had forgotten about the letter and the open door behind him as he listened to Shane's soft voice.

Shane went on: 'Oh, we Irish go up and down the world, looking at it, to see if there's a place we like better than our own. If we did we'd take it, but we never have seen one good enough yet.'

'You'd take the land of India if you wanted it, I suppose,' the Portuguese boy said with a short laugh.

'What would we be wanting with it? A dark land full of serpents.'

'Full of spices. Full of jewels. Full of silks and gold and ivory,' Joãn corrected.

'You make it sound pleasant,' said Shane, moving away from the wall against which he had been leaning. 'Maybe I'll have a look at it. Come on, Con.'

He started off again, the red dog at his heels, but a girl's voice from inside the house called his name and he stopped in the shadow beyond the house.

'Shane, Shane O'Connor!' the girl called, but seeing Joãn stopped at the open door.

'I thought you were Shane,' she said. 'Oh, can you catch him?

He's gone, and now my father's sorry. He didn't mean to turn him away. He knew Shane didn't mean to drop the astrolabe. He's a good boy even if his fingers are all thumbs.'

'Thank you for the compliment, Rachel,' drawled Shane, stepping out of the shadow. 'This is Señor Zacuto's daughter,' he added to Joãn. 'She'll hand the letter to her father, since I have important business down by the river.'

This girl, Joãn Coelho thought, must be younger than his sister Luisa, about thirteen probably, much too young anyway to be standing shivering at the door this cool evening and trying not to cry. The lantern that she held had red and yellow glass in it, so there were sometimes pink and sometimes yellow stripes on Rachel's white brocade dress as she moved the light. The pearl ropes twisted in her soft black hair looked pink when she lifted the lantern up to see Shane better. The two large tears that had rolled out of her dark eyes looked like pink pearls.

'Oh, Shane, you're not going to run away!' she said, so sadly that Joãn heard himself say, to his own surprise: 'He's not, because I won't let him.'

He grabbed Shane's arm and things became rather mixed up. Joãn felt one of his velvet sleeves rip at the shoulder. His feet went out from under him. There was red and yellow light in his eyes and something silky and furry on his chest.

It growled, and the girl in the white dress cried: 'Con, don't bite him. Make him get off, Shane. Go away both of you if you like.'

'Just for that I won't,' Shane said cheerfully. 'Come off him, Con.'

The dog got off Joãn's chest.

'The King's letter!' he thought and sitting up said: 'My letter, where is it?'

Shane helped him up.

'I'm sorry,' he said. 'Con thought you were going to hurt me. Here's your letter. And here's Señor Zacuto.'

A fat little man in a black robe with gold and silver stars on it was on the steps. He had a pointed cap on the back of his round bald head.

'I thought I heard a noise,' he said, looking around him vaguely. 'You have a lantern, Rachel. Such a good girl. Always know what is wanted. Hold it so I can see if I have straightened this properly.'

He had a flat round brass thing in his fat hand. It had an openwork plate of brass, fastened to a solid brass plate. It flashed in the red light from the lantern like red gold as Abraham Zacuto turned it over. There were letters and figures engraved on it, but not like any that Joãn had ever seen.

The fat little man in the star-sprinkled robe kept twisting the brass thing and saying the names of the signs of the Zodiac and the names of the stars.

'Aquarius... Pisces... Gemini... Orion... Jupiter...'

Joãn had heard the names often enough. King Manuel was always sending for astrologers and they always talked like that. Joãn thought this was the queerest one he had seen—this jolly round little man who kicked people downstairs and forgot about it; and who studied his astrolabe—that was what the brass thing was called—under a lantern on a night when there wasn't a star in the sky.

Abraham Zacuto said to Shane: 'So as I was saying, Shane O'Connor, when you interrupted me, we are entering a time very favorable for journeys.'

Joãn saw Shane try not to smile.

'When you interrupted me!' Joãn thought, almost smiling

himself. 'That's a funny way to describe kicking somebody downstairs because he dropped an astrolabe.'

The astrologer now noticed Joãn.

'A friend of yours, Shane?' he asked in a friendly voice.

'Yes, indeed,' Shane agreed. 'An old friend. Ten minutes I've known him at least. And he's brought you a letter.'

'Very kind of him,' murmured the astrologer. 'Yes, it's for me. "To the astrologer Abraham Zacuto by the hand of Joãn Coelho." Now, who could be writing to me at this time of night?'

'You might open it,' Rachel suggested.

'True. A remarkable girl! Isn't she a remarkable girl, Shane?'

Shane said she was, and Zacuto broke the scarlet seal.

He ran his round black eyes over the few lines of the letter and began dancing up and down on the stone steps. His black robe swung out around him so that the stars on it seemed to twinkle. His pointed hat fell off. He swung the astrolabe about his head by its brass chain. He laughed and panted and hugged Rachel and patted Shane on the shoulder.

'Didn't I tell you fame and fortune were coming?' he shouted. 'You're a good boy, Shane. You brought me luck out of those bogs of yours. Didn't I say this very day that I was Astronomer Royal once and I should not always be forgotten? Get my instruments, Shane. Get my charts. Rachel, what are you standing there for? Get my cloak. The black one with the hood. For I must cover my face and be secret.'

'Your cloak is here!' Rachel said, bringing it. 'But if it is a secret, my darling little fat father, hadn't you better shout a little more softly and not tell all our neighbors down there?'

The astrologer began to speak in a loud hoarse whisper.

'You are right,' he said. 'What a remarkable girl! Isn't she a remarkable girl, young Señor? Tell your mother I may be late,

Rachel. Come, Shane. Carry the bag. It wouldn't be dignified for me to carry it. I was Astronomer Royal under King Joãn the Second.'

He wrapped himself in the black cloak and bounced off down the Street of the Rat, followed by the red-headed boy with the bag of instruments slung over his shoulder.

The red dog Connemara sneaked along the wall with his silky tail drooping. He knew he would be sent home if the astrologer saw him too soon.

'You'd better go too,' Rachel said to Joãn Coelho. 'Aren't you going to show them the way?'

'Oh, everyone knows the way to the pal—' Joãn began, but stopped in the middle of the word with his mouth open.

'To the palace,' finished Rachel. 'I thought I'd find out. So King Manuel has sent for my father. Thank you for telling me.'

'I did *not* tell you,' Joãn Coelho said angrily, but he said it to the heavy oak door as it slammed in his face. He heard the bar drop into place.

Joãn Coelho pounded on the door.

A small window in the upper part of it opened and Rachel's face appeared behind an iron grating.

'Did you want something, Señor?' she asked politely.

'When shall I see you again?'

'Better ask an astrologer. There's a good one going down the hill, so trot along to the palace, Señor-who-never-tells-anything.'

She started to shut the window as Joãn said crossly: 'If I were to say what I think of you—'

'I wouldn't. I'm sure it's rude.'

'Not at all, I agree with your father. I think you're a very remarkable girl!'

CHAPTER 2

SHANE LEARNS TO PROPHESY

CONNEMARA followed Shane and the astrologer down the Street of the Rat. He slunk into a doorway as João Coelho's long black legs ran past him. The doorway had a delicious-smelling bone in it, but Connemara only gnawed it a little and went along.

The night was full of pleasant smells. Down by the Tagus, the wide river that runs below the towers and walls of Lisbon, there were smells of fish and spices and fat chickens. Connemara did not care for spices. A codfish head was nice to drag in front of Rachel's gray cat to make her back bristle and her eyes flash green sparks. Fish heads were too bony to eat, though; but a chicken—that was really tempting.

However, Con was on business that night. He turned away from the river and climbed another hill. There was a wide street. He could hear Shane's footsteps ahead on the black-and-white pavement. Abraham Zacuto had begun to puff and pant from the steep climb. Connemara decided it was time to show himself to his friends.

SHANE
QUINN

He frisked around in front of Zacuto waving his feathery tail, sniffing at the astrologer's black cloak, and barking joyfully.

'Now this is a fine thing!' puffed the astrologer. 'What we need is a dog to jump on us. Such a help in reading the stars! Go home, you savage!'

Connemara pretended that he didn't understand Portuguese. He chased a rat under a doorstep and joined his friends again.

'Don't send him home,' Shane begged. 'Didn't you say I brought you luck? And how could I bring you any and Con not bring it too? Didn't we come first in the dog days when the red star Sirius was rising? And you said it was my star and you called Con Procyon and me Sirius. For Procyon always followed Sirius and Con always followed me.'

'Let him come,' Joän said. 'The King likes dogs.'

'So I did,' admitted Zacuto, pleased by Shane's talking about the stars. 'Well, let him come, but make him behave himself.'

They were under the wall of the palace now. Joän led them past the main entrance where torches smoked in iron holders and armed guards paced up and down. The little man and the two tall boys edged along the curves and angles of the wall and came at last to a small door half hidden by a tangle of bushes.

Joän unlocked it with a key that he had on a cord around his neck. Zacuto and Shane, with Con close at his heels, followed Joän up a dark twisting stairway. At the top Joän shoved a heavy leather curtain aside and led them into a big room where smoking candles made a dim light. There were tapestries on the walls. In the flickering light of the candles the figures of men and beasts seemed to move.

Joän pushed aside a strip of faded crimson embroidered with the arms of Portugal and knocked on the door behind it.

A peevish voice inside called: 'Who's there?'

'The astrologer Zacuto, Your Majesty, and his assistant,' said Joãn.

'And none too soon!'

The door was jerked open and King Manuel stood in the doorway. Shane had seen him, splendidly dressed, riding through the streets, a grand figure on his prancing black horse.

'That can't be the King,' he thought, but seeing Zacuto bow till his pointed cap nearly touched the floor, Shane bowed too. Having his head so near the floor gave Shane a fine view of King Manuel's bare feet in their shabby velvet shoes, of his skinny ankles, and of the moth-eaten fur around the bottom of his gown.

'Oh, get up, get up,' the King said, yawning. 'The backs of people's heads are no treat to me.'

Shane looked up and saw the rest of the moth-eaten fur, a face with a mouth half-open, a short turned-up nose, narrow blue eyes, a bulging forehead, and a fluff of untidy light hair.

'Is the dog an astrologer?' the King asked. 'Here, dog, come here!'

Con moved forward, waving his tail.

'Down, Con,' Shane whispered. 'Set!' And the big red dog stretched himself on the floor as quiet as a dog carved out of copper with his red-gold eyes fixed on the King's face.

'This is no breed I know. Where did he come from?'

'From the west edge of Ireland, Your Majesty, where we hunt birds through the bogs. He's trained to lie quiet that way when he sees a bird.'

'And what are you and your dog doing so far from home?' asked the King, stooping and touching Con's smooth head.

'The O'Connors were kings in Connaught,' Shane answered. 'At Connemara we lived and the red dogs followed us. But Diarmid Macmurrough brought Saxon strangers into Ireland and the O'Connors were kings no longer. So my brother Dennis and the dog and I went seeking our fortune. Dennis is a scholar. At our own school at Tuam that Cathal O'Connor built they could teach him no more. With the pen and the brush there's no one his equal. So our parents being dead we came away to school here at Lisbon.'

'So the King your father died, did he? He's not a king we have heard of.'

'Not my father, Your Majesty. It was some few years ago Ruadri O'Connor was King. Three hundred or some such matter.'

King Manuel laughed.

'Well, we are sorry you lost your kingdom, brother,' he said pleasantly, 'whenever it happened. But if you study the stars, that is work for a wandering scholar—or a wandering king either, isn't it?'

'Since I am lucky enough to have a great master,' Shane said, waving his hand towards Zacuto.

The astrologer had been standing first on one foot and then on the other while the King talked with Shane. Zacuto did not really like being forgotten while the King asked about dogs and dead kings, but he knew better than to interrupt. Now he puffed up importantly, looking rather like a frog. At least if a frog ever wore a pointed cap and a robe with stars on it!

'We will hear some of that wisdom now,' said King Manuel. 'You, Coelho, and you, young scholar from the West, keep watch here. Let no one disturb us.' The door shut behind the King's thin figure and Zacuto's round one.

Joán Coelho said: 'I am afraid I'll go to sleep. Tell me something to keep me awake. Tell me about Ireland.'

Shane told him about hunting snipe and woodcock in the bogs, about bare mountains that looked like dark blue clouds against the western sky, about storms that roared into the little bays and tossed seaweed on the beaches.

'And the red-headed boys and the red dogs chasing the red deer,' Joán said sleepily.

'I could tell it better if I had my harp. Then you wouldn't yawn in my face.'

Shane yawned himself and began to walk up and down.

'Or if I had my guitar I could keep you awake,' Joán Coelho said. 'But we couldn't play outside the King's cabinet. Some day I'll bring my guitar to Zacuto's house and we can both play.'

'Not I,' said Shane. 'I was hungry last summer and I sold my harp. Down in Setubal. After they took Dennis away.'

Joán was going to ask about what had happened to Shane's brother, but the door of the King's cabinet opened and they heard King Manuel's thin voice saying: 'Take time. Come again and tell me whether the stars bid me engage in this discovery.'

The astrologer's voice boomed out a speech of thanks in which he mentioned the Bull, the Lion, and other beasts that were supposed to shine in the sky. He tossed the charts and instruments to Shane and bustled out, looking more important than ever. Muttering the names of more stars, he hurried down the dark stairway. He went on talking to himself softly all the way home, but Shane could hear little of what he said. It was not until they were safe in Zacuto's own laboratory that the astrologer began to speak clearly.

This laboratory was a room at the top of the tall house. It was full of parchment rolls with charts of the sky and land and sea drawn on them. Jars full of drugs were on tables, on shelves, even on the floor. A small furnace for casting metals was at one end of the room. On the opposite wall was a huge chart of a man's body with stars and animals around it.

Shane had studied this for many hours when he would have liked to be sailing with the sardine-fishers or loafing along the wharfs, or hunting among the heather with Connemara. Without looking at it he could repeat: 'Aries the Ram rules the head. Pisces the fishes take care of the feet. Gemini the twins look after the shoulders.'

Every part of the body had some planet or star or constellation that affected it. It was all drawn on the chart. Zacuto had a way of asking Shane questions about it when Shane was standing with his back to it.

Tonight, however, the astrologer never looked at it. Instead he patted Shane on the shoulder—he had to reach up to do it—and said: 'You did very well, Shane. The King liked you and the dog. It put him in a good mood. Now we must give him a good prophecy—one of our best.'

He walked up and down with his hands behind him, his starry robe tucked up over them, his face bent toward the floor. His pointed cap fell off. He whistled a sad little tune and kicked the cap and parchment rolls out of his way as he walked.

Shane knew the tune. It meant that Zacuto was thinking.

The astrologer spun around suddenly, almost knocking over a jar of burnt horses' teeth.

'Gemini, the twin brothers,' he panted. 'This very night we leave the sign of Taurus and enter that of Gemini. Does that mean anything to your thick head?'

'Not much,' said Shane honestly.

'Now listen, boy.' Zacuto perched on a high stool and wagged a fat finger at Shane. 'You may be such a dunce that you can't hold an astrolabe straight, but you haven't been here all these months and not learned *anything!* I've told you a hundred times what makes a good astrologer. Now you tell me.'

'Imagination and common sense,' said Shane promptly.

'Right! When a lady comes here because her hair is falling out, what do we do?'

'We use Cleopatra's cure for baldness, which is burnt mice, horses' teeth, bear's grease mixed with honey.'

'You needn't tell me,' interrupted Zacuto. 'There couldn't be a better medicine. Cleopatra wasn't bald, was she? No, indeed. She was beautiful. Ladies think they'll all be like her if they buy it. That's where imagination comes in. They stop worrying and their hair stops falling. But do I mix it for them and tell them how to rub it in—me with a head as bald as an owl's egg? Certainly not! You, Shane with your thick mop of red bristles, do that. There's common sense for you.'

'The King doesn't need any essence of burnt mouse rubbed into his head,' Shane said, laughing.

'He does not. But he needs common sense which no one has given him yet, and imagination so that he'll get a little courage into him. Sense first. Listen now—for years Spain and Portugal both have been trying to find a way to India by sea. Portugal had a great prince—Enrique the Navigator. Sense and imagination both Prince Enrique had. He tried to find a way to India by sailing around Africa. I was with him in Ceuta in Africa when I was a young man. We studied the stars and the winds and everything about sailing a ship. Do you know, Shane, what is the important thing about sailing a ship?'

'Why, the wind—no, the stars. Or perhaps a strong mast. But the sails must be right. And she mustn't leak—'

'All right. And all wrong! The most important thing is the captain. With a brave man in command, the ship may leak, the winds may roar, the stars hide behind a cloud, the sails be ripped to tatters, but still the ship will come safe home. That's where Prince Enrique was wisest. He knew men, so the men he sent along the coast of Africa brought their ships safely home, and knowledge of that coast and how to trade with the black men along it.'

'After the Prince died, did they stop sending ships to explore?' Shane asked.

'No. King Joãn the Second went on with the work. It was he who sent out Bartolomeo Diaz, the man who sailed around the southern tip of Africa. The Cape of Storms they called it at first, but now it is the Cape of Good Hope, for it has opened the way to India. It was King Joãn—and I was his Astronomer Royal, as you may have heard me say—that started building ships strong enough to finish the voyage to India. But this little king with the skinny legs, he listens to the counsellors who say: "You'll lose your money." He's stingy, Manuel is, so he listens to that. Then someone else says: "Columbus has been there already. If you go now, you'll have to fight Spaniards." He's afraid of Spain, so he believes *that*. Though I told him—if Columbus got to India I'll eat it, red savages and parrots and all.'

Zacuto stopped to breathe, but went on after a minute: 'So then some clever monk gives Manuel an idea. "Marry the Spanish princess and you'll get the throne of Spain and the land of India without spending a cruzado." Manuel likes that idea. It's both cowardly and cheap. What do you think of it, Shane?'

'Well, I never yet saw a mouse eating a cat,' Shane said.

'I said you were not a dunce,' Zacuto exclaimed, jumping up and thumping Shane on the back. 'Portugal would not rule Spain. Spain would eat up Portugal. And we poor Jews who have been well treated here would be tortured and burned again. Those ships that King Joãn started to build must be finished. They must find the way to India. Spices will come to Lisbon instead of to Venice. This land will be rich. Manuel will be called the Fortunate. And you and I, Shane, must make him a prophecy that will put courage into his mean heart and sense into his foolish head.'

Zacuto began to spin around again with his robe swelling out around him like a sail full of wind.

'Gemini,' he puffed again. 'It all hangs on that.'

'You keep saying that,' Shane yawned, 'but I don't know what you mean.'

'Imagination. Here's where the stars help us. The sign of the twin brothers, Castor and Pollux, is in the sky. Manuel must choose two brothers to guide his ships. If he puts one of those silly peacocks at the court in charge, we may as well say good-bye to India.'

'Do you know the two brothers who could do it?'

'I do. The very ones King Joãn himself would choose.'

'Tell him their names then and he'll send them,' said Shane.

'Now,' Zacuto groaned, 'you are being a dunce again. He must think he has chosen them himself. With the help of the stars, of course.'

'Well, tell me their names, then,' said Shane.

Zacuto bent forward and spoke in a low voice as if he were afraid that someone might hear him even in the high lonely room.

'Vasco da Gama and his brother Paulo,' he said in a hoarse whisper, and then more loudly: 'Don't stare at me with your mouth open like a—a king. Didn't you hear me?'

'I heard you,' said Shane.

PAULO
DA GAMA

IN THE KING'S PALACE

Dennis o'Connor, Shane's brother, had been Paulo da Gama's secretary. Shane himself had lived in Paulo da Gama's house until that hot night last August when they rode through Setubal.

Dennis had spent his days copying stories of travel and adventure for Señor Paulo, for his master loved books and loved, too, the sound of the harp that Dennis played so well. There was nothing, Shane thought, that Dennis couldn't do. He could speak and write in half a dozen languages. He could draw and paint in gold and colors. The manuscripts that he wrote were all decorated with patterns of vines and flowers and birds so that each page looked as if it were set in a border of jewels.

Dennis had taught Shane to play the harp and to draw. The harp, Shane had sold one hungry day. It was lucky he could draw. If his fingers hadn't been clever with brush and pen, he might still have been wandering half-starved around the stone wharves by the Tagus. He was drawing a map for a sailor when Zacuto found him and took him home to the Street of the Rat.

That was some weeks after the fight.

They were riding through Setubal when it happened. Paulo da Gama was ahead with Dennis following him. Shane was behind with the servants. In the narrow street outside the prison they had met the Judge of Setubal—a skinny old man with a beard like gray string called Nuno Calves.

Into that very prison with its thick gray walls and narrow slits of windows Nuno Calves had sent the father of Paulo and Vasco da Gama. Da Gama was imprisoned unjustly. Everyone in Setubal knew it. But he had died there before the King's letter came that said he was to go free.

And now here was Nuno Calves jostling Paulo da Gama against the wall and laughing in a voice that sounded like the neigh of a mule.

Shane heard the laugh and heard Nuno Calves say in that ugly, sneering voice: 'It is a pleasure to see you, Señor. We always welcome criminals in Setubal.'

The moonlight flashed on Paulo da Gama's sword. Nuno Calves had his sword out, too, and the two swords rang against each other. Above the ringing of steel and of the horses' feet on the stones, Shane heard the Judge's voice again. There were men behind him, but they could not pass him in the narrow street and attack Paulo da Gama's servants, so he was calling to the guards at the prison gate. His voice was loud and angry and his sword clanged on the stones. Paulo da Gama had disarmed him, and cut him in the hand.

Paulo da Gama could have killed the Judge then, but instead he wheeled his horse around and rode back towards Lisbon, calling to his men to follow him. Fernan Martinez, the big negro cook, and the two grooms tried to follow, but the prison guards ran out with their long spears and stabbed at the horses. The

Judge's servants rushed at them from behind. Calves himself had ridden his horse into the prison gateway and shrieked out his orders in his harsh voice that was louder than the noise of the fight.

Shane saw Dennis's horse rear as the guards rushed at him. Dennis fell and two of the guards hauled him into the prison. Shane rode at them, but the iron gate clanged in his face. One of the Judge's grooms, a man with a red face scarred by smallpox, dragged Shane from his horse.

'Shall I shove this one in too?' the man shouted to Nuno Calves, but the Judge only scowled at him for a minute and then said with one of his harsh laughs: 'No one would pay much ransom for such a ragamuffin, and he looks hungry. He wouldn't be worth feeding.'

They let Shane go, but they kept the horse. He ran north on the gray dusty road because Paulo da Gama had ridden that way. He slept behind a clump of bushes and woke to hear hoofbeats passing him. It was a dozen soldiers. One of them had a red cloak over his jacket of leather and steel.

There was a fork in the road, and the soldiers stopped for a minute arguing about which road to take. The man in the red cloak—they called him Veloso—said the right-hand road was the best.

'I tell you it leads past da Gama's door,' he shouted. 'I know all these roads the way I know the lines on my hand.'

The troop rode off down the right-hand fork. Shane watched them go, and then set off down the left-hand road.

'At least,' he thought, 'that red-cloaked boaster has put them on the wrong road. I am on the right fork myself. Perhaps if I run fast I might beat them.'

He ran as fast as he could, but he came limping and sore of

foot to Paulo da Gama's house. It was dark and empty. Señor da Gama had ridden up to the door the day before, the neighbors said. He must have gone away again that night. No one had seen him go.

Yes, someone added, there had been soldiers from Setubal looking for him only an hour ago. They had ridden off without learning anything. If Señor Paulo had given Nuno Calves a cut over the wrist, as the soldiers said, it wasn't half what the old villain deserved. Let him catch mice for himself and shut them up in his mouse-trap there at Setubal, and ask bags of gold for ransom. No one who knew Señor Paulo would help Calves catch him.

Shane thought that Paulo da Gama might have gone away on a ship. He was a fine sea captain. Shane went to every wharf along the Tagus, but he could find no trace of his master. The harp was heavy to carry and he sold it at last to buy food. After a while he stopped asking for Señor Paulo. He had never spoken about him to Zacuto since the day the astrologer had found him drawing a map in exchange for some fried sardines and a hunk of bread.

The astrologer had never said a word about Paulo da Gama in all the past months. It was no wonder that Señor Paulo's name made Shane open his mouth and stare at Zacuto.

'You can shut your mouth any time now, Shane,' Zacuto said. 'You'd better go to bed. Don't sleep with it open or you will snore. Or a mouse might run into it. It is annoying to find a mouse in the mouth when one wakes.'

He laughed and picked up a candle.

'Oh, wait, please!' Shane said. 'Did you know Señor Paulo all the time?'

'Of course. Why else do you suppose I brought you here? He sent me a letter asking me to find you and feed you. And he sent money to your brother in prison more than once.'

'I thought you brought me home because I could draw,' Shane said.

'That was how I knew you. By that and the red hair. You've been a good boy, Shane. Except for dropping things. And the dog eating enough for a man and making muddy footprints besides—which my wife often speaks of and not very softly. I know where Señor Paulo is and you shall know too before many days. Curl up now and go to sleep.' Shane unrolled his straw mattress, threw it down on the floor among the jars of drugs, and curled up on it under a sheepskin. Connemara, after turning around three times, lay down at his master's feet. Shane thought he could never go to sleep. There were so many things to think about. Joãn Coelho with the black eyebrows like a band of black silk across his forehead when he scowled.

King Manuel's fretful voice and skinny legs. And Señor Paulo... perhaps he would see him soon... perhaps he would see Dennis...

Shane opened his eyes and looked up at the window. There were stars shining now. He wished he weren't so stupid about stars. Those bright ones, he thought sleepily, might be Castor and Pollux—the stars in the sign of Gemini that meant good luck for King Manuel's ships.

Fortunately for Shane, Zacuto could not know that Shane had been looking at the wrong stars!

Shane wondered what Señor Paulo's brother was like. Shane had never seen Vasco da Gama because he had been away on a voyage while Shane was living in Señor Paulo's house.

'I hope he is like Señor Paulo,' Shane thought, yawning.

The next thing he knew there was bright sunshine coming in the east window and Zacuto was shaking him to wake him up.

For the next three days Shane sat at a table and drew charts. One was a map of the sky at the moment of King Manuel's birth. Another showed the stars where they were when the King had sent for Zacuto. The third was a map which showed how it was possible to sail around Africa and reach India. It showed, too, Zacuto said, how much easier it would be to bring spices to Lisbon all the way in the same ship than it was to send them to Venice partly by ship, then on land by caravan, and then in ships again.

Shane, who was just finishing copying Zacuto's rough map of the west coast of Africa as far as the Cape of Good Hope, said: 'There's a lot of space between Africa and India that we don't know about. What shall I put there—sea monsters?'

'Keep your sea monsters out of this,' Zacuto said crossly. 'Do you want to frighten the King? Put in some ships and some pleasant-looking ladies blowing winds from gold horns. You can give them fish-tails of gold if you like. And draw plenty of elephants on the land. Some dark-skinned natives with gold on too.'

Shane loved to paint with gold and colors. Generally Zacuto did not like to spend money on paint, but now he kept saying: 'Put on plenty of vermilion. It's rich-looking. Some good clear blue now on the sea. Draw some flowers and scrolls now in the corner. Take more gold. We don't draw maps for a king every day!'

Shane worked until his eyes ached and his fingers were stiff. At last Zacuto was satisfied. The three big parchments shone with gold and brilliant colors.

'They are the best,' he said, as he rolled them up. 'I was Astronomer Royal once, and I say they could be no better.'

'They could if Dennis had drawn them,' Shane said sadly.

'Oh, that wonderful Dennis! He is, of course, wiser and more clever than anyone. Shall I make a prophecy about him, Shane?'

Shane rested his aching head on his tired hands and muttered: 'I'm tired of fortune-telling and stars.'

'Suppose I tell you that I see by the stars that a prison gate swings open, and through it walks a tall young man with black hair and eyes like emeralds and a pencase and inkhorn swinging from his belt.'

'I'd not believe it,' Shane said. 'You always said that a Jew could do nothing to help him. That if you tried, you'd only find yourself in prison with a jailer tweaking your toes with red-hot tongs.'

'Perhaps times have changed. Be more cheerful, boy. If the King is pleased with your charts, we can ask him some favor for you.'

'He'll probably never look at them,' Shane groaned.

Rachel Zacuto, who had been running upstairs, stopped in the door and said: 'Shane is just like a sunbeam. Always so gay.'

'Shane is tired,' said her father. 'Be more kind, Rachel.'

'Too tired to go with that black-eyed boy with the long legs? He is downstairs waiting. The King wants you both—and the dog too.'

Shane jumped up forgetting his headache and gloom. 'What is that you have over your arm?' Zacuto asked Rachel.

'Shane's new suit,' she said, laying it on the table.

'I—I haven't any new suit,' Shane exclaimed, looking at the heap of brown velvet. 'It's a mistake.'

'Your orders are to put it on as fast as you can,' said Zacuto, smiling. 'No, don't thank me,' he added as Shane began to stammer out something. 'To have a well-dressed assistant when I go to the palace suits my dignity. Besides, my cousin Samuel the tailor made it for half price. The velvet I got free from Isaac Ben Abraham because of the fortune you told his daughter. You know you said a dark man would come on a ship and there would be a wedding. Sure enough, from Flanders came a ship and the bridegroom and this velvet too. So hurry, Shane, for we must not keep our little King waiting.'

Shane felt as if all Lisbon must be looking at his new velvet coat with the wide sleeves, at his gold-trimmed jerkin and the breeches that fitted so neatly around his knees. There was even a velvet cap with a turned-back brim that rested rather unsteadily on his red hair. Connemara kept sniffing at his master's new velvet shoes. He missed Shane's bare ankles and old leather sandals.

King Manuel, Shane thought, looked better dressed than he did the other evening, but his black satin and ermine wasn't really the latest style. The sleeves were too narrow, for one thing, and the coat too long in the skirt. Compared to Zacuto's cousin Samuel's masterpiece in brown velvet and gold, the King's clothes looked old-fashioned.

King Manuel's voice squeaked with excitement as he saw the charts unrolled on the table in his cabinet. Shane had expected the King's cabinet to be a splendid place. Instead he saw a little room with faded and ragged tapestries, with a dingy carpet partly covering the stone floor, and a table covered with papers. Maps pinned to the tapestry hung crookedly here and there. A tray with silver dishes stood on top of the papers on the table. One of the cups had a little wine in it. There was a mutton bone, picked almost bare, on the platter.

'I am sorry you are too late to share my breakfast,' said the King, 'but at least the dog can have something.'

He threw the mutton bone into the fireplace.

Con went over and gnawed it politely, but without much excitement. Con was used to bones with more meat on them.

After this hospitality the King said impatiently: 'Your search of the heavens, Zacuto—what does it tell you?'

Zacuto said solemnly: 'I have bestowed great care on the task, Your Majesty. The stars have spoken. India is a long way from Portugal. It is a dark land, rich, full of dark, proud people. There is danger, much danger. From rough and stormy seas. From sickness. From the treachery of savages. They will try to seize and kill your men. But your planet is great under the sphere. You will rule that dark land. King Manuel the Fortunate, men will call you.'

The King snapped his thin white fingers as Shane unrolled the charts. Zacuto ran his stubby forefinger over them, talking all the time.

'Riches and fortune await Your Majesty,' Zacuto said at last, rolling up the map of Africa. Then he let the chart showing the stars at the hour of Manuel's birth snap together again and added: 'But one must seize fortune at the right moment. The stars swing through the heavens without waiting for us to catch them. Seize the moment now, Your Most Excellent Majesty, while the sun is in the house of Gemini; while the great Twin Brothers look kindly upon you. See, on this last chart, it shows how Gemini, the brothers, are favorable to your venture. But the stars say something more.'

Zacuto paused, looking grave. The King, snapping his fingers again, said impatiently: 'Don't stand there looking like a boiled owl. What do they say?'

'Only this. Your venture depends on the man who commands it. He must be already experienced in handling ships and men. He must be as bold as a lion, as patient as an ox, as strong as a bull, as wise as a serpent. Also he must be a man who has loyal followers. Better still a loyal family. Best of all a brother at his side. The stars say that India will be discovered by two brothers. That is the meaning of the sign of Gemini.'

King Manuel said fretfully: 'And to find these two brothers would be like looking for two diamonds that someone had dropped into the Tagus.'

'True, Your Majesty, yet strange things happen. Down at the Tagus a few weeks ago a fisherman cut open a codfish and found a ring in its stomach. I bought it for my little daughter, but she— she's a remarkable girl—said: "Sell it again, father. You can use the money better." So I did, and gave the money to my cousin Samuel for a suit—for some work he did for me. Otherwise I might show the jewel to Your Majesty as a proof that jewels are found in strange places. When Your Majesty sees the right man to lead the fleet to India, you will know him wherever he is.'

'Perhaps,' said King Manuel bitterly, 'I may find him at my own court, among the people who croak about the storms that always rage between here and India. They say that beyond the Cape of Storms there is a black whirlpool of boiling pitch into which all ships are drawn and where they stick forever. Until you gave me courage, Zacuto, I believed them. Do you think that among them I am likely to find the man of whom you speak—wise as a serpent, brave as a lion—and all the rest of it? I'm more likely to find one wise as a donkey and brave as a rabbit!'

Zacuto burst into a hearty laugh. After a minute the King laughed too and said more cheerfully: 'Surely you who have so much wisdom can find me this jewel of a captain—no, two jewels, for he must have a brother as good as he is.'

'The stars have not said their names, Your Majesty,' Zacuto said, 'but you will find them.'

There was a knock at the door. The King's chamberlain announced that it was time for the King to speak to the counsellors and the nobles of the kingdom.

'Stay and see them turn as green as old cheese when I tell them that my mind is made up to send out the ships for India,' the King said to Zacuto. 'Perhaps among them you will see one who has red blood in his veins instead of buttermilk!'

There was a great crowd of splendidly dressed men in the throne room. King Manuel walked through them to the red velvet chair that stood behind a wide table. His secretaries began to lay papers in front of him. The King picked up a quill pen and began signing them.

Zacuto and Shane stayed in the corner near the door of the cabinet. No one paid any attention to them. All faces were turned to the King. That is, all but one. Not far from where

Shane stood was a window. A man was standing near it with his face half turned towards it. Shane could see his face—a proud dark face with a nose like an eagle's beak, large dark eyes, and a thick black beard that partly covered his tanned cheeks.

Zacuto, seeing that the backs of the courtiers were turned to him, moved over towards the window.

'The King,' he said softly, 'will hardly see you if you turn your back to him all the morning, Señor Vasco da Gama!'

CHAPTER 4

RIDING NORTH

VASCO DA GAMA shrugged his shoulders.

'I don't belong in that crowd of peacocks,' he said. 'I was a fool to come here.'

'Perhaps I was a fool to ask you to come,' Zacuto said, 'but at least since you are here you will pay your respects to His Majesty.'

Vasco da Gama still leaned against the wall scowling.

Zacuto said, almost in a whisper: 'Remember it's for Paulo's sake.'

Da Gama's look of fierce pride changed suddenly. He smiled kindly at the little astrologer and swung off down the big room towards the group of chattering courtiers.

He did indeed, Shane thought, look out of place among what he had called the peacocks. The plain suit of fine blue cloth, the rolling swing with which he walked, his sturdy shoulders and strong arms, all seemed meant for the deck of a ship. They looked strange among the silks and velvets of the throne room.

'He blows through their scents and perfumes like a salt breeze,' said Zacuto softly.

The courtiers moved aside, looking at da Gama in surprise.

Shane muttered: 'Not a breeze, like a ship plowing through waves. He makes his own path.'

Looking along that path, Shane saw the King signing a paper.

King Manuel looked up suddenly. Vasco da Gama thrust his head and shoulders forward in a bow so low that Shane could see, above his shoulders, King Manuel's narrow blue eyes and thin lips open wide.

'Thank Heaven,' the King squeaked in his high voice. 'I have found the man. Vasco da Gama, are you ready to undertake a task of danger?'

'I am your devoted servant, Sire. Whatever you confide to me shall be performed while I live,' said Vasco.

'You have a brother, I think. Would he help you?'

'Three, Your Majesty. One is a boy. One is a priest. The third—Paulo—is a man you could trust with anything.'

'Bring him here at once.'

'Unfortunately, Your Majesty, he had a quarrel with the Judge of Setubal. He is in hiding because the Judge would put him in prison if he caught him.'

King Manuel said: 'Out of respect for you, Vasco da Gama, I will pardon him. Write to him that I will do so. He must satisfy the Judge. If there are fines to be paid, I will help him.' King Manuel stood up and said loudly: 'To you, my counsellors, to the gentlemen of my court, and to the members of my household, I now say this: I give Vasco da Gama full command over the ships that will discover India.'

India!

At that word there was a buzz of talk among the courtiers, but it stopped as the King went on speaking.

'You are to choose the crews and train them and see to fitting out the ships. I give you charge of everything.'

'Sire,' said Vasco da Gama, 'I thank you for your confidence, but my brother Paulo is older than I am. He is the one who should command. I will gladly serve under him.'

'I like such feeling between brothers,' the King said. 'You may take counsel with your brother, but it is to you I give the command. Name him captain of one of the ships. There are two ships that were begun by King Joãn waiting to be finished. A third ship can be bought. Can you suggest another man for her captain?'

'I can, Your Majesty. Nicolau Coelho, the brother of your page here, is a good seaman and a good friend of mine. He has always said that the way to India can be found. I name him for the captain of the third ship.'

'Very well.' King Manuel turned to his counsellors. 'Gentlemen, he said, 'it is written in the stars that India shall be found by two brothers from our country. One of them stands here before you. I command you to do him honor, for he is going to bring great honor to our land of Portugal. Come to my cabinet in a few moments, Señor Vasco, for we have much to talk about. I bid you good day, gentlemen.'

The King went back to his cabinet. As he passed Zacuto he pressed a purse into the astrologer's hand. Shane saw gold shining through the network. Joãn Coelho followed the King. He looked solemn and important, but he found time to poke Shane in the ribs.

The courtiers were now gathered close about Vasco. Shane caught a glimpse of his face. Señor Vasco did not seem to be enjoying the society of the 'peacocks.' He looked fiercer and prouder than ever.

'We must go, Shane,' said the astrologer.

They slipped out by the dark stairway, but were not far from the palace when they heard running footsteps behind them.

It was Joãn Coelho.

'I am to ride north to find my brother,' he panted. 'Señor Vasco asks you to send a message to Señor Paulo to tell him to come. Here is a letter. Only a few words because everyone is talking to him at once, but enough so that Señor Paulo will know that it is not a trick. He says you are the only one who knows where his brother is.'

'Where are you going?' Zacuto asked.

'Towards Leiria. Nicolau has gone there to bring my sister home from the convent where she has been at school.'

'Shane can ride with you then, for Señor Paulo is not far from there.'

Shane stammered: 'Am I—? You mean me? Can I really—?'

Zacuto laughed. 'Yes, you are really going. Me, I am too old and fat for a fifty-mile ride. I trust no one but you with the name of Paulo's hiding-place. You know all that has happened as well as I do. You have only to change your clothes, for my cousin Samuel did not make that suit for riding and getting rained on and being slept in. I will get a horse—a swift horse, from my cousin Moses. How soon do you start, young sir?'

'In an hour.'

'He will be ready. Come Shane. And remember,' he added as Joãn Coelho ran back to the palace, 'you have seen a prophecy come true.'

Zacuto trotted off to the stables of his cousin Moses. Shane took long strides towards the Street of the Rat with Connemara running in circles around him.

The swift horse from the stables of Zacuto's cousin Moses turned out to be a chunky little gray beast with a strong affection for his native city. He kept turning his head towards Lisbon and had to be kicked hard to stir him into a jouncing trot.

Joãn's bay mare from the King's stables moved along as easily as if she were floating. Two of the King's grooms followed on mules with silver bells on their bridles. As they left the gardens and farms outside Lisbon and took a sandy road through tall pines, the gray horse made up his mind that it was no use looking back, and broke into a rough canter. Shane was lame from bouncing in the saddle when they came to the inn where they spent the night.

It was dark when they found it. The iron gate and the door stood open. From inside came the glow of a fire. Dark figures moved around it. There was a smell of fish and olive oil and onions. The innkeeper came running out with a torch. Its light made pink splashes on the walls. The feet of the horses and the mules rang loud on the stones of the courtyard.

The fish stew tasted good. The room was full of smoke. Shane could hardly see the strings of onions and garlic and the smoked hams that hung from the beams. The only light besides the fire came from a wick floating in a saucer of oil.

An old man muffled in a black cloak sat in the warm corner between the big chimney and the wall. It was dark there and Shane could not see his face. The other men seemed to be his servants. One of them, a big man, was already snoring on a bench with a brown cloak over his face.

There was no bedroom. After supper Joãn and Shane rolled themselves in their cloaks and lay down as close to the fire as they could get. Once a rat ran over Shane's feet, but Connemara chased him away, and soon both master and dog were asleep.

A cock crowing close to his ear woke Shane up. He opened his eyes and stretched. The cock was standing on the table facing the doorway. The sky was turning from gray to dull red. Two pink-eyed pigs came in snorting and grunting. One of them pushed his pink snout into Joãn's neck.

Joãn sat up suddenly and shoved the pig away.

'He thinks I'm a truffle,' he said, yawning.

Connemara nipped one bristly red ear and the pig ran under the table. Con chased the other into the fireplace. The rooster crowed and three hens came in, all cackling. The innkeeper woke up, shoved the pig out of the fireplace, and began to make the fire. The old man slept peacefully in his corner. He had the only mattress in the house and a pillow under his gray head.

Shane and Joãn were soon ready for the road again, but the mules did not want to start.

'Go on, my little angel,' said one of the grooms, beating his mule till clouds of dust rose from his thick coat.

The little angel at last started with a jingling of silver bells.

'I forgot my whip,' Shane said when they had ridden a little way. 'I must go back for it.'

There was light enough now so that he could see the face of the old man who was still asleep by the fire—a face like yellow wax with a stringy gray beard.

It was Nuno Calves, the Judge of Setubal.

Shane picked up his whip and went quietly out of the room. He stood for a moment at the door thinking. Could Nuno Calves be hunting Paulo da Gama? It did not seem likely after so many months. Yet the Judge was known to be a man who never forgot an injury. He was a long way from Setubal and on the very road that led to Señor Paulo's hiding-place.

'I must find out which way he is travelling,' Shane decided. 'If he's going towards Lisbon, it doesn't matter. If he's going north, it may be he is looking for Señor Paulo.'

He went over to the stable. The man who had been snoring on the bench the night before was watering the horses. Shane had seen that red, pockmarked face before. It was the groom who had been with Nuno Calves when Dennis was dragged into the prison.

Shane asked him about the road north.

'That I can't tell you,' the man answered, 'for we haven't been over it yet. We'll find out today.'

Shane had found out what he wanted to know. Nuno Calves was travelling north, and along the very road that led towards Batalha, where Señor Paulo was.

'He may not be looking for Señor Paulo, but at least we

won't walk into his mouth,' Shane thought as he rode out of the courtyard.

He gave such a thump with his heels and such a cut with his whip that the gray horse broke into a jerky canter and caught up with the cloud of dust that covered Joãn Coelho and the mules.

'Why do you keep looking over your shoulder?' asked Joãn after they had ridden about two miles.

Shane told him. Joãn gave a whistle.

'That is bad,' he said, his black brows meeting over his nose.

They rode on in silence for a few minutes.

At last Joãn said: 'We've got to make a plan, Shane, before we get to the fork in the road where I leave you. If the old man was still asleep when you left, they will not start early. So we need not worry about them now, but they may catch up with you this afternoon, or meet you tomorrow when you are on your way home. The Judge and his six servants would make short work of you and Señor Paulo.'

'I don't know about that,' Shane said. 'I could lick three of those little men myself.'

'Suppose you could lick all seven of them,' Joãn said seriously, 'that wouldn't help Señor Paulo. Would the King pardon him, do you think, if he gets into another fight with Nuno Calves?'

Shane grunted, but admitted that Joãn was right.

'The only thing is to keep out of his way until Señor Paulo can go to the Judge with the King's pardon in his hand. Señor Paulo must get back to Lisbon without meeting Nuno Calves. If they meet and there is another fight, Señor Paulo will be wrong whether he wins or loses. Isn't that true?'

'Oh, you're as wise as all the seven wise men of Greece!' Shane said.

'Then tomorrow you must meet my brother's party and

travel south with it. It will be too big for the Judge to attack it, and Nicolau will keep Señor Paulo from fighting. He is a sensible fellow, my brother. Señor Paulo knows that, because they have sailed together. I will get Nicolau to wait at the fork in the road until you come. We will be there early tomorrow afternoon, I think. Can you be there?'

'Unless Nuno Calves sees us first.'

'You must not meet him. If you get here before we do, hide in the pine woods until we come.'

Joãn and the two servants took the road that led uphill, and disappeared among the pines. The gray horse jounced along over the lower road that led down among olive groves. Con padded along in the dust. His red coat was gray with it. He tried to chase a big black and white billy goat, but Shane called him away.

'It's a long journey, old man,' Shane said to him, 'and no fights to make it shorter, but you and I must both attend to business.'

CHAPTER 5

BATALHA

AT A LITTLE whitewashed inn with pear trees around it Shane asked for Señor da Sousa. That was the name by which Paulo da Gama was known there, Zacuto had said.

An old woman smiled and pointed a brown finger down the hill.

'He is down there at the monastery, Señor. He goes every day to talk with the monks.'

Far down in the deep hollow Shane saw a church.

'It looks like ivory and gold, doesn't the Señor think?' the old woman asked. 'It ought to, for King Joãn the First and his Queen lie there. Yes, and Prince Enrique too.'

'Prince Enrique the Navigator?' Shane asked. 'Why is he buried in this lonely place? Has he been dead a long time? May I put my horse in your stable? Have you any oats?'

'So many questions at once,' grumbled the old woman. 'Yes, put him beside Señor da Sousa's horse, and look out for the black fiend's heels. While you rub him down and feed him I will tell you about Prince Enrique, for it is a shocking thing that a fine-looking young man like you should be so ignorant.'

'Thank you, Señora,' Shane murmured, taking the saddle off his horse.

'When the Spaniards came to take our country away, King Joãn the First said: "I will drive them out, and on the spot where I defeat them in battle, I will build a church, the most beautiful church in Portugal." So he did both. The Spaniards ran away and the church is down there. King Joãn is in his tomb with his Queen beside him. Prince Enrique loved this church. He was King Joãn's son, you know. He has left his horses often in that very stable when he went down there to pray. I have fed his horse myself. (Throw down some hay for yours, there is plenty.) But he went away to Africa, which is a hot country full of black magic and lions. He died, and they buried him down there near his father. Shall I give your red dog a bone, Señor? He will not kill my hens, will he?'

'He would like a bone. He would kill me as soon as he would a hen,' Shane said.

'Prince Enrique loved a fat hen roasted in front of the fire. With cream poured over it. And sprinkled with paprika. He would sit there carving a little ship out of wood for me—I was a child then, Señor—and smell the good smells of cooking. Ripe olives he liked, too, and eggs cooked a certain way that my mother knew. Eggs-like-stars, she called them. I have the little ship still. One day I asked him where it would sail. He picked up a piece of charcoal from the fireplace and drew a map on the wall of that hot African shore and lands beyond. It is still there, Señor, though a little smoky. We whitewash the rest of the wall, but never that. Will the Señor look at it?'

'Not now,' Shane said. 'I must go to Señor Paulo—to Señor

da Sousa. We must ride back to Lisbon in the morning. Will you cook us a chicken tonight the way Prince Enrique liked it? The ride and your tales have made me hungry.'

'I will wring its neck this moment, Señor. Perhaps you would like to choose it yourself.'

'That I leave to you,' said Shane hastily. 'And Señora, there is an enemy of Señor da Sousa's somewhere on the road. An old man with a face like yellow cheese and a goat's beard with six grooms, one of them red-faced and scarred by the smallpox. If he comes here will you send one of your servants to warn us?'

'I will do that, and I will cook eggs-like-stars for you, because though they may not be as good as those my mother cooked, Señor da Sousa has praised them. And on the chicken I will sprinkle paprika that my uncle grows in the south. From Hungary he brought the seeds many years ago.'

'Thank you, Señora.—Take care of the horse, Con.'

Connemara lay in the sunshine gnawing his bone and keeping one eye on the gray horse. Shane ran down the hill through air that smelled of rosemary and thyme and lavender.

The old woman was right. In the warm glow of the afternoon sun the monastery of Batalha looked as if it were carved out of ivory and touched with gold.

'It's like sea foam running over yellow sand,' Shane thought.

It hardly seemed possible that the pinnacles and flying buttresses and windows could be carved out of stone. The flowery crosses and the figures of saints looked so light and airy that it seemed as if a good strong wind might blow the whole thing away.

Most churches Shane had seen were dark and grim.

'Surely the little people made it,' he said out loud in Gaelic, stopping for a moment outside the great door. Unless he talked to himself, he never heard his native language now. Sometimes he was afraid he would forget it.

He could hear voices inside chanting. He went in. The monks were moving through the clusters of pillars to the altar. The gold and ruby light from the window above the door streamed in on the moving figures. Their white robes seemed to be painted with flowers. On the pavement, in the shadows near the altar, even on the top of the pillars, there were sparkling jewels of light.

People were kneeling near the altar—peasant women mostly, their bright handkerchiefs and bodices looking gayer than ever in the red and gold light. It gave color even to the men's brown homespun and sheepskin trousers. Nowhere among them could Shane see Paulo da Gama's tall figure and yellow hair and beard.

'He might be in the chapel,' Shane thought, and turned towards it.

The stone figures of King Joän and Queen Philippa lay hand in hand on their high tombs. Because Philippa was an English

Princess, the arms of England as well as those of Portugal were carved on each coffin. There was a wreath of wild English roses carved around the Queen's tomb. Shane moved over towards Prince Enrique's tomb with its cross and sphere—the Prince's device—and stood looking up at the quiet figure.

'He wasn't like other princes,' Shane thought. 'Fighting he didn't care for. He wanted to sail better than other men—not kill people better. At that he might be right. A good fight is pleasant once in a while, but to see strange lands—that's better than cutting and stabbing and getting bloody noses from someone's fist. And perhaps being shut up in a prison afterwards.'

The Prince's face looked peaceful and kind in the dim afternoon glow.

'I'd have liked him,' Shane thought. 'He liked stars and children and ripe olives. He worked as hard as any of his servants, but he had time to carve a boat for a little girl.'

'Dennis would be a prince like that,' Shane said aloud, speaking in Gaelic again.

He knelt down by Prince Enrique's tomb to say a prayer for Dennis, shut away out of the spring sunshine in that dark prison in Setubal; for Dennis, who liked birds and flowers and drew them so well.

'Kind Prince, help me to set Dennis free,' said Shane, bowing his red head.

A voice above it said: 'Shane O'Connor! What brings you here?'

Shane jumped up and found himself looking into Paulo da Gama's kind eyes. Señor Paulo looked thin and pale, but his smile was the same as ever and his hair and beard were still like yellow silk. No two brothers could be more unlike each other than Vasco and Paulo da Gama, Shane thought.

He handed over Vasco's letter and told his story, speaking softly. The chanting of the monks was still going on.

'There's nothing like a good brother,' Paulo da Gama said, and was silent, looking up at Prince Enrique's tomb.

'I heard you ask the Prince to help you,' he added gently, 'and he will do so, I know. I was on the other side of the tomb praying too. Your voice was my answer. I will make peace with Nuno Calves for Dennis and myself as soon as I have the King's pardon. The great navigator has cleared our road for us. Let us thank him now, Shane. Then I must say goodbye to the kind monks, for they have helped me to bear these long days.'

The voices of the monks were away in the distance. The peasants were moving through the rainbow light to the door. The church was empty as Paulo da Gama and Shane knelt before the high altar. They stayed there until the last note of the chanting voices had died away. Then Paulo da Gama led Shane through a quiet garden to the cloister.

The monks gathered around da Gama. They were sorry to see him go. There was an Irish monk among them, a fat, red-faced man from a Galway village not many miles from Shane's home. Brother Pedro, his name was. He took Shane into the great vaulted kitchen where the stone roof was black from the cooking fires and gave him bread and honey to eat.

'I keep the bees,' said Brother Pedro proudly. 'Here's apple-blossom honey. The first of the season.'

'Can you play the harp?' he asked, as Shane licked the last of the delicious stickiness from his fingers.

'If I had one,' said Shane.

'Take this, then,' Brother Pedro said, pulling something out from behind a door.

The leather case was worn and shabby. The strings were limp, the gilding dull and dusty, but it was an Irish harp.

'It belonged to one of our brothers. He gave it to me when he went away because I loved the music, but my fingers are stiff now and the skill is gone out of them,' said the monk as Shane blew the dust off it.

'It needs only for the strings to be tightened,' Shane said, doing it swiftly. He put his chin against it, half laughing, half singing. 'I'll make you talk in a minute, my beauty,' he crooned. 'Now what have you to say for yourself, my jewel?'

He swept his long fingers over the strings, listening, tightening a string, then loosening another.

'Speak pretty now for the good brother. Sweetly, sweetly. That's better.'

It was in tune now, and the notes ran out from under Shane's fingers like water sliding over smooth stones.

'Small children like to dance on the yellow sand to this tune. Do you remember it, Brother, and the blue waves splashing in?' he asked, thumping one foot to the beat of it.

Brother Pedro nodded. Then he set his foot thumping too. At last he whirled around with his white robe swinging.

'And you won't have forgotten this song,' Shane said, and sang:

> *'Diarmid was a traitor,*
> *A traitor to his prince.*
> *He brought strangers into Ireland,*
> *And they've been there ever since.'*

Brother Pedro kept on jigging up and down and joined in with a hearty voice:

'*Brought Saxons into Ireland*
To steal our fields of green'

'Is there a bull in the kitchen? What is this roaring?' came a voice from the door.

Brother Pedro stopped dancing and turned redder in the face than ever. Paulo da Gama and the Abbot of Batalha were standing in the doorway.

The Abbot laughed.

'I always said that one Irishman was enough for any monastery,' he said. 'When there are two, they fight or bellow these songs. Or others that sound like two cats on the cloister roof. Our young harper may like to know that the church was built by an Irishman. Huguet, his name was. He played the harp himself, I've heard, in this very kitchen, and the brothers making cakes and pies and singing like larks in a cornfield.'

'We must go, Shane,' said Paulo da Gama, with his kind smile, 'though it's a pity to spoil the music.'

'Take the harp,' Brother Pedro said. 'It will only gather more dust here. Take it, boy. I've no doubt you're a cousin of my own, if we'd just the time to figure it out. Neighbors we are surely. Take the harp. I like to think of its voice sounding across the far seas where you're going.'

'I'm afraid it's only to Lisbon I'm going,' Shane said.

'I thought you'd go with Señor Paulo, since it's a voyage he's making, but never mind—take it anyway for the sake of old Ireland.'

'It will go farther than Lisbon,' Paulo da Gama said. 'My brother shall find a place for you on the ships. The harp, as the good brother said, will cheer us on.'

Shane hardly knew how he got back to the inn again. He was so excited by the idea that he might go on the voyage to

India that he forgot about Nuno Calves. He stared at Prince Enrique's map of Africa as if he could really see the country and its strange people. Señor Paulo had sailed along that coast. In his soft, slow voice he told Shane about it—the hot jungles, the queer trees, the apes with hair as red and bristly as Shane's own.

The long ride, the chicken cooked as Prince Enrique liked it with cream and paprika, the warm room, and Señor Paulo's voice all made Shane sleepy. He lay down on a bench under the map.

Paulo da Gama's voice grew softer and softer: 'No more creeping along that hot shore an inch at a time. If I know Vasco he'll sail boldly across the South Atlantic to the Cape. And he'll get safe to India by paths no man has sailed...'

SHE RODE A WHITE HORSE

ON THE way back to Lisbon the next morning Shane saw an old goat trotting about under some olive trees and said suddenly: 'Nuno Calves!'

'Yes, he looks like him,' Paulo da Gama said. 'But why spoil a fine morning with that name?'

'I saw him on the road yesterday. I was so tired last night I went to sleep without telling you. Joãn Coelho said—' Shane hesitated, and Paulo da Gama laughed.

'Young Coelho! He's as wise as a judge himself. What did he say?'

'That you mustn't get into another fight with Nuno Calves, because then the King would not pardon you. He said I'd better watch out and make you hide if I saw the Judge coming.'

'Well, I've been hiding a good many months,' Señor Paulo said cheerfully. 'A little more won't hurt me. This is no time to be a hero waving a sword. I've had time to be sorry I ever drew one. To tell the truth, Shane, I was a fool. There are better things to do in the world than fighting. Once I get my pardon

NICOLAU
COELHO

from the King, I'll go to Señor Calves as meek as any monk and make my peace with him—the old rascal!'

They trotted on to the pine woods at the fork in the road where Joãn had told them to wait. The road by which Joãn would come twisted up hill through the pines. A brook tumbled down through the valley below. Paulo da Gama and Shane led the horses down to it and let them drink. The noon sun was hot. It was pleasant to lie in the shade of the pines and rest and listen to the singing of the brook.

Shane dozed, but woke suddenly to hear Paulo da Gama saying: 'I hear horses. Run, Shane. Hide in the clump of young pines at the top of the hill and see whether it is our friends or someone else.'

Shane hurried up hill through the woods and stopped behind a bushy young pine at the edge of the road. He could hear horses' feet, the squeak of leather, and the jingle of metal from across the road. There was another noise that he could not understand. It sounded like a pig grunting—a pig that had its nose buried in dirt. Yet he was sure it was not a pig.

A man's voice, not very loud, said: 'Stop that noise or I'll finish you now!' and the grunting stopped.

'They're coming. Keep still, all of you. Keep your horses quiet till they come over the top of the hill. The two men in front are Coelho and his brother. Knock them down and we're all right,' he added a little louder.

Shane cautiously pushed two branches aside and looked through. Across the narrow horse-track, well hidden by the pines from anyone coming from the north, were six men on horses. One of them was the red-faced, pockmarked man—Nuno Calves's groom.

'I can't see the Judge—the old robber. That's queer,' Shane

thought as he stole back down the hill. His feet made little noise on the slippery pine needles. Halfway down he met Paulo da Gama.

'Nuno's men!' gasped Shane. 'Waiting to attack the Coelhos!'

'We'll just fight them first,' said Paulo da Gama calmly.

Both he and Shane forgot that they were supposed to be avoiding fights.

'Make plenty of noise,' Paulo da Gama said. 'Sound like as many as you can,' and he began running up hill calling: 'Come on, men! Swords out! Forward, Martin, Enrique, Pedro, Joãn!' and a whole string of names and orders.

Shane yelled and roared like at least six men: 'Coming, sir, Coming!' in Gaelic, English, and Portuguese.

He reached the road just in time to hear the pockmarked groom bellow at his men: 'Come on, you cowards! Will you stand still and let them kill you?'

'No, we won't,' shouted another. 'Come on, men!'

He turned his horse into the road towards Batalha, over which Shane had travelled that morning. Two of the other grooms galloped after him. Two followed the pockmarked one into the road.

A tall man on a black horse rode over the hilltop. Behind him was Joãn Coelho. The pockmarked groom charged straight at the man on the black horse, but he might as well have ridden at a stone tower. The groom's horse reared. Shane saw its rider whizz into a tangle of blackberry vines. There was a sound of swords ringing. Joãn was fighting with one of the grooms. The man on the black horse rode at the third one just as the rest of the Coelho party rode up the hill.

There was a girl in black and scarlet on a white horse; a girl with straight black eyebrows like Joãn's. Shane grabbed the scarlet bridle and tried to lead the horse away from the fighting. The girl lashed Shane's cheek with her whip. The horse jerked his head and dashed off in among the pines where the grooms had been hiding. Shane still held onto the bridle, although the girl kept cutting at his face and hands with her whip. Connemara, barking angrily, tried to catch the whip in his teeth.

'Down, Con! Señorita,' Shane gasped. 'I'm only trying to keep you out of the fight. I'm Joãn's friend.'

The whiplash stung his cheek again.

'I'm Joãn's friend. I'm Shane O'Connor!' he yelled again.

The girl heard him this time.

She lowered her whip and said crossly: 'Why didn't you say so?'

Shane rubbed his face, on which there were several large red welts, with one hand, but he still held the bridle with the other.

'I was only trying to keep you from getting hurt in the fight,' he said.

'Yes, the first chance there is to see any fun! After I've been shut up in that old convent for months!'

She swung her whip again. Shane raised his arm, but it was the horse she hit this time. The bridle was yanked out of Shane's hand as the white horse bounded back towards the road.

Shane started to follow the white horse, but stopped suddenly. He heard again that sound like a pig grunting. Then it changed suddenly and sounded like a cat whining. He hurried towards it. Tied to a big pine with a gag in his mouth was Nuno Calves. His gray goat beard moved up and down as he grunted and whimpered. His yellow face had turned purple. His gray eyes stared at Shane as if they would pop out of his head. His own grooms had robbed him, bound him, left him to die while they robbed the Coelhos.

Shane pulled out a knife, cut the ropes that bound the old man, and pulled the gag out of his mouth.

Nuno Calves sank down on the pine needles breathing hard.

After a few moments he gasped out weakly: 'You—saved my life. Reward you—but grooms—robbed me. Tied me up. Come—Setubal—pay you.'

'You can pay me now, Señor,' Shane said. 'My master is Paulo da Gama. The King has pardoned him—only he said Señor Paulo must make his peace with you. My brother Dennis was with Señor Paulo that day. He hurt no one, but it's in your prison he is. Set him free, Señor, and there need be no talk of reward between you and me.'

Nuno Calves listened to Shane so quietly that Shane was not sure that the old man had understood him.

At last Calves muttered: 'Da Gama—let him come here.'

Shane went back to the road. The fight was over. The pock-marked groom had been picked out of his thorny nest and was now sitting backwards on a mule with his hands and feet bound. The one who had fought with Joãn was lying on the bank with blood running down his cheek. The third groom was on his knees in front of the tall man, who looked like a giant even off his horse. The tall man was Nicolau Coelho, Joãn's brother, and brother of the girl in black and scarlet. The girl stuck out her tongue at Shane as he appeared. There was another girl perched on a big bay horse. She was a tiny, fair-haired girl with enormous blue-gray eyes.

Paulo da Gama was standing beside her and she was say-ing in a quick, sweet voice that made Shane think of spar-rows chirping: 'Oh, I was so frightened, so frightened. Oh, Señor Paulo, we heard such noises like bulls. But no one is hurt except that poor man whose head is cut. And the one kneeling looks so sad. Tell Señor Nicolau to let him go. I'm sure he is sorry.'

'I'm sure he is sorry he didn't have a chance to rob you, Señorita Catarina,' Paulo da Gama said. 'This is Shane O'Connor, who frightened the robbers with those bellows of his. This lady is Señorita Catarina de Ataide, Shane. Her family and ours are old friends. And this is Joãn's sister, Señorita Luisa Coelho.'

'I have met the Señorita already,' Shane said, bowing politely.

'We are grateful to you for helping us,' said Catarina de Ataide, leaning over to look down at Shane, 'even if you did frighten us so. And you have been hurt in the fight. Your poor face!'

'Forgive me for frightening you, Señorita,' Shane said hastily. 'My face,' he added, looking at Luisa Coelho, 'got hurt while I was running away from a wildcat in the woods. At least I thought it was a wildcat.'

Luisa Coelho's cheeks turned slightly pink.

'And what was it really?' she asked, swinging her scarlet whip.

'That, Señorita, is something I must tell Señor Paulo in private, if you will forgive us.'

'What is this nonsense about wildcats, Shane?' Paulo da Gama asked.

Shane took his master aside and told him about Nuno Calves.

'He wants to see you. He's only a little way down this path. He knows you saved him. Oh, Señor Paulo, make him set Dennis free.'

'Go back and tell Nicolau Coelho to tie up those men. We'll see what the Judge wants to do with them. Perhaps he can make room for them in that prison of his.'

Paulo da Gama swung off down the path.

Shane gave Señor Paulo's message to Nicolau Coelho.

'So you're the boy Joãn keeps talking about,' the tall man said.

Like his sister and Joãn, Nicolau Coelho had straight black eyebrows that almost met over his nose, but they were thicker than theirs, his nose was like the beak of a hawk, and his eyes were blue-gray instead of brown like theirs. His face was sunburned where it was not covered with a silky black beard and a long drooping moustache. He smiled pleasantly down on Shane as he thanked him for helping them. He did not say anything about the red marks from his sister's whip that still decorated Shane's face. Shane was grateful for that.

When the party set off again, Nuno Calves rode beside Paulo da Gama, talking to him as if they had always been the best of friends. The grooms, guarded by some of Coelho's servants, followed.

'Take care of Catarina, Joãn,' Nicolau Coelho said, flinging himself on his tall black horse. 'Shane, will you escort my sister? The rest of you men follow Señor O'Connor.'

He rode forward to his place at the head of the little troop.

The whole line moved forward with saddles creaking, bits jingling, mule-bells tinkling, hoofs padding softly on the sandy road.

'Forward, my little angels!' cried the mule-driver.

'I suppose he meant me,' said Luisa Coelho, turning her brown eyes on Shane.

'No doubt,' Shane said coldly, and they rode on in silence.

'What's that queer thing thumping around on your back?' Luisa asked after a while.

'My harp.'

Shane wanted to go on and tell her about Brother Pedro, but he remembered that he was not going to speak any more than he could help. He rode on trying to look dignified. It is a little difficult to do so if you have rumpled red hair, a freckled face marked with the lash of a whip, old sheepskin riding-trousers, and a harp in a shabby leather case bouncing around on your back.

Shane thought: 'If I'd only worn my new suit she wouldn't laugh at me. How can Joãn and Captain Nicolau have such a hateful sister?'

'I thought only girls played harps!' Luisa Coelho went on. 'They tried to teach me in the convent, but I wouldn't learn. Harps are only for ladylike girls—like Catarina.'

'That shows all you know!' Shane burst out angrily. 'Why, in Ireland the harpers are so grand that kings are proud to have them set foot in their halls. My father had his own harper that could sing every tale of the old wars in Ireland. It was himself taught me. A big man as tall as your brother there, with a red beard that blew in the wind like a flame and a voice that could shake the stones on the mountains was Patrick. Harping's ladylike, is it?'

He paused for breath and the girl said: 'I thought I could make you stop sulking. Honestly, Shane, I'm sorry I hit you. And I wish I could have heard that harper.'

Shane could never stay angry long. He began to laugh.

'Oh, never mind that!' he said. 'No wonder you thought I was a ruffian and were afraid.'

'I was *not* afraid,' Luisa said, angry in her turn. 'I just wanted to see what was going on. It would take more than you with that red wolf at your heels to stop me!'

Shane did not like to hear Con described as a red wolf. He said stiffly: 'You'll get into trouble that way some day. It isn't proper for girls to be where there's fighting.'

Luisa's brown eyes flashed under the silky black band that her eyebrows made when she scowled.

'Not proper!' she burst out. 'You sound like the Mother Superior at the convent. How would *you* like it if all you were allowed to do was to work on tapestry and learn to hold a silver fork prettily, and how low to curtsy to a countess? When I want to be out hunting and hawking and climbing trees and swimming and fishing—how would you like it?'

'Not a bit,' Shane admitted. 'But I'm a boy and you're—'

'If you say that again I'm afraid I'll forget my pretty convent manners,' Luisa Coelho said, swinging her scarlet whip.

'Oh, do you remember them?' asked Shane. 'Indeed I'd like to see them.'

Fortunately at this point in the conversation Joãn Coelho rode back saying: 'Change places with me, Shane. Señorita de Ataide wants to talk to you.'

Shane took Joãn's place at Catarina de Ataide's side. She was very polite. She kept her blue and silver whip where it belonged. She admired Connemara. He was, she said, the most beautiful dog she had ever seen. How sweet it was, the way he always followed at Shane's heels! Dogs were man's best friends. Didn't Señor O'Connor think so?

She looked very pink and pretty, especially when she asked if Shane had ever seen Señor Vasco da Gama's gray wolfhounds. They must have missed their master. Didn't Señor O'Connor think so? It was just a year and three months that very day that Señor Vasco went to Africa. It was her birthday-that was how she happened to remember. She wished Shane would play his harp. Music, she said, was the greatest of arts. Didn't Señor O'Connor think so? And to think that Señor O'Connor's father had had his own harper! He must have been a great prince then—was he like King Manuel? It was sad that he had died and someone had stolen his lands. Joãn had told her that. But of course it was pleasant for Joãn that Shane had come to Lisbon. Joãn admired Shane so much!

In fact her manners were a great credit to the convent. Yet somehow Shane found himself listening with only one ear. The other was trying to hear what Joãn and Luisa were laughing at behind him. By the time the party reached Lisbon, Shane felt as if that ear were a foot long and twisted back of his head.

Somehow he found the last part of the journey very dull.

Chapter 7

PRISON IN SETUBAL

Dennis O'Connor wiped the sweat off his forehead and put down his pen. The day had been hot and the stones of the prison seemed to have shut all the heat inside his cell. The light from the iron-barred window above his head was fading. The square of sky changed from blue to pearl color as he looked at it.

Dennis rubbed his tired eyes and lay down on the heap of rushes that softened the hardness of the stone floor a little. His head ached from writing all day and from the stuffiness of his cell. He looked very thin as he lay there. His face in the fading light was almost the color of the paper on which he had been writing.

A key grated in the lock of his door and the jailer's voice roared: 'Come into the court, King O'Connor. The banquet is ready for Your Majesty.'

The prisoners ate at a rough table in the courtyard. Dennis sat down on a bench beside a huge negro. The banquet consisted of wooden bowls full of a sour-smelling, greasy stew and hunks of soggy gray bread.

The jailer said: 'Your Majesty is not eating anything. You don't seem to like our roast peacock.'

Dennis did not like being called 'Your Majesty.' It had never seemed very funny and he'd been tired of the joke for a long time. He had lost his temper once and said to the jailer that his—Dennis's—ancestors had been kings in Connaught when the jailer's grandfathers were already jailers. It was a foolish speech and he had paid for it in many ways. Being laughed at was only one of them, and far from the worst. Being forced to eat the jail food was bad. It was not safe to leave anything in his bowl. It would only be served to him next day, tasting worse than ever. And if he refused then, the jailer might take away his pen and papers. Dennis dreaded that worse than being kept in his cell all day, or being lashed with a whip, an exercise the jailer enjoyed.

He dipped his piece of bread into the stew and tried to eat it. When the jailer turned his head away, Dennis slid his bowl along to the negro and whispered: 'Eat it, Fernan. I can't.'

The negro, Fernan Martinez, had been polishing his bowl with the crust of his bread. He pushed the empty bowl to Dennis and began on the full one. He dipped his huge black fingers into the bowl, crammed the meat and onions into his mouth, then tipped his woolly head back and poured the liquid down his throat. He finished by sopping up the last of the juice with Dennis's bread. He chewed loudly, showing enormous white teeth and turning every now and then to smile at Dennis.

Down at the other end of the table a man with a ragged red velvet cloak slung over one shoulder was talking loud and pounding the table with his fist.

'Believe it or not, Machado,' he said to the tall, brown-bearded man next to him, 'they were four to one against me, but the first I ran through with my sword, the next I cut across the fingers so that he dropped his club and ran howling, the third I knocked down with my fist. I tripped and threw the fourth into the water, and the fifth—'

'You said there were four!' Machado remarked.

'Oh, the fifth was so small I forgot him,' the man in the red cloak said. 'I just picked him up and squeezed him till his ribs cracked.'

'Didn't any of them get away, Veloso?' asked a fat, bald man named Rodriguez who was sitting beside Machado.

'It might be there were one or two,' Veloso said carelessly. 'It was dark at the time. The King's enemies they were, every one of them, yet he lets me, a soldier just off Vasco da Gama's ship, be thrown into jail for any such trifling cracking of ribs and heads! Is that justice? I ask you, is that justice? Why, I saved King Manuel's life when he was a boy. A wolf attacked him and I fought it with my bare hands. It was like this:'—Veloso got up from the table and stood up swinging his cloak in front of him—'I saw the wolf coming and I said to the little chap who's King now, "Get behind me, little one," I said. "Don't be afraid," I said. "Veloso's in front of you."

'So this wolf runs in, snapping his teeth, and the eyes—such flashes of green fire they shot they lit up the dark place we were in. Well, I had my cloak. I've fought bulls with it. This very cloak here. Would a wolf trouble me? Even though he came in snarling with foam dripping from his gray jaws? Not me, not Veloso!

'I swung my cloak—so. And so. A wolf is quicker than a bull. A bull would have plunged past me. But the wolf ran straight into the cloak—which was just what I planned. I simply wrapped it around him and choked him at my leisure. He bit through it—here's the place!'

Veloso ran his fingers through the hole and sat down.

'I wouldn't wear another cloak even if the King himself gave it to me. Not that he offered me one. Just lets me be thrown into prison,' he grumbled.

'Veloso fine liar,' the big negro whispered, grinning at Dennis. 'Best liar in Portugal, I think. You think?'

'I haven't heard them all,' Dennis said. 'But I think he must be one of the best!'

Veloso went on bragging. Machado and Rodriguez squatted down on the stone pavement and began throwing dice. Fernan Martinez walked around the table picking up bread crusts. Fernan never got enough food for his big body. He was bare to the waist and his ribs looked as if they would cut through his dark skin. He owned no clothes except a ragged pair of brown homespun breeches and a shirt that Dennis had given him. The shirt was not made for a giant. When Fernan wore it—he did so only on Sundays when the priest came to the prison—it left a large band of black between the bottom of it and the top of the breeches. The sleeves reached only a little below his elbows.

To Fernan, however, it was a splendid garment, because Dennis had given it to him. The other men might joke and call Dennis 'King O'Connor' and 'Your Most Worshipful Majesty,' but to Fernan, Dennis really was a king. Everything that Dennis did was wonderful to the negro. He could not read, but he would take Dennis's writing and—as likely as not holding it upside down—run his black eyes over it, nodding his woolly head wisely. When Dennis drew a bird or an animal that Fernan had seen before, he would put his thick black finger on it, laugh, dance up and down on his big flat feet, and tell its name in Portuguese, Arabic, and his own language. Dennis was learning Arabic from Fernan and also the language of the African jungle from which the negro had come.

Fernan swallowed the last crumb of bread and walked over to Dennis, who was sitting on a bench in a corner of the courtyard looking up at the sky. The clouds that were drifting across the sky had turned to a bright new gold. Fernan waved his hand towards them and said: 'Gold ship, sailing away. Señor Dennis and Fernan sail in it.'

The cloud did look a little like a ship with red flags flying from the masts.

Dennis smiled, but he said wearily: 'We'll never get out of here, Fernan. Everyone's forgotten us.'

The negro looked so gloomy at this that Dennis added hastily: 'I didn't mean it. Of course they'll be letting us out sometime. I'll sing to you, Fernan, some tale you'd like to hear. That way the time would pass a little quicker. Would you like to hear how Ruadri O'Connor met a leprechaun? A little man no higher than your knee, Fernan, that made Ruadri a grand pair of boots as tall as the shoemaker himself? It goes this way—'

Dennis began crooning softly. It was quiet in the courtyard except for the click of dice on the stones and the rise and fall of Dennis's low voice.

Suddenly Fernan held up his hand.

'I hear horses—many horses,' he said.

Dennis listened, but he could hear nothing but Rodriguez rattling the dice in his fat hand and snores from Veloso, who had put his head on the table and dozed off.

'Many horses,' Fernan repeated. 'They come fast up the soft road. Ker-thumpety, thump, their feet go in the dust. Now they turn by the wineshop. The road is hard there. Ker-lippety, klop, go the hooves... Now they go slow over the bridge. Kloom. Kloom. Kloom. Faster now over stones... Ker-langety, klank... klank... Kling, kling, kling.'

'I hear them now,' Dennis said.

Rodriguez and Machado got up, forgetting the dice. Veloso shook himself out of his sleep and slung his red cloak around him. Everyone in the courtyard stood still, listening.

A troop of horses might mean nothing to them. It might be only a party of merchants late on the road. But it might be more prisoners, or soldiers. No one dared to think it might mean freedom.

'I think they're going by,' muttered Dennis, but as he spoke the horses slowed up with a slow kling, kling, kling on the stones outside. Then came pounding on the gate and loud shouts for the jailer.

Dennis saw him hurry towards the gate, swinging the big key. A boy ran behind him carrying a torch. It was dark now in the court, pitch black under the arched gateway. The jailer looked out through the peep-hole. Then the door turned on hinges that screeched.

'Only, Judge, more prisoners,' Fernan said in a disappointed growl, and moved close to Dennis in a dark corner.

The torchlight fell on Nuno Calves's face, turning it orange. Behind him were soldiers and three men with their hands bound.

Dennis leaned against the wall in the shadows. A visit from Nuno Calves was not a happy event. Calves had an unpleasant habit of holding a red-hot iron close to your hand as he asked you questions. Dennis still had a red scar on his hand from a burn. The Judge had brought the iron down hard, because Dennis would not tell where Paulo da Gama was hiding. Luckily it was his right hand. Nuno Calves did not know that Dennis was left-handed, so Dennis could still draw and write while his right hand was healing.

The scar on it seemed to burn again as he saw the Judge's face in the torchlight.

'Anyway, I didn't tell him where Señor Paulo was,' Dennis thought proudly.

The jailer's boy ran around sticking lighted torches into iron holders. Riders jumped off their horses and left them to drink at the watering trough. The whole courtyard was full of light and noise and smoke.

Suddenly through the smoke Dennis saw a face he knew. It was his brother Shane. Behind Shane, sitting quietly on his horse and looking around the court with his gentle gaze, was Paulo da Gama.

Dennis said hoarsely to Fernan Martinez: 'He's caught Señor Paulo and Shane. You said there were more prisoners, Fernan. You were right. There they are.'

Dennis leaned his head against the wall and shut his eyes for a moment. The wound on his hand was for nothing, he thought.

Then he heard Shane's voice calling: 'Dennis! Dennis! There he is, Señor Paulo. I see him.'

Dennis looked up, saw Shane throw himself off his horse and run towards him; saw Paulo da Gama following; felt one of Shane's strong arms around his neck; heard Shane's voice in Gaelic say: 'You're free, Dennis lad. Free to sail the seas and travel the wide world entirely!'

Dennis stared at Shane, only half believing him.

Then Paulo da Gama's kind voice said: 'It's true, Dennis. I have made my peace with the Judge. You are to come to India with me—if you like.'

'India!' Dennis muttered. 'India?'

'Yes, India. Listen if you don't believe me.'

The jailer was bellowing above the sound of voices and the noise of moving horses: 'Silence! Listen to our lord, Nuno Calves!'

Nuno Calves, still perched on a big gray horse, rode into the middle of the courtyard and began to speak. He told how King Manuel had decided to send ships to discover India; how he had chosen Vasco da Gama to be Commander of the Fleet; how Paulo da Gama had been pardoned by the goodness of the King and would be captain of one of the ships. Calves did not say anything about how he had been found tied to a tree half-choked, or about the money that Paulo had paid him to make peace between them, but Shane whispered to Dennis about it as the Judge's voice brayed along.

'And to the judges of his prisons His Illustrious Majesty sends this word,' said Nuno Calves. 'His Majesty says that since there will be many dangers on this voyage such as visits to savage peoples and exploring strange places, he will send on the ships some men from his prisons. They will be sent ashore on dangerous errands. If they come home safely, the King will pardon and reward them. Now in this prison are certain followers of Paulo da Gama. His Majesty graciously offers these men a chance to follow Captain da Gama if they wish. Those who prefer our comfortable prison here at Setubal to being eaten by savages and crocodiles are welcome to stay here until their fines are paid.'

Nuno laughed in his mule's bray, and went on to read the names of the prisoners who might be freed for dangerous service with the expedition to India.

'Step forward,' he called, 'those who are anxious to be crocodile meat.'

Dennis heard Veloso's name and saw the soldier swagger forward with his red cloak swinging. Machado and Rodriguez followed him. Other names were called, but no one moved.

'Fernan Martinez,' called the Judge.

Fernan's big figure moved out of the shadow. Except for his white teeth and the whites of his rolling eyes, he looked like a bronze statue as he stood in the flickering torchlight.

Last of all Nuno Calves screeched: 'Dennis O'Connor,' and Dennis followed Fernan into the ring of light and smoke.

Nuno Calves grinned at the prisoners and creaked out: 'Well, it seems all the fools are not yet dead! You are free to go and sail across seas of boiling pitch, to die of strange fevers, to be swallowed by serpents, or be boiled for dinner by savages. Good-bye, gentlemen, and—a pleasant journey to you!'

CHAPTER 8

ROSES AND THISTLES

THE weeks before the ships sailed slipped by quickly. When Paulo da Gama and his party came back from Setubal, Nicolau Coelho's ship, the Berrio, was ready for the voyage. The Berrio had already sailed along the coast of Africa and had proved to be a swift and steady ship. Vasco da Gama's ship, the San Gabriel, and Paulo da Gama's ship, the San Raphael, had been lying half finished in the King's shipyard. Now the carpenters, blacksmiths, and sailmakers were busy fitting them out.

Each ship was given two sets of sails, ropes, and cables. Cannon and powder and shot were put on board. There was also merchandise to be used in trade—cloth of different kinds, gold necklaces and bracelets, silver bowls and pitchers, swords, daggers, and shields, mirrors and little bells. All these things and food for a hundred and seventy men took up so much space that Vasco da Gama bought a fourth ship for a store-ship to make the first part of the journey with them. He ordered the sailors to learn rope-making, sail-making, carpentry, and black-smithing while they were waiting for the ships to be finished.

VASCO
DA GAMA

Shane, instead of studying the stars, came home to the Street of the Rat with his hands covered with pitch, because he had been learning how to fix the seams of a ship so that she would not leak.

Zacuto groaned over Shane's pitchy hands.

'You do work that any loafer on the wharves could do, while in these few weeks I might still knock some wisdom about the stars into that thick head of yours.'

'My thick head has all the wisdom it can hold now,' Shane said, laughing. 'And indeed I am grateful and will not forget what little I know. Besides,' he added proudly, 'Señor Vasco himself has seen the charts I drew for the King and so has Señor Nicolau. And I am to be cabin-boy on the Berrio and help Señor Nicolau with the charts besides. He says I know more than he does!'

Zacuto groaned again.

'The stars help the Berrio, then! With your help she's as likely to land at the North Pole as India. I thought you were going with Paulo da Gama on the San Raphael.'

'I wish I were,' Shane said. 'Everyone would like best to go with Señor Paulo, but Dennis goes with him. One wild Irishman on a ship is enough, Señor Vasco says. I hoped Joãn would be with me on the Berrio, but he is to be Señor Vasco's cabin-boy. I don't envy him.'

'Why not?'

'Señor Vasco da Gama is enough to frighten the hair right off your head. When he looks at me out of those black eyes of his, I feel as if he knew what I've had for dinner and what I'm thinking. He's like an eagle ready to pounce with that hooked nose, and those hands like steel hooks. And when he's angry his voice is like an eagle's scream. How the men hop when they hear it! I wouldn't be Joãn for all the pearls in India.'

'You talk foolishly,' growled Zacuto. 'What would you like for a captain-major? One of those pretty young men at the court who write verses and smell like lilies and roses? They coo and chatter like pigeons. They hate rough men. The sea makes them sick. Before this voyage is half over you'll be glad you have a man in command, a man with an eagle's scream and courage, not a poet with a dove's heart.'

'I know he's a brave man, but so are Señor Paulo and Señor Nicolau,' Shane said. 'They don't frighten their men half to death.'

'Yes, they are brave men and good captains. But the voyage to India needs something more than ordinary courage. You will see.'

'Is that a prophecy? Do the stars say so?' Shane asked with his impish smile.

'Yes, you rogue! The stars say so and you have seen that I know how to read them,' Zacuto said good-naturedly, pulling Shane's red hair.

Rachel, who had been listening quietly, asked: 'Did you hear what Father has given Señor Vasco, Shane? The big wooden astrolabe—his best one; two small brass ones—the one you dropped, but Father had it straightened; a fine compass, and a copy of Zacuto's Perpetual Almanack. One of the new printed ones.'

'It is a present any king might be proud to give,' Shane said.

'Nonsense,' the astrologer said hastily. 'I'm just a stingy old Jew. I gave the things because it is good to have powerful friends.'

'I suppose you took me in when I was starving for the same reason,' Shane remarked.

'No. It was because you could draw. And you are to bring me back maps of the east coast of Africa and of India to pay me for all my trouble and for your food. For you have eaten like a wolf—no, two wolves—not to mention your red dog, who eats like three more.'

Zacuto spoke crossly, as he always did when Shane tried to thank him for his kindness.

'And what will happen to the red dog when you are gone?' Zacuto went on. 'Because my wife says he brings in too much mud and shakes himself all over her best tapestries and her velvet dress from Flanders, and though I don't mind mud in my laboratory and having him knock over jars of drugs with his tail—'

Shane blushed and said that Joãn's sister was going to keep Connemara for him.

'She likes Con. So do her uncles, who are fond of hunting birds. Luisa is to live with them while her brothers are gone. She has no mother and father. Her uncles are not married, so Con will not be bothering any ladies with his muddy paws. I will take him to the Coelhos the day we sail.'

'And speaking of the Coelhos,' Zacuto went on, 'tell your young friend with the long legs that he is not to play the guitar under my daughter's window. There is already enough noise down in the Street of the Rat. Cats we have plenty of them. Also fish-sellers screaming. Milkmen bellowing we have, and driving cows and goats and milking them on my doorstep. Musicians we don't need. If there is any more singing about how my daughter is like a fair, white rose, then it is time she wore a veil and married some respectable old man. Tell Señor Joãn Coelho that, please. Cabin-boys—guitars—squawking—' Zacuto bounced out of the room.

'Was this what he sang?' Shane asked, picking up his harp.

He touched the strings gently and sang the words gently enough not to offend the astrologer's sensitive ears:

> *'High on that thorny rose-tree*
> *There is a fair white rose.*
> *Down here no one can reach it;*
> *Above there no one goes.'*

'Yes, that was it,' Rachel said. 'He looks like a black spider under my window. He is very silly.'

'He sent you this,' Shane said, 'but I don't suppose you want it.'

He held out a big blue thistle.

'Why should I want a prickly old thistle?'

'Perhaps because you're prickly yourself. Or perhaps because this is the evening when all the girls in Lisbon set their candlesticks in their windows and burn thistles in them. If the edges of the flowers are still blue in the morning, then their lovers are true.'

'I think such things are very foolish,' Rachel said, but she took the thistle.

Shane looked up at her window as he went to work early the next morning. The thistle was there, and there was still a little blue fringe around the flower.

Shane ran down the street humming the tune of the song about the fair white rose. He added a new verse and sang it as he went past Señor Affonso Coelho's house.

> *'My thistle burned till morning*
> *And yet it still shows blue.*
> *Now that the sun is shining*
> *I know my love is true.'*

There was no thistle in Luisa's window, but there was someone standing at it. Shane thought it was Joãn and called up to him.

Luisa Coelho's voice said crossly, but not very loud: 'If you just please won't wake up the whole house,' and then added more pleasantly: 'Wait, I'm coming.'

Shane waited. He heard a door shut quietly at the side of the house. Inside the garden wall there was a scrambling sound. The branches of a tree near the wall began to wave and rustle. Luisa, dressed in an old suit of Joãn's, appeared on top of the wall. She swung herself down, landing on the stone pavement as lightly as a cat.

'You ought not to be here,' Shane said sternly.

'Now, don't talk like my new governess,' Luisa said. 'You sound just like her—when she's awake, that is. Fortunately she's a fine sleeper. She hates to get up in the morning, and eating makes her sleepy too. She always sleeps after lunch and dinner. Otherwise I'd have no peace. So let's come along.'

'Come along where?'

'I only want to go down and see them building the ships. Nicolau says it's no place for a girl, but now I'm a boy, so it's all right, isn't it?' Luisa jumped up and grabbed some cherries from a branch hanging over the wall, and began tossing them up and catching them in her mouth... 'Open your mouth and I'll give you some. I'm a good shot. No? Well get your own then... I don't want to wait to see the ships when they're all painted and trimmed with flags. I want to hear the hammers pound and smell the hot pitch and see the smiths making the big anchors.'

'Your brothers won't like it.'

'That's not your business. I'm going anyway. If you don't

want to walk on the same street with me, you don't need to. It's my only chance. Nicolau and Joãn both have to go to the palace this morning. I'll be back in plenty of time to do my embroidery. I'm doing a dove's toenails now. Wouldn't you love to sit indoors a day like this doing a dove's toenails, Shane?'

Shane gave in. There was no use doing anything else!

Work was just beginning in the yard. The San Raphael, launched, rigged, and partly loaded, lay beside the dock. Men were still pounding oakum into the seams of the San Gabriel and covering it with pitch. The little Berrio was anchored out in the river.

The watchman of the San Raphael knew Shane and let them go on board. Shane showed Luisa everything—the figure of the saint on the bow; the towering 'castles' where the guns were and where the officers had their cabins; the javelins and spears and axes; the big water barrels and the coils of rope. He even took her down below where the provisions and goods for trade were stored. It was dark among the bales and casks.

'There are lots of hiding-places down here—for rats, I mean,' Luisa said.

'They'll have to get a cat. Every ship has a cat. Rachel has given me one already for the Berrio. A striped cat named Hepzibah. She's caught two rats already,' said Shane.

'Then I shall give Joãn my black tomcat for the San Gabriel. His name is Señor Patapito. Though I must say I think it's hard that the cat can go to India and I must stay at home.'

Shane said it was hard, but that Luisa had better go home now before the fat governess woke up.

'Yes,' sighed Luisa. 'It's nice of you to think of it! I must go back to my doves. Good-bye, Shane.'

'That's one of the young Coelho boys, I suppose. They all look alike,' the watchman said as Luisa's thin black figure slipped through the gate. 'Will he be going with his brother?'

'No,' Shane said. 'Too young.'

'Oh, all those Coelhos are born in the water like dolphins. They swim and sail before they can walk. This one won't want to be left behind.'

'True enough,' Shane remarked, and went over to help the caulkers work on the flat bottom of the San Gabriel.

It was Saturday, the seventh of July, 1497, when the ships sailed. There was a hot south wind blowing up the Tagus. The city, steaming in the heat, was no place for King Manuel. He had gone to a cool palace in the hills, but there were plenty of people to watch the ships spread their sails and start down the river. As they moved slowly against the head wind, they were a fine sight with the red crosses on their new white sails, and the banners flapping at their mastheads. Everything about them shone in the hot sun as they cut across the silver ripples of the Tagus.

The Berrio, swiftest of the ships, was the last to leave her moorings. Her three-cornered sails made it easier for her to sail against the wind than it was for the heavier square-rigged ships. Shane was one of the last to go on board. He had stopped to leave Connemara at the Coelhos' house.

Con must have known that he was going to be left behind. Shane called and whistled all through Zacuto's house and garden, but there was no sign of the dog anywhere. At last Shane found him lying under a chest in a dark corner. Con gazed up at his master with a miserable look in his soft golden eyes. Shane could hardly bear to meet Connemara's gaze nor watch the feeble thumping of the dog's long tail.

'Come out, Con,' Shane said.

His throat felt tight and sore as the dog came out from under the chest, dragging his hind legs and drooping his tail so that its tip touched the ground. There was no one else in the house. Everyone had gone down to the docks. Shane knelt down and put his arms around Con for a moment.

'We'd better—say good-bye here, old man, as long as we're alone,' he said.

Con seemed to understand. He put his cool nose against Shane's cheek for a moment, but he made no sound. When Shane got up and moved towards the door, Con followed him with his head up and his tail waving proudly.

The only person left at the Coelhos' was the old lame cook. She said the family had all gone to see the ships sail. The governess had slept late and had just now gone running down the street, after scolding the cook because she couldn't remember whether the Señorita had gone with Captain Nicolau or with her uncle, Señor Affonso.

'I told her that it was my business to cook and hers to chase the Señorita,' the cook said. 'If I cooked no better than she does her work, we'd all starve.'

'This is the dog the Señorita is going to keep for me,' Shane said. 'He eats—'

'Run if you don't want to miss your ship.' The cook waved her fat hands towards the river. 'I fed dogs before you were born. Go through the garden out the back gate and past the warehouse. It's nearer.'

Shane ran through empty alleys and streets. As he came to the docks he heard a sound of wailing and moaning. The wharves and the river shore were crowded with people, and most of them were sobbing or crying. Afterwards people called that shore the Place of Tears. Shane had to push his way through a crowd of weeping women.

'They will be burned in the Sea of Pitch!' groaned one.

'Not one of them will ever return!' another cried.

'Sea monsters will swallow them,' wailed a third.

Shane thought: 'Well, a cheerful send-off this is! If I'm not drowned in tears before I start, I'm lucky.'

The Berrio's boat was still at the end of the dock. Fernan Martinez was standing up in the bow looking at the crowd.

'Whoopee! There he is!' Fernan called, showing his big white teeth in a wide grin. 'There's Señor Shane! Almost went to India without you, Señor Shane!'

'Coming!' Shane shouted.

He looked around for Luisa Coelho, but she was not there. He saw Rachel Zacuto and her father standing at the top of the stone steps where the boat was lying.

'I told you she was a remarkable girl,' the astrologer said proudly. 'The only girl in Lisbon who isn't dropping tears into the Tagus.'

'I don't see anything to cry about,' Rachel said. 'Shane's coming back.'

'Of course he is,' said Zacuto hurriedly. 'Here, boy. These may help.'

He thrust a compass and a small astrolabe into Shane's hand.

Shane tried to thank him, but Zacuto said quickly: 'Nonsense, they are no use to me. I don't want them. Notice at what point the Pole Star disappears from the sky, and when you see it again. Don't keep the boat waiting. You will see some fine stars—especially the Southern Cross, which you will please draw carefully. You've been a good boy, Shane.'

The astrologer turned away and blew his nose on a star-spangled silk handkerchief.

Shane said: 'Good-bye, Señor. Good-bye, Rachel. I'll take care of the cat,' and jumped into the boat.

The pilot, Pero Escolar, growled: 'One more minute, my young rooster, and you'd never have seen India. Shove off, there. Row, and put your backs into it.'

Shane dug his oar deep into the water. The wailing and sobbing on shore grew louder. Then it began to fade away, but just as they drew near to the Berrio it changed to shouts. Shane heard Rachel's voice calling him. He turned his head. Everyone on the dock was pointing at something that was moving through the water, something rusty-brown that pushed across the ripples more and more slowly.

It was Connemara thrusting his head bravely through the water, but swimming more and more slowly as he reached the choppy waves made by the wind blowing against the tide.

Shane gasped out: 'Oh, Señor Escolar, wait, please. It's my dog following me. The current is too strong for him. He will drown.'

The men all stopped rowing and looked back at Con.

Pero Escolar said gruffly: 'Let him catch up if he can,' and then added impatiently: 'Oh, back water and take him in. It will save time.'

Con, dripping and shivering, was dragged into the boat. He whimpered with joy and waved his wet tail so that he soaked Shane and Fernan Martinez. After shaking the water off his curly ears, he stood up in the bow and sniffed the south wind.

'Not dog. Sailor!' Fernan chuckled over his shoulder.

Con's career as a sailor was a short one.

Captain Nicolau Coelho, who had been watching impatiently from the deck of the Berrio, was not pleased with this addition to his crew.

'I'm sorry, Shane,' he said, 'but a ship's no place for a dog. We'll have to put him ashore at Belem. With the wind the way it is that's as far as we'll get today. We'll find someone there to take him home.'

The anchor chains rattled. The Berrio's new sails snapped in the breeze. The mournful sounds from the shore swelled louder. Then they began to soften and fade. Soon all Shane could hear was the creak of ropes and the slapping of waves against the side of the ship.

Behind them lay Lisbon, growing fainter in the mist. In front of them, thousands of miles away, lay India.

Chapter 9

DENNIS BEGINS HIS DIARY

ALL sailors knew the monastery at Belem. It was not a beautiful building like the one at Batalha. At Belem there was only a little old stone church and a row of plain whitewashed cells, but there was a light always burning in the tower and another on the rocks below. By those lights many ships had been saved from being wrecked. The church was a landmark for home-coming ships both by day and night. Sailors leaving Portugal stopped there to pray. If they came back, they stopped too. Sometimes only to pray; sometimes to be warmed and fed by the monks.

It was in the church at Belem that Vasco da Gama spent his last night in Portugal. It was a short night. Darkness came late and dawn came early. During those hours of darkness Vasco da Gama knelt before the altar watching his armor and the King's banner.

To Shane, kneeling in the shadows at the back of the church, it seemed as if the night would never end. The dim light from the candles on the altar, the smell of incense, and the low chanting of the monks all made him sleepy. He dozed and woke to find himself lying on the cold stone floor with his head on Connemara's shoulder. The open door behind him showed a faint gray light. He heard the monks still chanting and the sailors praying. Vasco and Paulo da Gama still knelt near the limp scarlet and white folds of the King's banner. Nicolau Coelho was near them with his black head bowed.

Here and there a sailor, like Shane, had fallen asleep. Fernan Martinez was lying as quiet as a bronze sailor on a tomb. Veloso, his bragging tongue quiet, was curled up with his red cloak over his face.

The pink light of the dawn turned the candles pale. People moved at the front of the church. Vasco and Paulo, their head and feet bare, with candles in their hands, followed the priest through the crowd of kneeling men. One by one the sailors, each holding a lighted candle, followed the captains to the wharf below the church. There, with the candle flames burning clear in the still air, the men knelt down, confessed their sins, and were forgiven them by the priest.

Crowds of people spent the night outside the monastery. The men looked pale and the women's eyes were red with weeping. Among the crowd Shane saw Catarina de Ataide. She was standing at the end of the wharf with her father, a thin little man splendidly dressed.

Vasco da Gama stopped and spoke to them before he stepped into the boat that was to take him to the San Gabriel. Da Gama, with his coarse homespun robe and bare feet, looked strange beside Señor Ataide's crimson and gold silk, yet no one could doubt which was the Commander of the Fleet. There was something about Vasco's fierce dark face and strong figure that made him look more splendid than the most richly dressed man there.

He said something to Catarina de Ataide that made her

smile in spite of her tears, and jumped lightly into his boat. As he did so a hard puff of wind blew his candle out.

'Wind from the north,' Vasco da Gama called in his ringing voice. Everyone on shore could hear him above the moaning and crying.

'Wind from the north—the wind he wants,' people began to say.

All the candle flames began to flutter and smoke and go out. Women stopped crying and watched the men on the ships setting the sails. The men of the San Gabriel and the San Raphael and of the store-ship had gone on board. Only the crew of the Berrio was left on shore. Shane, with Con close at his heels, walked through the crowd looking for Luisa Coelho. At last he went up to Catarina and asked her where her friend was.

'She was going to keep my dog for me,' Shane said, 'and now I can't find her.'

'Oh, he's the darling, beautiful angel that swam after you yesterday!' Catarina said. 'But as for Luisa—it's strange about her. I asked her uncle, Señor Martinho, where she was and he said with Nicolau. And I asked Nicolau and he said with Joãn. When I asked Joãn, he said he wasn't sure, but she ought to be with her governess. And when I asked the governess, she said Luisa was with her uncle, Señor Affonso Coelho. But there he is over there coming towards us with Señor Martinho, and she is not with them! Oh, I am afraid she is lost in this crowd! Poor darling, and she will not see the ships sail!'

'I'll speak to Señor Affonso,' Shane said.

He was just walking towards Luisa's uncles, two stately old men with black beards turning gray and the straight Coelho eyebrows gray-frosted too, when a noise from the deck of the

San Raphael made him turn towards the river. Angry voices and the sound of scuffling feet sounded clearly across the water.

Then Paulo da Gama's pleasant voice said: 'What's this? What's this?' and the pilot, Coimbra, answered: 'Stowaway, Señor Captain. Found him in the storeroom, sleeping on the bales of cloth.'

Coimbra was dragging a slim black figure towards Señor Paulo.

'Stop scratching me, you young leopard!' the pilot roared, and then added hastily: 'Pardon, Señor, but what shall I do with the young gentleman?'

Paulo da Gama laughed and said: 'You will take *the young gentleman* to Captain Coelho, who is saying good-bye to his uncles on the dock. I think they will know what to do with him.'

The stowaway, still kicking, was put into a boat and rowed to the dock. He hid his face in a fold of his black cloak, but not before Catarina and Shane had seen it.

'Luisa!' gasped Catarina. 'Oh, poor dearest little angel dove! Now her governess will shut her up like a prisoner!'

Luisa Coelho did not look much like an angel—or a dove—as she was presented to Nicolau and her uncles. Her suit—Joãn's suit—was wrinkled. Her black curly hair was tumbling down from under the knitted cap that she had pulled over it. Her face was red and her black brows met angrily above her nose. The laughter of the people on the dock did not add to her sweetness and ladylike appearance.

Shane wriggled his way through the crowd to Captain Nicolau's side and panted: 'I'm sorry, Señor Captain. It was my fault. I showed her over the ship.'

A voice behind him said: 'No, it wasn't. It was my fault. I

lent her the clothes and told lies to the governess. Honestly, Nicolau, why can't she come? She's as good a boy as any of us.'

This was Joãn Coelho speaking. He had seen the excitement and rowed back from the San Gabriel.

Nicolau Coelho said good-naturedly, but firmly: 'You're a set of young idiots. Take her home, please, Uncle Martinho and Uncle Affonso. If you think you can stand it. If you can't, there's always the convent.'

Luisa sobbed: 'Oh, Nicolau, don't make me stay shut up all my life embroidering doves' toenails.'

'Promise to behave yourself till I come home?' Nicolau Coelho said, putting his big arm around her shoulders.

'Yes, yes, I will.'

'All right. No embroidery and all the riding you like. Hunting and hawking, too, if our uncles will take you,' said her brother. 'Is it a bargain?'

'Yes, I'll be an angel. I promise.'

Señor Martinho Coelho, who had been trying not to laugh, said: 'After all, she's an olive off the old tree. A real Coelho. We'll get a governess with some sense. Doves' toenails indeed! You shall have hawks of your own. The finest in Portugal.'

Señor Affonso said mildly: 'What did you do with your governess, Luisa? You didn't drown her, I hope!'

'Oh, no, uncle. I just saw that she had a good dinner. She loves eating and she sleeps afterwards like a bear in winter. She was having a wonderful sleep when I saw her last,' said Luisa.

Then she saw Connemara and said: 'Oh, Shane! I forgot Con. I am so sorry, but I will take good care of him. Really I will.'

'He will take care of you, won't you, Con?' Shane said.

The dog seemed to understand. He rested his head for a moment against Shane's knee, and he watched him with sad eyes as the Berrio's boat left the shore, but he stayed close by Luisa's side. When the four ships had grown so small that they looked like white gulls far down the river, the girl in the black suit and the red dog were still standing on the dock gazing after them.

Thousands of miles from Lisbon, Dennis O'Connor sat writing one November morning in Paulo da Gama's cabin. The long voyage had done Dennis good. Nuno Calves would hardly have recognized his prisoner of six months before in this sunburned young man who whistled while he wrote. He had drawn ships at the top of a clean sheet of paper and was copying his diary on it. At the left was a large letter 'I' surrounded by flowers and leaves and dolphins all in gay colors.

This is what he had written:

'In the name of God, Amen!

'In the year 1497 King Dom Manuel, the First of that name in Portugal sent four ships to search for India. Vasco da Gama was Captain-Major of this Fleet and commanded the San Gabriel. Paulo da Gama commanded the San Raphael; Nicolau Coelho, the Berrio; and Gonzalo Nunez, the store-ship.

'We left Lisbon July 8, 1497. May our Lord God let us finish this voyage in his service. Amen!

'On Saturday, July 15, we saw the Canary Islands. On July 16 the fog at night was so thick that Paulo da Gama lost sight of the Captain-Major, although all the ships carried colored lanterns. We then sailed for the Cape Verde Islands as Vasco da Gama had ordered. The wind fell and we were becalmed, but on July 26 we sighted the San Gabriel. We showed our joy by firing our cannon and blowing our trumpets.

'On August 18, in a storm, the Captain-Major's mainyard

broke. We lay to for two days and a night while it was repaired. On the twenty-second of August we saw birds flying southeast as if making for land.

'On October 27 we saw many whales and seals.'

(Here Dennis took a fresh sheet of paper and drew pictures of whales spouting at the top of it.)

'On November 1 we saw gulf weed which grows along the coast. That meant land was near, and we were very tired of the great waste of water we had sailed over. On Saturday, November 4, we sighted land. We then drew near to the other ships. We put on our best clothes, trimmed our ship with flags, and saluted our Captain-Major with our cannon.

'We found a broad bay and anchored there. Saint Helena Bay we called it. The men cleaned weed and barnacles from the sides of the ships and mended sails which had been torn in some great winds that we met. We went ashore to get wood, and the beach seemed to tip under our feet because we had been so long at sea.

'The people of this country are dark brown, as dark as Fernan Martinez. They are short—no taller than Sancho Mexia. They eat seals, whale meat, and roots. They are dressed in skins and have pointed spears. Their dogs bark like the dogs of Portugal and look like them. The birds are like Portuguese birds. We have seen gulls, doves, and larks.'

Dennis stopped writing and began to draw gulls on his paper. Gulls flying. Gulls squabbling over a fish. Gulls bobbing up and down on the waves as if they were carved out of wood. Gulls standing on a rock and looking wise.

Then he began again:

'On the day after we anchored, we landed with the Captain-Major and captured one of the natives. He was gathering honey. The Captain-Major fed him at his own table and the man ate everything that was given him. Then the Captain-Major gave him some fine clothes and sent him ashore.

'The next day more natives came to the beach near our ships. Captain Vasco da Gama landed and showed them cinnamon, cloves, pearls, and gold. Fernan Martinez, who speaks their language a little, asked them if they had any such things, but they said no. The Captain-Major gave them bells and tin rings and copper coins. The natives gave him some of the shells they wear in their ears, and a fox tail on a handle. They use these to fan their faces.'

'Dennis! Dennis!'

It was Shane's voice outside.

Dennis left his writing and went on deck. The Berrio's boat was alongside the San Raphael. In it were Captain Coelho, Veloso, Fernan Martinez, and Shane.

'Dennis, you old owl! You stay inside writing this fine morning, as soft and sweet as any in Ireland itself! Come on with us and meet our friends on the beach. It's a party they're giving us.'

Shane pointed to the shore. There were forty or fifty small brown figures standing there, staring at the ships. A boat from the San Gabriel with Vasco da Gama steering was near the beach.

Dennis swung himself down into the Berrio's boat.

'I'd like it just as well if they wouldn't bring those spears with horns on the ends with them when they come to call,' he remarked.

Veloso laughed loudly.

'They'd better not tickle *me* with them,' he said. 'Why, those men are just little brown beetles. I'd be afraid I might hurt them by stepping on them.'

He was the first one out of the boat. He looked very big in his red cloak as he swaggered up to the little brown men. The natives crowded around Veloso, feeling the velvet of his cloak and making the hissing noises that were part of their language. Their fuzzy heads hardly came above his elbow.

They began tugging at Veloso's cloak and pointing. Fernan, who had to stoop down to hear what they were saying, said they were asking Veloso to go with them.

'It would be a fine thing for me to see their houses, Señor,' Veloso said to the Captain-Major. 'They may have gold hidden there. I may find out important things about them.'

'Go if you like,' Vasco da Gama said, 'but do not go too far. Come back at once if they seem unfriendly.'

'No fear of that,' Veloso said. 'They've taken a great fancy to me, as people always do.'

He started off, taking enormous strides, with the natives trotting after him.

Vasco da Gama, with Shane's help, used the astrolabe that Zacuto had given him to find out how far south they had come. He went back to the San Gabriel and, by studying Zacuto's book, decided that the southern tip of Africa must be about thirty leagues south of them. This was the place once called the Cape of Storms, but, since Bartolomeo Diaz had sailed around it, now known as the Cape of Good Hope.

Coelho's men stayed on shore collecting wood. Shane and Joãn Coelho caught some lobsters and cooked them over a fire they made on the beach. Afterwards they lay on the warm sand sucking lobster claws and talking.

'Do you know, Shane,' Joãn said, 'that we've made the longest voyage anyone ever made out of sight of land? Longer than Columbus even? Didn't you get sick of the sea? Isn't it grand not to hear ropes creaking and waves going thump, slap, bubble, thump against the ship? Aren't these lobsters good? Don't you hate salt pork?'

'Yes,' said Shane to all these questions.

'Do you really think there's a sea of pitch on the other side of Africa? Do you wish you were back in the Street of the Rat? Does Nicolau scare you till your knees shake when you serve his dinner? Would you like to change with me and be cabin-boy on the San Gabriel?'

'No,' Shane said, throwing a stone up high and listening to it splash.

Joãn said disgustedly: 'I believe it's more fun to talk to these Africans than it is to you! The first time I've seen you alone for months and all you say is yes and no!'

'What do you want me to say?' Shane yawned.

'Tell me what it's like on the Berrio.'

'Why, just the way you'd think. We carve little ships of wood. We sleep and eat. We watch your sails by day and try not to get too far ahead of your nice old washtub—stop putting sand down my neck or you'll be sorry you ever saw Africa!—and by night we watch for your lanterns. We have salt beef and biscuit for dinner one day and salt pork and biscuit the next. And salt fish on Fridays. The men talk about what they'll do with all the gold they get in India. Most of them are going to open little country inns. They say anyone can run a country inn—all you have to do is to talk with the guests and your wife does the cooking.'

Joãn said in a low voice: 'Aren't the men on the Berrio afraid? They are, on our ship.'

'Afraid of what?'

'Everything. Storms. Sea dragons. The strange stars in the sky. If they weren't more afraid of something else, they'd mutiny now and try to sail back to Portugal.'

'You mean they're afraid of the Captain-Major?' Shane asked.

'Yes. And you would be too. I dropped his fork the other day. It wasn't such a bad thing to do—we have three forks. The way he looked at me scorched the hair off my head—nearly.'

'Seems to be plenty left,' Shane observed. 'I don't think the men on the Berrio are afraid. Except for Machado, who sulks behind his beard, and Rodriguez, who always looks about as gay as a dinner plate and who always puts me in mind of a bald jellyfish—though come to think of it I've seen no jellyfish with much hair—they seem jolly enough. They sing enough. And dance, too, when I play my harp for them.'

'I've heard it across the water,' Joãn said.

'And it's you I heard twanging away on your guitar once—

> *'Down here no man can reach it:*
> *Above there no one goes.'*

—or was it that black cat squawking?'

Scuffling in the sand followed this remark. It ended with Joãn sitting on top of Shane and pouring sand into his friend's red hair.

'I apologize,' Shane gasped, 'to the cat. To Señor Patapito. A fine voice he's got. But Hepzibah pays no attention to him. She's a hard-working, sensible cat. Rats she thinks about all day and most of the night, not about some black velvet-coated yowler with a grand white shirt and gloves, and long black eyebrows... Dennis! Dennis! Will you see your only brother murdered and sit there as heartless as a hunk of salt pork?'

Dennis, who had been sitting some distance away drawing maps on the sand, strolled over and looked down at his well-sanded brother.

'It would be a sad thing if we lost him!' he remarked. 'How

should we ever get to India without him squinting at the sun and looking wise? Do not kill him today, Joãn.'

'As a favor to you, then, I won't,' Joãn said laughing.

He stopped using Shane for a cushion. Shane sat up shaking sand out of his hair.

'Besides, I wanted to ask you something,' Joãn said to Dennis, and began asking much the same things he had asked Shane. The answers were not very different. The voyage on the San Raphael had seemed long. There had been many dull days, but the men seemed happy enough. They grumbled about the food, of course, but there was little talk about sea monsters and whirlpools of fire. Captain Paulo was gentle with the men, and they liked him and obeyed him cheerfully.

Joãn looked down the beach. There was a crowd of sailors from all four ships gathered around a fire.

'Pero d'Alenquer and Gonzalo Alvarez are doing a lot of talking over there,' he said.

Pero d'Alenquer was pilot of the San Gabriel. Alvarez was the master.

'It's natural for the men to talk together,' Dennis said.

'Yes, but those two always have queer stories to tell. I think they are cowards. I know they hate the Captain-Major. When they eat together, as they do sometimes when the sea is calm, they sit there scowling over their food as if they expected to find poison in it. You know how the Captain-Major looks through you as if you weren't there? He does that to d'Alenquer and Alvarez and they don't like it. If I were Captain Vasco da Gama, I wouldn't turn them loose with the crews of the other ships.'

Trumpets sounded from across the water. It was the signal for the men on the beach to leave the shore.

The boats made several trips. Shane was among the last to leave.

'Veloso hasn't come back yet,' Shane said as he took his place at the bow oar in the Berrio's boat.

'Let him swim, then!' the boatswain snapped. 'My orders are to go back at once.'

The boat had almost reached the Berrio when Veloso's tall figure appeared in the distance. He was running with his red cloak sailing out behind him. He vanished in a hollow, then he came sailing over the top of a sandy hill shouting as he ran.

From the San Gabriel came the sound of Vasco da Gama's voice.

'Send your boat back, Coelho. The savages are chasing him.'

Nicolau Coelho tumbled into the boat himself and the men started to row for the beach. A boat from the San Gabriel with Vasco da Gama standing up in the stern started too, but it had taken a few minutes to launch it and Veloso was already on the beach. A whole swarm of little brown figures was buzzing down the hill behind him.

Above the angry hum of their voices came Veloso's roaring: 'Hurry, you fools! Do you want me to be killed?'

'I know who's the fool,' muttered Machado.

Captain Coelho called out: 'Into the water with you, Veloso. Are you afraid to wet your clothes? Speed up, men.'

Veloso waded into the water up to his knees and stood there helplessly with his cloak trailing in the ripples. A shower of darts whizzed into the water around him.

Vasco da Gama roared: 'Swim, you double-dyed popinjay!' But Veloso only hunched up his shoulders and stood shaking, with the darts making little fountains around him.

Tears were running down his fat cheeks and his teeth were

chattering when Fernan Martinez and Shane at last hauled him on board.

Two of the rowers were hit by the darts, but their yells were not nearly so loud as Veloso's.

'Back to the ship, Coelho,' Vasco da Gama called. 'I'll settle with these wasps.'

The Berrio's crew swung the boat out of range of the darts and carried the wounded men back to the ship. Veloso collapsed in the bottom of the boat.

The boat from the San Gabriel was now close in shore. Shane saw Vasco da Gama jump into the water, sword in hand, and splash towards the savages on shore. His men followed him, and the savages, seeing their swords and crossbows, started to run back up the sand hill. As they did so, they threw the last of their darts and sharpened sticks.

Three or four of da Gama's men were hit by these. They were like arrows and the wounds they made were very painful. Just as the Captain-Major reached the shore, one of these arrows hit him. It was thrown with such force that it cut through his boot and pierced his leg. He still tried to follow the savages, but they disappeared over the hill, throwing stones as they went.

Three men lay groaning on the beach. A fourth, also wounded in the leg, had fallen while he was still in the boat. Vasco da Gama was injured as badly as any of the others, but he took care of the men, washed their wounds in sea water, and tore up his own shirt for bandages. Joãn Coelho, who helped him, thought his Captain looked pale.

'Let me wash your wound, Señor,' he said, but Vasco da Gama only laughed.

'It's just a sting,' he said. 'Another time we must look out for the bees. This happened because we looked upon these people as men of little spirit and went ashore unarmed. We shall know better after this.'

It was not until he reached his own cabin that the Captain-Major looked at his own wound. Joãn Coelho helped him off with his boot. It was full of blood.

Vasco da Gama might be stern and severe, but he was also brave. He was patient, too, with Joãn's handling of his wound, and never complained of the pain of it.

'He got hurt,' Joãn thought, 'saving that loud-mouthed Veloso, who isn't worth one drop of Captain Vasco's blood. The coward had better not let me hear him boasting again!'

Chapter 10

MUSIC ON STORMY SEAS

THE ships sailed the next day, so Joãn Coelho did not have a chance to tell Veloso what he thought of him. The crew of the Berrio, when they heard Veloso's story and found that his only wound was a pin-prick in one arm, attended to laughing at him, however.

The savages, he said, had been very friendly to him. They had caught a young seal on the beach and roasted it. When they offered him some, Veloso was so disgusted with the smell of it that he refused it, and started back for the beach. The savages all went with him. He got frightened and began to run. The Africans laughed and ran too. Then the trumpets sounded from the ship. Veloso began to run faster and to shout. It was then that the savages began to throw their stones and arrows.

The whole thing was in fact Veloso's fault. The two men of the Berrio's crew who had been wounded pointed that out to him clearly and often as the ships sailed southwest for the Cape of Good Hope.

There was no sea of boiling pitch anywhere near the Cape.

Veloso was one of those who had always believed firmly in the sea of pitch. He had also boasted that he could swim through it easily.

'Veloso perhaps swim better in pitch than in water,' the negro, Fernan Martinez, said.

The sailors, who remembered Veloso's bawling in the water while the savages buzzed their darts at him, laughed loudly at this remark.

Some of the crew believed that there were always storms raging around the Cape so that no one could sail past it. Others thought there might be a wall of ice in their way. And of course there were some who expected sea monsters to swallow up the ships. Pero d'Alenquer, the pilot of the San Gabriel, said he had seen a sea serpent once that could twist itself around the Berrio and crush it as if it were a walnut. Alvarez, the pilot of the store-ship, preferred the idea that a mountain of ice would fall on the ship and sink it.

They were all wrong!

Dennis O'Connor wrote about it in his diary, but he mentioned none of these wonderful things.

'We stood out towards the south-southwest,' wrote Dennis, 'and late on Saturday, November 18, we saw the Cape. On that same day we stood out to sea again, but turned towards the land in the night. We tried to round the Cape again on Sunday, the nineteenth of November, but we could not. The wind blew from the S.S.W. and the Cape juts out to the southwest. We then stood out to sea again. The Cape was still there, east of us. We thought we never should pass it, but on Wednesday the wind changed. So we sailed around the Cape and ran north along the other edge of Africa.'

No hot pitch. No mountains of ice. No dragons that chewed

up ships. Just waves and winds that didn't always blow the right way—like the winds of Portugal!

On the east coast of Africa the fleet anchored in the Bay of San Braz. There they broke up the store-ship and transferred the things in it to the other ships. They burned the hull to get the nails out of it. Nails were precious and were saved in case the other ships needed mending. Some men from the store-ship were taken on board each of the other three ships.

The Portuguese met more negroes at San Braz, but this time Vasco da Gama took with him a party of soldiers armed with crossbows. He gave the savages red caps and small bells. They gave him some ivory bracelets. The negroes played on their flutes and danced. The men on the ships sounded their trumpets and danced too. Shane played his harp and Joãn his guitar.

The negroes sold the sailors a black ox for three bracelets. It was roasted over a big fire on the beach.

'This meat is as good as the beef of Portugal,' Joãn Coelho said to Shane.

'Better. It's as good as the beef of Ireland!' Shane said, licking his fingers. 'I'm wishing Con were here to take a gnaw at these bones.'

He tossed a bone into the fire made of driftwood and the store-ship's timbers and picked up his harp.

> *'Diarmid was a traitor,*
> *A traitor to his prince...'*

he sang, thrumming away at the strings.

Joãn followed the tune on his guitar. The sun had gone down behind the hills to the west. There was a silvery twilight along the beach. Green and blue flames licked along the salty driftwood. The sailors began to dance and sing, stamping their feet hard on the smooth sand. The two boys, sitting on a rock some distance from the fire, played all the tunes they knew. At last the sailors grew tired of dancing and sat down in small groups around the fire.

Joãn still kept on twanging his guitar strings. He spoke softly to Shane, chanting the words. To the men around the fire it sounded as if he were still singing, but the twang and thump of the guitar covered the words.

'We sail, you know, tomorrow,' Joãn said—twang, thump, thump—'this may be our last talk. I don't like the new members of our crew.'... Tinkle, tankle, tank... 'How are things with you?'

Shane answered, sweeping his fingers over the strings of his harp: 'Veloso, the brave Veloso, looks sulky and talks in dark corners with the men from the store-ship.' The harp sounded like ripples running over smooth pebbles... 'Have you spoken to your brother? What does he say?'

'My brother,' Joãn hummed, 'thinks I am silly. As silly as these birds here that bray like donkeys and can't fly. He advised me, oh, kindly and very politely, to be a good boy and keep the Captain's silver bowls nicely polished.'

He played his guitar for a minute without speaking and then went on: 'He knows the men were afraid when we were rounding the Cape, but he says'... thump, thump, twank... 'that now they see this ocean is like any other they are happy again. The other captains think the same.'

'The men would not dare mutiny on one ship unless they knew those on the others would help them,' Shane hummed. 'Cannon from another ship could always shoot them down. They would think of some way to signal. They may be planning it now—look at d'Alenquer's face in the firelight. He is plotting something. With lanterns they could signal and all rise at once. But you and I have a better way. If there is trouble play this to me.'

Shane broke into the tune of 'Diarmid was a traitor,' and Joãn joined in on the guitar.

'To show I understand I will play 'The fair white rose,' he added, and swung into it, singing the verse he made up the morning he saw the half-burned blue thistle in Rachel's window.

Joãn nodded and began playing it too.

> *'If we could only hear*
> *What they say around the fire,'*

he chanted softly.

'These men are too clever to talk when we're near them,' Shane said, playing more runs on his harp.

Into the middle of his melody burst the sound of trumpets. It was the signal to leave the beach for the night.

'Every night before I go to bed, if everything is all right, I will play this,' Shane said.

He walked down the beach singing, the harp strings sounding sweetly under his long fingers:

> 'Sing, for a road that's long
>> Shortens with singing;
> Reapers with happy song
>> Set their scythes ringing.
> Sing when night turns the day
>> Darker and colder;
> Song makes a faint heart gay,
>> Stronger and bolder.'

Joãn took up the tune on his guitar and went on:

> 'Sing in a prison grim,
>> Song turns it brighter;
> Chains bind and scar the limb,
>> Song makes them lighter.'

'Dennis says that's true,' Shane said. 'He used to sing in that prison in Setubal. It made him keep on hoping.'

Both boys were in the firelight now. One of the sailors kicked the glowing timbers together. Sparks flickered through the shadows. The fire blazed up brightly for a moment, shining on Shane's red hair and on the dull gold of his harp.

Shane's clear high voice and Joãn's deeper one rang out together as the fire died down.

> 'Sing as the rain drop sings
>> "Sunshine tomorrow":
> Song to each toiler brings
>> Peace for his sorrow.'

'Come on, you nightingales,' called a voice from the darkness.

The boys ran down the beach to their boats.

'Remember, Diarmid,' Shane said. 'My fair white rose.'

Joãn slapped him hard on the shoulder. Shane scrambled into the boat.

'Who's Diarmid?' asked Pero Escolar, the Berrio's pilot.

'Someone a grandfather of mine knew in Ireland a while ago,' Shane said, and went on singing.

Veloso and d'Alenquer, the pilot of the San Gabriel, were still talking farther up the beach. A third man was with them. He had been in the store-ship, but now was one of the San Raphael's crew. They moved slowly along, but started running as the boatswain's whistle pierced the air. The men jumped into their boats. Pebbles grated. Oars plopped into the quiet water. The ships' lanterns were spots of green in the darkness. On shore the fire had died to a faint orange glow. From somewhere back in the hills came the notes of a native pipe.

Lisbon seemed a long way off.

Before the ships sailed the next day, Shane saw Dennis and told him what Joãn had said about the discontent of the crew of the San Gabriel and his fears that all three crews might mutiny. Dennis had noticed nothing wrong on the San Raphael. He said the sailors had been afraid while they were rounding the Cape, but now they were all right. He laughed at the idea of Shane's signaling with his harp, but promised he'd listen for it.

'Tell Señor Paulo what I say, will you not, Dennis?' Shane asked.

'Not unless I see what makes me think you are right. I'll not go tattling about nothing.'

He was sitting at his table in the San Raphael's cabin. He began to draw pictures of penguins.

'That's how they look, isn't it—those braying birds that can't fly?' he asked.

'More or less,' Shane said. 'Listen, Dennis: put your pen down. Do you know a man named Pedro Diaz?'

'Yes. He's one of the men that came from a prison in Lisbon. He was freed so that he could be sent on dangerous errands for the fleet.'

'A criminal, you mean?'

'The same as I am—yes! I was in prison, you know. What about him?'

'Only that I saw him talking with Veloso and d'Alenquer last night. Joãn thinks they were plotting something.'

'Fine imaginations the two of you have!' Dennis said. 'But I'll keep my eyes open. There's no harm in that, I suppose.'

'I wish I could stay with you, Dennis.'

'With Señor Paulo, you mean! Well, it's the best ship, no doubt.'

'The Berrio can outsail her,' Shane said loyally.

'We'll see who's first in the Tagus,' Dennis said. 'It is the end of the race that counts.'

Dennis had a chance to see how the Berrio sailed that very morning. His cabin was needed for one of the officers of the burned store-ship. Dennis was ordered by Vasco da Gama to move to the Berrio.

Within a short time of his talk with Shane, Dennis, his chest of books and papers, his pen, brushes, and colors, and a small bundle of clothes arrived on board Nicolau Coelho's ship. By the time the ships set sail, Dennis was at work at the table in the Berrio's cabin.

He was still writing when Shane came in to set the table for the Captain's dinner.

'Did you speak to Captain Paulo?' Shane asked as he polished Nicolau Coelho's silver drinking cup.

'I did not then,' said Dennis whose green eyes looked angry. 'How would I have time when the Captain-Major stamps in and roars: "O'Connor, move your things to the Berrio at once. Your cabin's needed for Gonzalo Nunez"? I'd hardly time to pack up my chest, much less be breathing tales of blood and slaughter. As it is I lost a quill that I'd cut to a point so it would draw a line the width of your eyelash. If there's a mutiny, I'll be in it.'

Shane set wooden trenchers on the table.

'I wouldn't talk like that, Dennis. Someone might hear you.'

'Let them, then,' Dennis grumbled.

He took up a small knife and began to trim another quill. After a minute, the quill being sharp enough so that it pleased him, he smiled up at his brother cheerfully, saying: 'Never mind, young man. It'll be fine to be together anyway. That's something. I hope you've got a good dinner for us. I'm hungry enough to eat the mainsail and one of the anchors.'

For the first few days after they left San Braz everything went well on the Berrio. But on the San Gabriel there was grumbling among the men from the very first. The voyage had already taken longer than they had expected. They had been gone six months and no gold, no jewels, no spices. India, where they thought they would pick up rubies off streets paved with gold, seemed as far away as ever. They were homesick for their wives and children. The voyage home would take at least six months. Every hour they sailed was making it longer. Worst of all, the winds were light, and the currents along that coast were so strong that sometimes they would see the same wooded point of land in the evening that they had tried to pass in the morning.

Joãn used to go on the upper deck in the evenings and play the guitar. There was so little wind and the waves were so quiet that he could hear Shane's harp clearly as it answered him, and his friend's voice.

> 'Sing when night turns the day
>   Darker and colder'...

The sullen faces of Vasco da Gama's crew made it hard to answer cheerfully with the same tune. Still, Joãn knew nothing more than that the men grumbled about their food and that they stopped talking when they saw him coming. They obeyed the Captain-Major briskly enough, but there were dark scowls behind his back.

Unluckily, when the wind came, it came in a tempest. All but the foresails were reefed. The ships ran north before a stern wind that sent great waves that looked like mountains following them. The clouds were so black that even in the daytime the ships could hardly see each other. Towards night a sudden lull in the storm left the ships lying hopelessly battered and wrecked by the waves.

As they lurched about with water breaking over the decks, the timbers creaking, the pumps useless, the pilot, Pero d'Alenquer, went to Vasco da Gama and asked him to order the ships back to San Braz.

Da Gama said quietly: 'I vowed when I left Lisbon that I would never turn back one hand's breadth. Back to your post, d'Alenquer. *We are going to India!*'

Both men were drenched to the skin. D'Alenquer was shivering, but the look in the Captain-Major's eyes seemed to burn into him. He went back to his post at the stern. Da Gama had not slept for twenty-four hours. He went to his cabin to change his clothes and rest for a few minutes.

The ships were close enough together so that the men could shout from ship to ship. The sailors on the San Gabriel began to call to their friends on the other ships that they would see the bottom of the ocean before they ever saw India. D'Alenquer made no attempt to stop them.

A sailor from the Berrio—Joãn thought it was Machado's voice—called out that they were many men and their captain only one. D'Alenquer laughed bitterly and said to Alvarez, the master of the San Gabriel, that what the men said was true enough.

Joãn Coelho had lashed himself to the railing near the stern, so that he would not be washed overboard by the waves. He was close to d'Alenquer, but the pilot paid no attention to him. Joãn waited until the waves were less violent. Then he went below and got his guitar. His fingers were cold and wet as he tuned it. He went back to the deck and began to play, but this time it was the tune of 'Diarmid was a traitor.'

At first there was no answer from the Berrio. It was so dark that all Joãn could see was her lanterns swaying up and down as she wallowed and pitched. Once a wave larger than the others broke over her, splashing the spray so high that it turned green in the light of the lantern. He could hear only the creakings and rattlings and groanings of the San Gabriel and the sizzling and slopping of the waves.

Then above all the tumult came faintly the sound of Shane's harp, and his voice singing,

> *'Down here no man can reach it:*
> *Above there no one goes.'*

He finished the song and then struck into 'Diarmid was a traitor.'

> *'They brought strangers into Ireland*
> *To steal our land so green,*
> *And they eat our fattest cattle,*
> *While we have to take the lean,'*

came Shane's voice across the stinging white crests of the black waves.

'There's trouble on the Berrio, too,' thought Joãn.

He played a verse of 'The fair white rose' so that Shane would know that he understood. D'Alenquer interrupted him with one of his sharp laughs. He was a little gray-faced man with a sharp nose, usually red, now purple with cold and fear.

'It's a fine thing,' he screeched, 'to be thumping and braying when the ship's going down. Can't you find anything more useful to do?'

'My watch is over, Señor,' Joãn said. 'I always play, you know, at this time. The men like it usually.'

'Well they don't tonight,' d'Alenquer said roughly, 'and if your watch is over you'd better get out of the way. Go and make your noise below.'

Joãn still had the guitar in his hand as he knocked at the door of the Captain-Major's cabin.

Vasco da Gama was getting ready to go on deck again. The heavy cloak that he flung over his shoulders was the one he had worn during the day. It was still wet.

Joãn was wet too. Water dripped off his guitar.

'It's time for your supper, Señor,' he said. 'The cook is sick and the fire in the galley has gone out—the waves came in there—but I can get you something. Some biscuit and honey, perhaps.'

'No matter,' said Vasco da Gama. 'I must get back on deck. It's where I belong in this sort of weather.'

'Wait, please, Señor,' Joãn said, speaking softly. 'Shane O'Connor has sent a message. They are planning mutiny on the Berrio. And I think d'Alenquer and Alvarez are in it too.'

'Sent a message? How?' da Gama asked, turning his piercing dark eyes straight on the boy.

'On his harp, Señor. We arranged the signal.'

He then told da Gama everything that he and Shane had noticed, and how the sailor from the Berrio had called out that the men were many and the Captain only one, and how d'Alenquer had answered.

'I think Pedro Diaz on the San Raphael is in it too, Señor Captain,' he said. 'And the men from the store-ship.'

'Haven't I any friends then but you and your guitar?' Vasco da Gama asked with one of his rare smiles. It lighted up his

fierce dark face for a moment, but faded while he stood thinking in silence.

As he wrapped his wet cloak around him and turned toward the door, Joãn said timidly: 'Won't you arm yourself, Señor? And let me go with you? I can use a sword if there is need.'

'And let them know I am afraid? Oh, no! Your guitar is a better weapon. And your sharp eyes. Thank you for using them. Wipe the guitar, boy, so the salt won't spoil it, and go to bed. I hear the wind coming up again. It's going to carry us towards India.'

He swung out of the cabin. The gale howled louder than ever. The San Gabriel drove forward through thunder, lightning, and the wild black water.

CHAPTER 11

MUTINY

ON THE San Raphael the sailors were afraid, too, but they were not ready to mutiny against Paulo da Gama. He was their friend. He nursed them when they were sick, sharing his own stock of medicines with them. He remembered all about each man, where he lived, whether he was married, the names of his children. Paulo's friendly smile made unpleasant orders easy to obey. They were not afraid of him, but they liked him and looked up to him for his courage. During the worst of the storm they begged him to turn back. His refusal made them sad rather than angry.

The crew of the Berrio had good reason to be afraid. The little Berrio, swifter than the other ships in a fair wind, seemed in the gale like a chip tossed about by the waves. Most frightened of all was Veloso. He groaned at every lurch of the boat, moaning that he wished he were back in the prison in Setubal. In fact, several of the Berrio's crew remembered how Nuno Calves had told them they were fools to leave his jail. The idea of any place that stood on dry land seemed better than a ship that plunged and pitched and seemed ready to sink at any moment.

It was these former prisoners who planned the mutiny.

Machado and Rodriguez, once grooms of Paulo da Gama's, had been in that prison in Setubal. They were glad that Dennis had been transferred to the Berrio. After they had seized the ship they would need someone to help sail it. Dennis and that red-headed brother of his who had a compass and astrolabe of his own would be able to tell them how to steer for Portugal.

Machado did not think Dennis would join them. Veloso was sure he would. By this time, Veloso said, Dennis must see that they would never reach India. They would either be drowned or else be wrecked among the savages. It would be better to be hanged at home than be eaten by fishes or savages. The King was a good fellow. When they told him the dangers they had been in, he would pardon them. Dennis would be the one to go to him, being a gentleman and a scholar. He would think up a good story for the King. As for the rest of them, if they found out the King was angry, they could go to Spain and sell the ship there and live on what they got.

Machado said that Veloso seemed to forget that they hadn't seized the ship yet, or even told O'Connor about their plan.

Veloso agreed that they must get hold of Dennis. When they had done that, they must get the other crews to join them, because if they tried to leave the fleet, the Captain-Major would surely chase them and kill them all. They had better wait till the storm was over because it was better for the captains to take the ships through it. After that, the mutiny. Then home, and never look at water again except in a pitcher.

After making these plans they spoke to Dennis secretly. Dennis listened to them quietly and pretended that he would help them. Luckily the others were called to the pumps just then. Dennis hurried on deck and found Shane alone near the bow. He was listening for Joãn's guitar.

'You are right. They will mutiny, but not till they can get the other crews into it. Tell the Captain,' was all Dennis stopped to say. He did not like to be seen talking to Shane by the crew. He did not know how many of those who were on deck might be among the mutineers. If they saw him speak to Shane and then saw Shane go to the Captain, they might suspect them both.

Shane went to the stern. Captain Coelho was there, but the pilot and the boatswain were with him. While Shane was waiting to speak to him came the sound of Joãn's guitar. Almost as soon as Shane had answered him, the wind came up again. The Berrio was whirled along after the other ships. During the thunderstorm she lost sight of them entirely. The flashes of lightning sent their green glare over an empty sea. The white things on it were not sails, but only the crests of waves.

Shane stayed on deck until he saw Captain Coelho alone at the helm. He was steering the Berrio himself as she pitched and heaved from wave to wave. Great fountains of spray shot into the air and splashed down on the deck. Shane crawled along the wet deck holding on sometimes by the rail, sometimes by a rope. The Berrio pushed her nose down into a dark valley so that the deck was a slippery mountain above him. Then she tried to climb a mountain herself. Shane slid downhill and landed at Nicolau Coelho's feet.

Captain Coelho towered above him like a giant. He looked as calm as the ship's figurehead.

'Nice little breeze!' he roared cheerfully above the screaming wind.

Shane shouted in his ear the news about the mutiny. Nicolau Coelho received it with his usual calm.

'Sailors are always like that,' he said, shoving the tiller over and sending the Berrio neatly through a wave that broke and boiled alongside. 'When the sea's calm, they'll be whimpering because the wind doesn't blow us to India quicker. I was half expecting it from some sour looks I saw on the faces of Machado and Rodriguez. Thanks to you and your brother, though. It's just as well to know what's going on. Tell the cook to fry me some salt pork. This air makes me hungry.'

Shane had not been any too soon with his news. A crowd of sailors came to the Captain shouting at him to turn back to San Braz.

Nicolau Coelho's big voice boomed above the wind and rushing water: 'Brothers, let us strive to save ourselves from this storm. As soon as I can get speech with the Captain-Major, I will ask him to put back. You will hear me ask him.'

The sailors had to be content with that.

The Berrio caught up with the other ships the next day. The wind had gone down, but the sea was still rough. As soon as he got near enough to the San Gabriel, Coelho called out to Vasco da Gama: 'Captain-Major, our ships are wrecked by the storm. We have death every moment before our eyes. It would be well to put about. My crew are begging piteously with tears and cries. If we do not turn back, they might kill or arrest us, and then they would put back and save their lives. We ought to save ours also, so let each look out for himself, for so I mean to do.'

Vasco da Gama heard what Nicolau Coelho said, because his ship was near the others.

Vasco da Gama shouted that he would consult with his pilot and master and then tell the other captains what he meant to do. He understood that Coelho was warning him and that Joãn was right about the mutiny.

He called the crew together and said: 'I am not so brave that I do not fear death as you do. I am not so cruel that I do not feel grieved by your tears and prayers. If the storm rises again, I will put back, but I must give the King good reasons or he will hang us all. I will draw up a statement and we will sign it.'

The men cheered.

'There is no need for the signatures of all,' Vasco da Gama said. 'The names of those who understand the management of the ship best will do. Then the King will know that the storm was too great for safety.'

D'Alenquer and Alvarez pointed out three seamen.

'Very well,' Vasco da Gama said. 'My clerk and I will draw up the document. I will send for you when I am ready. Go down, Joàn, and get the table ready.'

Joàn Coelho cleared the table and was spreading out paper and pens when Vasco da Gama and the clerk came in.

'Go, Joàn, and bring Palha and Pirez here. They are at the pumps,' the Captain-Major said hastily. 'Write what you like,' he added to the clerk. 'King Manuel will never see this precious paper.'

Palha and Pirez, two loyal followers of da Gama's, hurried after Joàn to the cabin.

'Stand behind the door,' Vasco da Gama said. 'Here are ropes to bind the scoundrels and gags to stop their mouths. Don't use your daggers unless you have to. I don't want to hurt them, but this nonsense about going back to Portugal is going to stop. Go up on deck now, Coelho, and tell d'Alenquer I am ready for him. Follow him, stand outside the door. When you hear me say "Sign," watch till he has finished writing, then shut and lock the door. Do you understand?'

'I do, Señor.'

Joàn went on deck and gave d'Alenquer the Captain-Major's message.

D'Alenquer said boastfully to the men around him: 'You see! I told you I would frighten him in to turning back,' and swaggered off to the cabin.

Joãn followed him to the door and stood ready to shut it. The key was in the lock.

Vasco da Gama said sternly: 'Think before you touch that pen. Are you bent on this cowardice and treachery to your King, d'Alenquer?'

'If you call it that!' the pilot said.

Vasco da Gama looked at d'Alenquer for a moment, pride and scorn in his dark eyes.

'Very well, then,' he said quietly, 'sign.'

D'Alenquer took the pen. Joãn could hear it sputter as it pushed hard across the paper.

The pilot drew a line under his name with a hard scratch and threw down the pen. Before he turned, Joãn had shut the door. He heard d'Alenquer start to cry out, but his voice ended in a choking gurgle. There were scuffing sounds. Something—the Captain's chair, perhaps—went over with a crash.

Then the cabin was silent.

At last Vasco da Gama's voice said: 'Unlock the door, Joãn.'

Joãn unlocked and opened it. Palha and Pirez came out carrying d'Alenquer bound and gagged.

'Take him to the blacksmith,' da Gama said. 'His fetters are ready by now. We'll receive Alvarez next, Joãn, as soon as Palha and Pirez come back. Do just as you did before.'

When Alvarez and the three seamen were all strongly bound and in the dark prison below, Vasco went back on deck.

Joãn followed him carrying a large astrolabe. Palha and Pirez were behind him with a small chest.

The men put the chest down near where Vasco da Gama

was standing. There was a compass near him—the one that Zacuto had given him.

Da Gama wrenched the compass from its fastenings and flung it into the sea. He snatched the astrolabe from Joãn's hand and threw it after the compass. Then he opened the chest and showed the staring, frightened sailors what was in it—maps, small astrolabes, and Zacuto's almanac. He picked up the chest and hurled it into the water where the compass had sunk.

The papers scattered as it fell. The brass of the astrolabes flashed and slipped through the foaming crest of a green wave. The wooden astrolabe still floated near the San Gabriel's side. The chest struck it. For a moment chest and astrolabe disappeared. When they came to the surface again, the astrolabe was only two broken sticks.

The San Gabriel sailed on, leaving the papers and the empty chest tossing about behind her.

'Your pilot and master and everyone who knows how to sail this ship are now in irons,' Vasco da Gama said calmly. 'All our means of navigation are in the sea. You have no one but me to show you the way. Those traitors are going back to

Portugal in irons. I need neither master nor pilot, nor any man who knows the art of navigation. God alone is our pilot and master. He will deliver us if we deserve it. If not, let His will be done. Pray to Him for mercy, not to me. Do not speak to me again of putting back. *We are going to India!'*

A great wailing went up from the frightened crew. They knew that they were now completely in da Gama's power, since he was the only one who understood how to sail the ship. Some of the men begged him to set the master and the pilot free, but most of them quickly forgot that they had ever meant to mutiny. They trimmed the sails as Vasco da Gama directed. A few of them even sang as they did it.

Da Gama then sailed along close to the other ships, shouting that he had put the pilot and master in irons and flung all the instruments into the sea.

'My ship is safe and I sail for India,' he called. 'Do what you like for your own safety.'

He steered off without waiting for an answer.

The crews of all the ships had been quiet while da Gama

was speaking. His voice was low, but he could make it carry across the water clearly. When he was silent, there was wailing and moaning from the Berrio and the San Raphael as the men begged that the Captain-Major would not keep d'Alenquer and Alvarez and the three seamen below decks.

'They will die before we reach Portugal—or India either,' sobbed one man, and the sailors repeated: 'They will die! They will die!'

Nicolau Coelho said good-naturedly that he would ask the Captain-Major to forgive the prisoners. The crew begged him to do so, and promised to follow the flagship around the world wherever it went.

Paulo da Gama spoke in much the same way with the men of the San Raphael. He promised them that he would beg his brother to spare the prisoners.

'Thank God,' he said, 'for sparing our lives. We have come safely through the worst storm I have ever seen. Ships that can stand this can sail through anything. Let us all have courage and all will end well.'

These words, and Paulo da Gama's friendly way of speaking them, made the crew forget their fears.

The ships all needed repairs, and they were short of drinking water because the barrels had been broken by being tossed about in the storm. Vasco da Gama sailed towards the land and the other ships followed him. After sailing north along the coast for several days, they found the broad mouth of a river. The Berrio went in first to see if it was safe to anchor there, and the other ships came in with the tide.

Dennis wrote in his diary about this place:

'The country is low and marshy and there are many tall trees. The people who live here are black but well made. The young women have their lips pierced and wear bits of tin in them. Men and women are dressed in skirts of cotton cloth. They took much delight in us and brought us food in their canoes.

'Their chiefs came to see us. Haughty men, they were, and liked nothing we gave them. One of them wore a silk cap with fringe. The other had a cap of green satin. Fernan Martinez understood a little of their talk. They told him they had seen ships like ours before. That made us glad because we thought the ships might have come from India.

"We stayed thirty-two days in this place. We keeled the ships over by putting all the heavy things on one side so that the other side was out of the water. Then we cleaned the weeds and shells off the planks and took out the caulking because it was rotten and had let in much water during the great storm. The caulkers put in new oakum and put pitch over it. We had a stove in a boat near-by and boiled the pitch in it.

'When we had finished one side we keeled the ships over the other way and worked on the other side. The mast of the San Raphael cracked in the storm and we repaired that too. Many of our men fell sick here. Their feet and hands swelled and their gums grew over their teeth. The Africans gave us fresh fruit and after drinking the juice of it the men felt better.

'We called the river the River of Mercy. We left there February 24, 1498.

'Just before we left, Paulo da Gama and Nicolau Coelho begged the Captain-Major to set the prisoners at liberty. They were ill with that sickness of which I have spoken—scurvy, Paulo da Gama called it—and he said the men might die in the dark hole below decks where they were.

'Captain Vasco da Gama always listened to what his brother said. Great love he had for Captain Paulo, as all of us did, for there was not one of us who had not had some kindness at his hands. He looked angry at first, the Captain-Major did, but then he smiled at his brother, and ordered Palha and Pirez to bring the prisoners on deck.

'I should not have known them for the same men.

'Vasco da Gama looked at them with that gaze he has like an eagle about to pounce. Then he looked at Captain Paulo and smiled—the smile he kept only for his brother.

'"I obey your commands, Paulo," he said. "I told the King I would, and it is right that the younger brother should obey the older."

'I stuck my finger into Shane's ribs at that, for he is entirely too proud of himself lately. He and young Coelho think they put down the mutiny with their harp and guitar!

'The Captain-Major went on: "What happened was because of faint-heartedness. It caused treason and that always brings a bad end to those who engage in it. I know that fear was at the bottom of it and I forgive you all. God has delivered us from the danger we were in and we ought to trust him to lead us safely to India. When we return to Portugal, the King will give us great honors and favors.

'"The smith shall strike off your chains, but you shall wear them when I present them to the King, so that he can see what dangers we have suffered. Let us all take courage for the rest of the voyage and ask God to protect us."

'The men with tears of joy all cried: "Amen! Amen! May the Lord so will it of his great mercy!"

'Then we weighed anchors and went out of that river with a land breeze.'

MOORS AT MOZAMBIQUE

IT WAS Shane who saw the sail.

At first it looked like an eagle, then like a dirty piece of paper. Then, as the south wind sent the Berrio forward over the rolling blue waves, the sun flashed full on it.

'A sail!' Shane yelled from his perch halfway up the mainmast, and whistled screechingly through his fingers.

The sailors below began climbing ropes and masts. On the other ships the men began to climb too.

From the San Gabriel Vasco da Gama's voice called: 'Give chase, men! We must overtake her!'

The pilots headed their ships to the west, for the strange vessel was between them and the land. Her crew must have seen the Portuguese fleet. She seemed for a moment to stand still with her sail flapping in the breeze. Then she swung eastwards and slipped out to sea. The Berrio, which could change her course more quickly than the square-rigged ships could, started after her, but lost sight of her when night came.

Captain Coelho was gloomy at supper that night.

FERNAN

'That ship might have known the way to India,' he grumbled to Shane, but added more cheerfully: 'Oh, well! Tomorrow's another day. Better luck perhaps.'

The next morning as the Berrio was passing the mouth of a small river, 'There's your luck, Captain,' Shane called. 'You can catch her this time. She's anchored!'

'What are you talking about, you impertinent monkey?' shouted Nicolau Coelho.

'The ship we saw yesterday. She must have come inshore at night. She's anchored in the river,' Shane said.

Someone on the San Gabriel had seen the ship too. Vasco da Gama had already started one of the boats for the shore. As it reached the mouth of the river, a canoe with seven men in it left the side of the ship. The San Gabriel's boat soon overtook it. Six of the men threw themselves into the water and swam away. The man who was sitting in it could not swim. The San Gabriel's men took him into their boat and rowed back with him to their ship.

Vasco da Gama called to Nicolau Coelho to come aboard the San Gabriel and bring Fernan Martinez with him. Shane managed to get into the boat that took Martinez over to the San Gabriel.

'You'll be staying to dinner, Señor Captain,' Shane said hastily, seeing Captain Coelho looking at him. 'And besides, I saw him first.'

Nicolau Coelho, whose mouth was opened to order Shane to stay on board the Berrio, laughed instead.

'So you did! Come along, you red-headed ape!' he roared.

The Moor was standing on the San Gabriel's deck looking quietly about him. He was a tall man with a skin the color of old ivory. He had on a robe of white stuff with a wide silk girdle. A colored cloth was folded around his shoulders. On his head was a cap made of squares of silk of many colors and sewn with gold thread. He had small gold rings in his ears.

Vasco da Gama gave him sweet cakes and olives to eat, and offered him wine. He would not touch the wine, but he ate the food. He was given a long red robe, with which he seemed much pleased. When they showed him spices, the Moor said to Fernan Martinez, who understood him and told the Captain-Major what the words meant, that he could get them plenty of such things. He was a trader, he told Fernan, and knew where to buy cinnamon and cloves.

'Ask him his name, Fernan, and tell him I will pay him well if he will go with us and help us find the way to India,' Vasco da Gama said.

'Moor says name Davane. Says he will go with us to help trade, but we must get pilots. He is trader, not sailor. India is part north, part east of us. But he can't sail ships there,' Fernan said after he had talked with the Moor.

Fernan stayed on the San Gabriel so that he could tell the Captain-Major what Davane said. Nicolau Coelho had dinner with Vasco da Gama before going back to the Berrio. Joãn Coelho and Shane waited on the captains at dinner. The boys hurried from the galley with the dishes of hot fried fish. They poured the wine without spilling a drop, as the San Gabriel pitched along over a choppy sea. They brought silver bowls and pitchers and poured water over their masters' hands between courses. They set the dishes of olives and nuts and the silver plates of honey cakes and the preserved pears neatly on the table and watched hungrily while the captains ate.

Nicolau Coelho always had a good appetite. Paulo da Gama was there too, but he ate little and sat playing with a walnut shell, floating it in his cup of wine. The boys watched anxiously as Captain Coelho ate olive after olive. However, the dish was a big one and there were still some olives in it when he stopped eating, picked up his olive stones, and began to place them around the table.

'Here,' he said, 'is the Cape of Good Hope. Here,' plunking down another olive stone, 'is the River of Mercy. If this Moorish fellow speaks the truth, India is over there by your wine cup, Paulo. Why, we shall be there before we know it!'

Captain Coelho put down another olive stone which, he said, marked the river where they found Davane, and began cheerfully on the cakes and pears.

Vasco da Gama scowled at the olive stones.

'If I had my astrolabe back again,' he said. 'I could tell better whether we have sailed far enough north. If we turned east now, we might sail to the south of India and never find it. No, we must go on along the coast until we can find pilots to guide us. There are cities to the north of us, he says. What do you think of this fellow, Paulo?'

Paulo da Gama put a crumb of cake into his walnut shell for a passenger.

'He's a fine-looking man,' he said. 'I like the way he sat calmly in the boat when his crew left him so suddenly. And I like his grave way of looking you straight in the eye as he speaks. Nothing seems to frighten him.'

'I wish we'd found one who knows the winds and the currents along this coast,' Vasco da Gama said. 'There are too many shoals. If we run on one, we shall be no better off than your walnut shell, Paulo, after you have drunk your wine. I'd like to turn east now, but without the astrolabe—'

'Señor Captain-Major, your honor,' stammered Shane. 'I

have a small astrolabe and a compass. My master Zacuto gave them to me. Shall I bring them to you?'

The Captain-Major raised his eyebrows and whistled in surprise.

'I'd give a ton of cinnamon for a squint of the sun with your astrolabe,' he said, 'but I won't touch it, Shane. The crew would think I was a liar—that I knew you had those things all the time when I threw the others overboard. No, Shane, I swore I'd sail to India without any instruments, and I will!'

Nicolau Coelho swallowed a honey cake almost whole and groaned: 'He was always like that. Compared to him, a mule is gentle and sweet-tempered. Will you throw Shane's toys overboard now you know about them? And is the sun your private property, or may Shane and I be allowed to look at it?'

'What you do on your own ship, Captain Coelho, is your own affair,' Vasco da Gama said gravely, but there was a twinkle in his dark eyes as he spoke.

'Don't look so down-hearted, Nico,' he added, getting up from the table and putting his arm around Captain Coelho's shoulders. 'Come, let's go on deck and talk some more to Davane. These boys are so hungry that I can hear their teeth grinding together. Give Shane plenty of food, Joãn. We must make friends with the only man in the fleet who knows how to navigate.'

The three captains left the cabin. Shane and Joãn fell to work on the food in silence. Shane, proud because Vasco da Gama had called him a man, thought: 'You don't need to be afraid of the Captain-Major unless you've done something wrong.'

With his mouth full of nuts, he said to Joãn: 'He's a seagoing man, your Captain. And so are your brother and Captain Paulo. Deep-water sailors all of them.'

'From a salty old dolphin like yourself, that's high praise,'

Joãn said solemnly, and found himself on the floor with Shane on top of him. 'Hey, stop choking me, you wild Irish sea serpent. Let me up. Got to—wash—dishes.'

'Gently, gently, my velvet-coated cabin-boy,' crooned Shane from his position on Joãn's ribs. 'Talk of serpents, would you? Stop squirming, then, or I'll think you're one my cousin Saint Patrick chased out of Ireland. Into Portugal they went, no doubt, and took their forked tongues with them, the way they'd speak sharp words to their betters!'

'Saint Patrick was your cousin, was he? I thought all your family were kings.'

'Not all,' Shane said calmly. 'Saint Patrick was a Connemara man or thereabouts. It might be his name was not O'Connor, but a man as good as he would surely be related to us some way or other. If I've sat on you long enough to make you respectable, we'll wash the dishes. Even a kinsman of Saint Patrick's and Ruadri O'Connor's need not be ashamed to be washing dishes for those captains, for as I said before, they're three seagoing men.'

Joãn got up and brushed crumbs off his velvet coat.

'I feel safe indeed now that I know Your Honor is going to pilot us to India,' he remarked.

'Have no fear, little man,' Shane said grandly. 'I'll bring you back safely to Lisbon.' He wiped off the table, and then, forgetting his dignity, added: 'Oh, Joãn, what do you suppose your sister is doing now? More embroidery—poor girl? Only think, if we'd been girls and had to stay at home! We must take something fine from India for her and Rachel, for I expect it's dull for them, waiting for us to come home.'

Joãn rubbed the Captain's silver cup till it shone and said gloomily: 'They probably never think about us at all.'

The ships sailed north. Towards the end of March they reached a place that Davane told the Captain-Major was called Mozambique. Davane had said he was not a pilot, but he warned the Portuguese that there were shoals and sand bars outside the harbor. Thanks to him they found their way safely among some small islands, and came at last into a safe harbor among green hills. The houses around it had roofs of straw. People hurried out of them at the sight of the fleet, ran to the beach, and stood staring and pointing at the strange ships.

Four ships that looked strange to the Portuguese were lying at anchor near-by. Davane pointed to them and said something to Fernan Martinez. The big negro came up to Vasco da Gama rolling his eyes and smiling.

'Davane says those ships from India, Señor!' he said, and began joyfully to shuffle his enormous feet and to snap his fingers.

'If they can sail to India in those things, we need not be afraid,' Vasco da Gama said. 'Ask him how they are made, Fernan.'

The planks, Davane said, were fastened together with cords made from coconut husks. The flabby-looking sails were mats woven from palm leaves. Though there were no decks, the traders carried silk and jewels and spices safely from India.

'Our ships look just as strange to them, I suppose,' Vasco da Gama said. 'Everyone in the town seems to be on the beach. We must make friends with the ruler of this place.'

Davane offered to go on shore and talk with the natives. The Captain-Major sent him ashore in a boat. The people crowded around him, chattering and pulled him along with them towards the town. It was a long time before he came back, but when he did it was in a canoe loaded with chickens, coconuts, figs, and mutton.

The Sheik of Mozambique had sent them with a message that he would visit the ships that afternoon.

Everyone set to work decorating the San Gabriel. Shane and Joãn hung flags and streamers from the masts. Sailors scrubbed the decks and spread carpets on them. Fernan helped Veloso to set up a tent on the deck. Veloso knew exactly how it ought to be done, he said. Fernan had an idea too. The result was that they both were found rolling on the deck covered with canvas. However, the tent was at last ready and the boys hung it with colored ribbons and set chairs and benches under it for the visitors.

There was a great polishing of swords and spears and breast-plates. The Captain-Major ordered the sick men to stay below where they could not be seen. The able-bodied men from all three ships gathered on the San Gabriel dressed in their best clothes and with their weapons in their hands.

Shane put on the brown velvet suit that Zacuto had given him. It was many months since he had worn it, but Zacuto's cousin Samuel had made it with room to grow in. It was still a good fit.

'You look very grand, Shane!' Joãn said as Shane and Dennis followed Nicolau Coelho to the San Gabriel's upper deck.

'I feel like boiled mutton,' Shane said.

'With carrots,' Joãn agreed, tweaking Shane's red hair.

'Behave yourself,' Shane growled, 'for it is not convenient for me to fight you now, because of the honor of our fleet which I must uphold at all costs. Besides which I'd rather look like a carrot—which is a sturdy and honest vegetable—than to have legs like two green string beans.'

João, who was dressed in bright green, only grinned at this insult and said cheerfully: 'Well, they look cool, anyway. You know so much about vegetables, Shane—what does Veloso look like?'

'A boiled beet,' Shane chuckled.

Veloso, in his crimson cloak, his face about the same color under his steel cap, the sun shining hot on his polished breast-plate, strode over and said gruffly: 'If you're grinning at *me*, you young imp—'

Just what Veloso intended to do Shane never found out, for the lookout called: 'The boats are leaving the shore,' and Vasco da Gama's rich, deep voice said: 'To your places, men.'

Followed by Paulo da Gama and Nicolau Coelho, the Captain-Major took his place on the deck near the tent. All three men were dressed in velvet coats edged with fur and jerkins embroidered with gold. Their stockings came up over their tight breeches and were kept in place by gilt cords. They had velvet shoes on their feet and stiff velvet caps turned back from their faces. It would be harder to say which looked hotter, Vasco da Gama in purple velvet or Nicolau Coelho in black. Paulo da Gama in dark blue somehow managed to look cool. He had grown pale and thin during the voyage. His long slender hands seemed made of bone and blue veins. There were hollows in his cheeks above his golden beard, and his blue eyes looked larger than ever.

From his place behind Captain Coelho, Shane could see the boats. Two canoes were lashed together and boards had been laid across them. Under an awning of palm-leaf nets sat the Sheik on a low stool.

As the Sheik's raft reached the San Gabriel, the Portuguese blew their trumpets. In a moment the Sheik appeared on deck.

Veloso and the other soldiers led him and his followers to the place where the three captains were standing.

The Sheik's tall thin figure moved slowly along the deck. His black eyes looked keenly at the faces around him. He kept his hand on the hilt of a silver-mounted dagger that was stuck into his sash. As he moved, a blue cloak embroidered with gold and silver swung from his shoulders. He wore also a red velvet jacket, thin white breeches, and a silk turban of many colors. Unlike his Portuguese hosts, he looked comfortable and cool.

The Moors with him were also splendidly dressed. Some of them were fair-skinned like their leader. Others were brown. Some were nearly as black as Fernan. The darkest of these were the musicians. They played on strangely shaped horns and trumpets and drums.

The Sheik looked haughtily about him. Then, seeing Davane, he began to speak. Davane, who had learned a little Portuguese while he had been with the fleet, told Vasco da Gama what the Moor said and made the Captain's answers to the Sheik.

'You have many things I have not seen before,' the Sheik said. 'From what country do you come?'

'From a far country called Portugal where we are subjects of a great Christian King.'

'You are so fair-skinned, I thought you were Turks, but it appears you are not,' said the Sheik. 'What do you want here?'

'We are trying to find India, but our pilots do not know which way to steer. We would like to buy goods there and here too.'

'If you do not find India, what will you do?'

The Sheik still spoke haughtily, but Shane thought there was a smile under his heavy black moustache.

Vasco da Gama answered: 'We will go about the seas till

we die, for our King would be angry and we should not dare go home.'

The Captain-Major then ordered some cinnamon and pepper and ginger to be brought. He showed them to the Sheik saying: 'These are the things we are looking for.'

The Sheik laughed, nodded at his followers, and said: 'Oh, you can find plenty of such stuff. I will give you pilots to take you where you can fill your ships, but what will you give in exchange?'

'We have gold and silver.'

'With gold and silver you can buy what you like anywhere. Will you make your men blow those things again? And let me see those bows and arrows that those guards carry.'

Vasco da Gama ordered the trumpets to be sounded again and told Veloso to show the Sheik his crossbow.

The Sheik took it and ran his thin fingers over it, looking at it keenly. Then he went ashore, promising that next day he would send pilots who would guide the fleet to India.

'Do you trust this man, Vasco?' Captain Paulo asked his brother.

The three captains were in the cabin. Outside the sound of the Moorish trumpets rolled over the water and died away, but the drums still throbbed and boomed.

'Why not?' the Captain-Major said. 'Help me peel off this jerkin, Joãn, before I boil to death... We will pay him well for the services of his pilots. He seems friendly and willing to trade with us.'

'I would trust him just as a flock of sheep ought to trust a wolf,' Paulo da Gama said. 'But then I am timid—like an old sheep. Pay no attention to me.'

'An old sheep who has more sense than all the rest of us,'

Vasco da Gama said, smiling at his brother. 'Tell us, Paulo, what you saw about our visitor that was like a wolf.'

'The look in his eyes when he saw the white crosses on our flags. The tightening of those thin lips of his when he heard that the King was a Christian. The smile he gave when you said you did not know which way to steer for India. His laugh, too, when you showed him the spices. Real laughter comes from under the ribs and rings like a bell. This was a wolf laugh. Yap, yap, snap, from just behind the teeth. I think they are teeth that would gladly bite Christians. I am sure he will not help Christians to take the trade with India away from his own people. And I see no reason why he should.'

'Except our cannon,' Vasco da Gama said angrily. He had taken off his hot clothes, but his face was red. 'We could blow their straw and mud town to the stars with a few huffs and puffs.'

'And have the news spread all along this coast that we were robbers and pirates,' Paulo da Gama said with his kindly smile. 'I never heard yet that it was wise for businessmen to kill their customers!'

'Oh, you are right, of course. You are always right!' Vasco said impatiently, but in a moment he added in the gentle tone that he used only to his brother: 'Shall we sail away, then, and try somewhere else for pilots? We need fresh water and food for our sick men.'

'Send Davane on shore tomorrow to buy more food,' Paulo da Gama said. 'He is loyal to us, I feel sure. Perhaps he will find out something about the Sheik's plans. Let us keep a good watch on our ships tonight. It would be an easy matter for the Moors to cut our cables and send us drifting on one of those sand bars. Trust them like wolves, for that is what I mean to do.'

LUISA

CHAPTER 13

LUISA GOES TO CHURCH

CONNEMARA! Here, boy! Here! Where *is* the dog?'

Luisa Coelho tugged at the bridle and the horse stood still. The wind on the hill above Lisbon set his long silvery tail swaying. It whistled through the scarlet reins and through Luisa's black curls. Far below it was beating the Tagus to a gray and white froth, and tossing the gulls about as they screamed and wheeled.

There were boats scudding up the Tagus ahead of the wind, but no square-rigged ships from India. Vasco da Gama's fleet had been gone many months. He must either, people said, have found India by this time, or have been swallowed up in those dark seas. But Luisa still rode to the top of the hills around Lisbon and watched the Tagus. Sometimes she rode as far as the monastery at Belem and prayed there for the safe return of her brothers.

The monks of Belem had grown used to the sight of the brown-faced, gray-bearded groom holding the horses while the tall girl with the red dog at her side prayed in the church.

They knew that she was thinking of her brothers who had gone with da Gama, and they cheered her by telling her of sailors who had journeyed for years, but who had come home at last. They did not know what Con was thinking of as he lay beside Luisa on the chilly stone pavement with his head on his paws, looking with sad eyes at the candles flickering on the altar. Still they spoke kindly to him. Once one of them gave him a bone with several bits of meat on it.

Probably the monks needed the bone more than Con did! It was a long time since Prince Enrique the Navigator had built the church and the shelter for sailors. The Prince had always given plenty of money to the brothers, but King Manuel was busy with great plans and seemed to have forgotten them.

Their little garden and the pennies given to them by grateful sailors kept them alive. But though sailors sometimes came home rich and gave money for Masses and candles, oftener they were poor and hungry and ragged. The monks looked carefully at a bone—one that with a little barley and a carrot or two, and onions and cabbage and a handful of dried peas, would make a fine soup—before they gave it away. Dogs they generally chased away, but this dog with the patient golden eyes was different.

On this windy afternoon, Luisa thought, the river looked as angry as those miles and miles of ocean between Lisbon and India might look. She shivered in the raw wind and called again: 'Connemara, you red rover!'

She whistled, but the wind blew the sound back between her teeth.

The groom hunched up his square shoulders. His bristly gray beard wagged as he spoke. His big hands were blue with cold.

He waved one of them and said: 'He's hunting rats, perhaps, Señorita. He went over towards that old house there on the next hill. The Street of the Rat ends just below it, and it's well named. There are grain-sellers' shops lower down. A dog can always find a plump rat there. We'd better go on, Señorita, for the light is going fast and your uncles will pull the hairs out of my beard for me one at a time if we are late.'

Luisa said: 'If you had hairs pulled out every time I did something my uncles didn't like, you'd have no beard at all by this time, Damian, and be as bald as an egg besides! You have a hard life, don't you?'

'Serving the Coelhos has always been like a hen taking care of a nest of young hawks,' growled Damian, 'but I've always done it, no matter how they pecked and scratched!'

Luisa laughed. There was not much like a hen about the grim-faced old groom.

'I'll race you to that old gray rat house,' she said tightening her reins. Damian grumbled something about a race between an Arab horse and a three-legged donkey not being much fun for the rider of the donkey. However, he urged his brown horse—which seemed to have the usual number of legs and was certainly not a donkey—after the white Arab.

The day was ending in a cold gray twilight. The white horse rushed through it towards the tall gray house. It was a gloomy-looking place. There were lights showing along the narrow street that twisted down the hill below it, and smoke blew out of chimneys there, but the gray house stood like a dark tower without either light or smoke.

Luisa would have ridden past it into the Street of the Rat, but above the whistling of the wind and the noises of the city below she heard a bark. It was Con's voice, and there stood the dog himself barking outside the iron-barred oak door of the quiet old house.

Luisa called to him, but he did not turn his head. His eyes were fixed on the door, his tail was swishing back and forth, and his bark had a pleading 'Let-me-in' note.

'He isn't chasing a rat,' Luisa thought.

Then the big door swung open. She heard a voice that was more like a sob say: 'Oh, Con! Con, darling, is it you?'

Connemara's voice changed to a happy whimper. A girl, younger than Luisa, had her arms around the dog and her face against one curly red ear.

'I've missed you. Oh, Con, I've missed you,' Rachel Zacuto said softly.

Then she looked up and saw the girl on the white horse looking down at her. Rachel got up from her knees. She looked up into Luisa's dark, handsome face with its black brows drawn together in a straight line above the short, straight nose, then said gently: 'Go with the Señorita, Con. You mustn't run away.'

She smoothed the head that was pressed against her knee and added: 'He comes sometimes. Perhaps you have missed him, Señorita. But I always send him away and without feeding him, so he will go home to you, though his golden eyes look so sad. He used to live here. With Shane, you know. Rachel Zacuto is my name.'

'Mine is Luisa Coelho.'

'Yes, I know, Señorita. Because you look so like your brother. He used to come sometimes—to see Shane. And because of what Shane said.'

'What did he say?'

'Your brother told us that one of the nobles at the court had said you were as beautiful as Cleopatra. Shane said—you remember his voice, Señorita, lazy one minute and quick the next—'

'Yes, I remember,' Luisa said.

'"Cleopatra!" he said. "A fat woman lying on cushions and playing with snakes. Don't tell me she wasn't fat. How would she be anything else—the way she lived? Rowed about in boats! And eating lying down! Why, she couldn't fan herself even, but had black men waving ostrich feathers around her. Of course she was fat. How would *she* look riding a white horse? Why, you wouldn't have been able to see the horse! You should slap the face, Joãn, of the man that had the impertinence to say that."'

Luisa Coelho started to speak, but Rachel went on: 'But you must go, Señorita. We are Jews, and it is not safe to be seen talking to me. I have talked too long already. Ride on, please, and take Con with you, before any of our neighbors see you.'

Luisa did not ride on.

'I'm not afraid of your neighbors,' she said.

'But I am, Señorita. They might say my father had put a spell on you, and stone us again. It is too dark, I hope, for you to see the bruise on my cheek. I spoke to a little boy down there and he slipped and fell. It was a cold morning and there was a little ice on the street. They called me witch and stoned me.'

Luisa said indignantly: 'Why, I know who you are. Your father was once Astronomer Royal, and he gave the compasses and things to Vasco da Gama. Everyone knows he is good and wise.'

'Yes, but now,' Rachel said, 'people think Vasco da Gama and all his ships have been burned up in a sea of fire and that it was my father who sent them into it. The compasses were magic and led them straight to their deaths, people say.'

'It is true,' said a melancholy voice.

A small figure slipped along the wall and stopped at the doorway. It was Zacuto, but so thin and with such lines of fear in his face that even Shane might not have known him. He had a basket in his hand. He set it down on the steps and began to speak in a low voice.

'I sneak out at this time of day when all my good friends and neighbors are at supper, so that I can buy a little food without being beaten or tripped up, or stoned. You had better go, Señorita. I know you. You are the sister of Shane's friend. Even in this light I can see how you look like him. We should not like to drag you into our troubles.'

Damian, who had now caught up with his mistress, said: 'Quite right, Señorita. Your uncle—'

'My uncle shall know about this and speak to the King,' Luisa said angrily.

'Better not, Señorita,' Zacuto said quietly.

He leaned against the wall wearily. He was still breathing hard after his climb with the heavy basket.

'The less His Majesty Dom Manuel remembers us, the better. You don't understand, Señorita. I will tell you, for the street will be quiet a little longer. Forgive me for not asking you to cross my doorstep. If you should do so and later—six months later even—you fell from your horse or had a fever, I might find myself being boiled in oil. I will speak quickly—no one will see us in this darkness. Then you must ride home and never come here again.'

'Boiled in oil!' Luisa exclaimed. 'You can't mean that.'

'Perhaps not exactly. But it is not very pleasant to have hot oil dropped on your hands till the skin has been burned off them. That happened to a cousin of mine only a few weeks ago, because he would not tell where his money was hidden. He was a tailor—such a good tailor. But he will never sew again with those hands. He made a suit once for a boy I knew, brown velvet

it was—but no matter. I was going to speak about something...
Speak quickly. What was it, Rachel? I forget everything these
days. But my daughter—a remarkable girl—she will remember
for me.'

'About all the Jews being sent out of Portugal,' Rachel Zacuto
said patiently. 'But we are Christians now, Father. You must
not forget that. My mother died, so she did not have to be
baptized, or stoned in the streets. But you and I are *maranas*
now—new Christians.'

'Yes, yes,' sighed the old man. 'I forgot. They threw my
candlestick with the seven branches into the river. I am a
Christian now.'

Luisa could no longer see his face. Damian tried to make her
go home. The white horse stamped and snorted impatiently, but
she sat still listening to the voice that came out of the darkness.

It told about how the Jews had left Spain, where they were
badly treated, and had settled in Portugal. There the kings had
protected them. They could live in any part of the city, wear
what clothes they liked, go into any business or trade. Then
King Manuel wanted to marry a Spanish princess. He hoped to
become King of both Portugal and Spain some day by making
the oldest daughter of Ferdinand and Isabella of Spain his wife.

King Ferdinand said that King Manuel could not marry his
daughter unless King Manuel sent all the Jews out of Portugal.
They must go, King Manuel said, before October, 1497.

'But where could we go, Señorita?' Zacuto's trembling voice
asked. 'If we left our houses and shops and trades, how could
we get new ones in some other country where they hate us? In
Spain they would kill us. In England they pull out Jews' teeth
when they want to borrow money. Here it is hot oil falling
on you. Drop by drop. Hot wax is good, too... Even if we had

known where to go and had the money, there were not ships enough to take us. You have not heard of this, Señorita?'

'No. I sit at home reading or making tapestry. Except when my uncles take me hunting, or I go to church. I do not like the Court. One of the courtiers, a friend of my uncles', comes sometimes, but he tells only court gossip. He does not think girls ought to know about public affairs. He started to teach me to play chess, but I beat him, so he decided it was unladylike.'

Zacuto went on: 'King Manuel had some mercy on us. We could leave Portugal—if we could swim or fly!—or we could become Christians. They baptized us—thousands of us. What else could we do? I am as good a Christian as I know how to be. But I wish they had not thrown my candlestick in the river. And the boys in the street still call me Jew and spit at me. Also there are men—they pretend to be of the King's household, but I do not know—who come and say: "Give us a gold noidor and we promise not to tell that you refused to eat pork on a certain day. Or that you gave money to this tailor whose hands were burned." So in that way my money is almost gone. And no one comes to ask about the stars... I was Astronomer Royal once...'

Rachel said: 'But it will be different when Vasco da Gama comes home. You will be a great man then, Father. And he must come soon. You think it will be soon, don't you, Señorita?'

'I—I hope so,' Luisa said.

'She would like to cheer me, you see,' Zacuto said gently. 'So would you, Señorita, but I know better. They are in danger. There is treachery around them. Vasco da Gama will find India. The stars say so. But the road is a long one, and the hour of his return is dark and uncertain. Perhaps I shall live to see it, but I cannot tell. It is hidden from me... hidden. You have stayed too long, Señorita. Go—and forget that you ever knew us.'

The door shut behind the shadowy figures of Zacuto and Rachel.

'If I were to tell your uncle—' Damian began crossly as the horses, followed by Connemara, clattered down through the dark curves of the Street of the Rat.

'Don't bother to do that,' Luisa Coelho said. 'I shall tell him myself.'

Her voice sounded strange to the old groom.

'You're not crying, are you, Señorita?' he asked, more gently than he usually spoke. 'I didn't mean—'

'I suppose I have a right to cry, haven't I?' Luisa sobbed. 'Poor little man—he was so good to Shane. And they threw his candlestick in the river.'

Chapter 14

TREACHERY

THE Berrio's boat with Shane at his place in the bow rowed Davane to the shore of Mozambique Harbor. The Moor carried a bundle of presents for the Sheik—pieces of satin, sharp Flemish knives, Portuguese caps, and a bag of money for the pilots.

The Sheik looked at the goods haughtily and asked why the Christian captain had sent no scarlet cloth. Shane, who had been busy adding Arabic to the other languages he spoke, understood some of the Sheik's questions. There were a great many of them.

'Why did Davane sail on a ship with the Christian dogs? How many men were there on the ships? It was said that some were sick—were there many sick ones? What kinds of merchandise did they have? Were the holds of the ships well filled? Was there much gold and silver? Could the men hit things with those strange bows? How many soldiers were there?'

Davane answered that the Portuguese were Christians, but they were brave and good men who had been kind to him. It was true that some of the sailors were sick, but there were plenty of strong armed men. They could shoot a flying bird with their crossbows. They had cannon which spoke with a loud voice and could tear a house apart as easily as the Sheik could tear a fig. They needed water. If the Sheik would lend them pilots who could guide them to a good stream and then show them the way to India, the Portuguese would go away quietly.

'Go back to your captain. Ask him to bring his sick men ashore. Our doctors will cure them.'

The pilots, two dark-skinned Moors, went back to the San Gabriel when Davane carried the message to Vasco da Gama. Davane advised the Captain-Major not to accept the Sheik's invitation, but to go away at once.

'He wants your silver and gold, Captain,' Davane said. 'And since you are a Christian, he will take it without any trading.'

'He's right, Vasco,' Paulo da Gama said. 'I have been watching the Moorish ships. There are more men on them than there were yesterday. They must have come on board last night. I think they mean to attack us.'

'I would blow them out of the water,' Vasco da Gama said, his face turning red, 'only I do not want to get a bad name here. I would sail with the tide, Paulo, but we must have water. Go back to the Sheik,' he added, turning to Davane. 'Thank him for his kind offer to care for our men, but tell him they are better and need no medicine. I'd as soon have them all bitten by snakes, but you needn't tell him so! Ask him where the best watering-place is. In the meantime Fernan Martinez shall question the pilots. We shall see if they say the same thing.'

When Davane came back from his second errand, it was clear that the Sheik meant treachery. The watering-place was not the one the pilots described, and it was a place where it would be easy for the Moors to attack the Portuguese.

'Paulo, you and I will watch the Moorish ships tonight,' Vasco da Gama said. 'Nicolau Coelho shall take his boat and one of the pilots and try to get water. We'll sail with the morning tide.'

The night was quiet. The ripples sounded loud against the bow of the boat. Shane, leaning back as he swung at his heavy oar, felt a cannon behind him, cold against his back. There was another at the stern where Captain Coelho sat steering with the pilot beside him. Soldiers with crossbows, the other nine rowers, and the empty water barrels crowded the big boat.

It moved smoothly through the quiet water. The squeaking of the oars, the chunking sound they made as they scooped into the water, the tinkle of drops dripping off them, all seemed to echo from the black shore. Even the low mutterings of Davane and the pilots seemed like shouts.

Shane could hear the pilot's: 'No. Not here. Farther! Farther!' and Davane's voice telling Captain Coelho what the man said.

The pilot had a thin sharp voice. Davane's was as soft as the rippling water. Nicolau Coelho's was like the deep rumble of a drum a long way off.

Shane heard him say: 'The man's cheating us, Davane. The tide will go down and leave us stuck on some sand bar. Tell him so.'

Davane spoke to the pilot who squeaked: 'No, no, plenty water. Deep water.'

At that very moment Shane felt the bow of the boat grate on something.

'We're ashore, Captain,' he gasped. 'Back water, men! Quick!'

The men rowed desperately and succeeded in getting off the shoal. The tide was now running out swiftly. They rowed back to the bay, the sailors crying out angrily to Nicolau Coelho that the pilot ought to be killed.

'I'll take him back to the Captain-Major,' Coelho said. 'Then he will find out how traitors are treated.'

The rim of the sun flashed suddenly out of the water as they were crossing the bay. As Captain Coelho turned to look at it, the Moorish pilot leaped overboard.

'Row after him! Catch the traitor!' Coelho roared, but the man had dived deep and he swam for a long time under water.

'Shoot him when he comes up,' Coelho shouted to the soldiers, but when the man's black head showed on the pink water, he was too far away to be reached by the crossbows.

The sailors rowed after him, but as they got near him a crowd of angry Moors appeared on the shore, shooting arrows and throwing stones from slings.

'Turn the cannon on them, Captain,' said Machado, who was rowing stroke with his friend Rodriguez next to him.

'Do that, Captain,' Rodriguez added. 'It's a fine town, and we could take it and live there at our ease.'

Nicolau Coelho said: 'The Captain-Major must decide whether our cannon are to speak. Back to the San Gabriel, men.'

Vasco da Gama was angry at the treachery of the Sheik and the pilot. The men were angry, too, and shouts of 'Take the town! Blow the black devils to pieces!' went up from the decks.

For a moment da Gama hesitated, then, still scowling, he said: 'It must not be told that we Portuguese have come to fight and plunder. Put that other pilot in irons. We'll leave this place.'

While they were making sail, a canoe pushed out from the shore. Four negroes were paddling. A Moor sat in the stern and waved a white cloth fastened to the end of a pole.

The Moor came on board the San Gabriel.

'The Sheik my master,' he said, 'is grieved that you should try to kill his pilot and go away so suddenly. If our people have done anything wrong, he will punish them, but the Captain must come ashore and tell him why he is angry.'

Vasco da Gama asked Davane to go back with a friendly message, but Davane begged da Gama not to send him.

'He will know I have warned you, Señor, and he will kill me,' Davane said.

'It is true,' Vasco da Gama said. 'Machado, I think I heard you shouting that you would like to see the town. You shall have your wish.'

Machado's handsome tanned face turned suddenly a yellowish brown. The red lips under his brown moustache grew purple and they twisted strangely as he said in a hoarse voice: 'Don't do that to me, Captain-Major. Let's sail away quickly, just the way you said. The town's not worth shooting.'

Vasco da Gama said coldly: 'When you were freed from prison, Machado, you agreed to do any dangerous errand that I might order. The smith has plenty of chains. You can go back in them to the prison in Setubal, or you can visit this pleasant town of Mozambique as an ambassador, stay there, and do your best to make friends with the Sheik and make him understand the power of our King. Palha, get his chest and put it into the canoe. Pirez, help him over the side if he is not able to go himself.'

'I'll go,' Machado said.

The color had come back into his face.

'I'll be lying on silk cushions sucking oranges while the rest of you are at the bottom of the sea with the fish sucking you,' he said, swinging himself over the side. 'So good-bye, fish-food!'

The canoe started towards the shore. The San Gabriel's anchor came up with its chains clinking. The red cross on the mainsail bulged as the sail filled. The Berrio's crew rowed quickly for their ship, with Rodriguez taking Machado's place at the stern oar.

Suddenly Rodriguez stood up in his place, leaving his oar trailing.

'I won't leave Machado,' he said, and threw himself into the water.

The crew watched with open mouths at the splash and the circle of ripples from his dive. In a moment his bald head appeared.

'Shall we row after him, Captain?' Shane called from the bow, but Nicolau Coelho only looked at the sun shining on the bobbing wet bald head for a minute. Then he moved to the seat that Rodriguez had left, seized the trailing oar, and said quietly: 'Let him go if he likes. He isn't so useful to us that we need to miss the tide. It will turn soon. Back to the Berrio, men!'

At the town of Mombaza the Portuguese met with more treachery. It was a pleasant place, with stone houses high on a rocky hill and fruit orchards in full blossom around it. The King sent out boats full of lemons, chickens, sugar-cane, and oranges.

'Sweeter than the oranges of Portugal,' the sick men said, and were better after eating them.

The presents, however, were sent only to make Vasco da Gama trust the Moors. The Sheik of Mozambique had sent a swift boat along the shore to tell the King of Mombaza that the Portuguese were Christians and that he must use every trick to get them on shore and kill them. Helped by Davane, Vasco da Gama found out the plans that the Moors of Mombaza had made against him, and he refused to go on shore.

He tried again to get pilots who could show him the way to India, but they were as treacherous and useless as those at Mozambique, and did their best to drive the whole fleet on a shoal where the Moors could seize and plunder it.

Vasco da Gama managed to get the ships safely away from Mombaza. The fleet went on sailing north along the coast.

'I think,' Shane said to Dennis, 'this is the worst part of the voyage. We know India is near. These people have spices and all sorts of Indian goods—I saw them when I went with Davane to the market—but we can't get there. It's like stumbling around a room in the dark looking for a candle. Right under your very nose, it may be, but find it you can't.'

The next day they reached the city which was the 'candle in the dark' for which they were looking. This was the city of Melindi.

The page on which Dennis wrote about Melindi had a picture of a negro playing a great horn of ivory as tall as himself.

'This is a friendly city,' wrote Dennis. 'It looks a little like part of Lisbon. There are high white houses along the shore. Fine houses they are, with plenty of windows. There are palm groves around it. When we first saw it, a few oranges were still on the trees, like balls of gold among the dark green leaves.

'Messengers came from the city to tell us that the King would make peace with us and help us. The Captain-Major sent Davane to say that we would enter the port. There is a reef of rocks that guards it and we were anchored outside in rough water. Davane went, looking fine in his new red robe. He carried presents for the King—some coral, three wash hand basins, a hat, some bells, and two pieces of cloth.

'I went with Davane, for I was a convict in Setubal and I had promised to go on dangerous errands. Indeed, I think there wasn't so much danger to this one as there would be in riding down the street of Setubal some fine morning! And besides, I wished to see the new things. I was very weary of the ship.

'We were taken to the palace. The King was sitting in his garden on a bronze chair with damask cushions under a round sunshade of crimson satin. His page had a short sword in a silver sheath. Two trumpets of ivory, richly carved, and of the size of a man, were blown by two black men. Through a hole in the side they blew, and it was a sweet noise they made.

'The King wore a fine robe of damask trimmed with green satin. On his head was a rich turban. We gave him the presents that the Captain-Major had sent. He was pleased, and gave us two silk cloths with fringes of gold and a ring with a blue stone, very pretty to look at, to take to our Captain. When we went back to the ship, a boat followed us. In it were large copper kettles full of boiled rice, very fat sheep all cooked, much good butter, thin cakes of rice and wheat flour, chickens roasted and stuffed with rice, also figs, coconuts, and sugar cane.

'The crews ate that day until they could not move. Not since we left Portugal have we had such a feast. When the Captain-Major sent his thanks to the King, he sent Shane to carry two silver basins with some preserved pears in them and a silver gilt fork. The King, Shane said, looked at Shane's red hair with as much surprise as if it had been green or blue with pink spots! And indeed red hair like Shane's is no commoner than blue in this part of the world!

'The King said that he would give us a pilot to guide us to India. There were ships from India in the harbor. Davane called the men on them Hindus. They were tawny men with little clothing, and long hair which they wore braided. One of them came on board the San Gabriel to be our pilot.

'The Captain-Major would have started at once for India, but the King and Davane and the pilot all told him that he must wait for the monsoon. Monsoon is the name they give to the winds that blow across this ocean. From October till April they blow from the northeast and bring rains and storms. From April till October they blow from the southwest. The Hindu ships were waiting for the wind to change. We had

Not many days later the wind changed as the King said it would....and we left the harbor of Melindi with a South~West wind. The day was the twenty~fourth of April of the year 1498.

never heard about these winds, but it was true that lately we had found that the wind was always against us. We had hard work to sail from Mombaza to Melindi for that very reason.

'We decided to wait, for the pilot and all the Hindus told us that when the wind changed it would blow us straight to Calicut on the coast of India, but that if we started now we would only battle with storms and head winds all the way, and perhaps never reach India at all.

'One day, while we were still in the harbor of Melindi, the King came to visit our ships. That was a great honor, so we cleaned our ships and trimmed them with green branches and flags, and sprinkled perfumes about. We trimmed the quarter-decks with carpets and rugs and figured stuffs from Flanders.

'A fine sight our ships were with the lances in stands with their points polished, the naked swords hung up with splendid breastplates and the arms of the captains. There was a table set out with dishes of silver and attendants grandly dressed. The captains went ashore in their boats to meet the King. In Paulo da Gama's boat they placed a chair for the King. It was covered with crimson velvet with a gold fringe and silver nail-heads. A carpet covered the floor of the boat and in the bow was a banner, forked, of red and white damask with the cross of Christ and a fringe and cords of gold and crimson.

'The King's own boats came with the King, and his men played on their drums and horns and flutes. Only when our trumpets blew, the King's men kept silence. The cannon saluted the King with a great noise and the captains helped him up a ladder to the deck of the San Gabriel. There they led him to a table spread with napkins from Flanders of the finest linen, and preserved almonds from Portugal, and jars of olives and marmalade. The silver dishes shone in the sunshine so brightly that the King said: "If these men use silver, their King must use only gold."

'The King and his people ate the food. They liked the olives more than anything else. When the King had finished eating, the Captain-Major brought a rich wash-hand basin, chased and gilt, and a pitcher to match, and poured water for him. Vasco da Gama gave them to the King's Moorish servant, but they were so heavy that the Moor needed two hands to carry the basin, and the same with the pitcher.

'The Captain-Major then told Shane to empty them of water and put them in their cases and give them to the King's man for his master. The King thanked him very much, and said that no King in India itself had such things.

'Not many days later the wind changed, as the King had told us it would, and we left the harbor of Melindi with a southwest breeze. The day was the twenty-fourth day of April of the year 1498.'

Dennis did not write again in his diary for a long time. There was a half-finished picture of a negro blowing one of the huge trumpets of copper and carved ivory at the bottom of the page, and a blot where the pen had fallen out of his hand that evening...

Chapter 15

DINNER IS LATE

SHANE came whistling along the deck. He had an earthen jug full of the red wine of Portugal—port they called it, and it was the color of the lantern at the left of the helm—in his hand. He was swinging the jug of wine, which was for Nicolau Coelho's dinner, around his red head. He was also dancing a jig-step to a little tune he had made up and swaying neatly as the Berrio pitched from the top of one long silver wave into the dark green hollow of the next one. Also he was looking at the stars.

Only a few moments before, the sun had rushed down into the sea. Darkness came suddenly on that gently rolling ocean between Africa and India. It was as if someone had drawn a dark blue curtain over the pale blue sky—a curtain with bright gold spangles on it.

Shane stopped jigging and swinging the jug. He had remembered—a little late—that Captain Coelho thought his wine had already been shaken enough by the sea, and did not need any more stirring up. Before going down to the cabin, Shane paused for one more look at the sky. Then he gave such a jump into the air that Captain Coelho at the helm thought for a second that Shane meant to jump overboard.

'Polaris! Polaris!' Shane yelled, bounding towards the Captain.

'What's the matter—you ambling elephant? You bouncing baboon! You rabbit-footed crocodile! You flea in the coat of a red-headed bear cub!' roared Nicolau Coelho, in a voice like a whole gale of wind and half of another.

'Polaris, Captain!' Shane yelled again. 'The North Star, Captain, sizzling up out of the sea. We're north of the Equator, Señor!'

He danced another jig-step and knocked over the wine jug. The cork came out and the good port made a dark pool on the clean deck. Shane snatched a rag from Fernan's hand—the negro had been cleaning the port-colored lantern—and began to swab up the wine, talking fast.

'Will Zacuto be proud when he hears that it was I, Shane O'Connor, and no other at all that saw the North Star first? Ha! I believe it's an astronomer I am, after all. On the twenty-ninth day of April in the year 1498, four days' sail from the good town of Melindi! I'll put it on my chart. There'll be no spot on the deck, Señor Captain. And after all you wouldn't mind sparing a few drops of wine to old Father Neptune now that we're north again, would you?'

He tossed the wine-soaked rag into the sea, and began talking in Arabic to the pilot from Melindi.

'It's true,' he said after a moment. 'He says it's the star they steer by to reach India. So *now* am I a flea and a baboon, Señor Captain?'

'You're a seagoing astronomer with as many eyes as the peacock has in his tail!' Nicolau Coelho said. 'Go on, astronomer-peacock with a thousand eyes, and get me my dinner, or I'll eat you roasted and stuffed with stars and with port wine poured over you! Scamper!'

Shane scampered.

He must tell Dennis. But why was Dennis in that stuffy cabin instead of on deck under the starlight?

The lamp was swinging from the ceiling with the pitch of the ship. It threw first light, then shadow on the dark figure at the table.

'He's gone to sleep,' Shane thought, 'over his writing.'

But Dennis was not asleep. He lifted a pale, heavy-eyed face from the drawing of the trumpet-player and stared at his brother.

'My head,' he muttered. 'Someone—put—iron band—around it. Trumpets blowing in—my ears. Ink—on—paper.'

He gazed down at his paper again. There was a blot that his pen had made. And something else besides.

'That's not ink, Dennis. It's blood,' Shane said quietly. 'It's all over the table. There's a cut here under your hair. What's happened? Can't you remember?'

Dennis said slowly: 'Sitting here drawing... Marmalade... Hepzibah...'

Shane tore a clean napkin into strips, poured water from the Captain's silver pitcher, washed the cut, and bound it up.

'It's almost stopped bleeding,' he said. 'Lie down, Dennis. Don't try to talk.'

He helped his brother over to the Captain's bunk and stood looking anxiously down at him. Dennis's face was as pale in the greenish glow of the lamp as a sheet of paper on which his dark eyebrows and lashes had been scrawled by his own pencil.

DENNIS

Shane knelt down and put his fingers on Dennis's limp wrist. His pulse was beating slowly and faintly.

Dennis half opened his green eyes and said again: 'Marmalade... Hepzibah.'

He smiled up at Shane. Then he dozed off and his pulse began to beat a little more strongly.

Hepzibah, the striped cat that Rachel had given Shane, came purring and waving her tail, and rubbed against him.

The purring grew louder. Then she jumped up on the bunk and lay down beside Dennis. Her eyes blazed green out of the dark corner of the bunk.

Shane stood up trying to think what to do. He did not dare to leave Dennis alone. If he went for help, the man who had hit Dennis might come back and finish his work. Shane hunted for the key of the cabin.

It must be in the Captain's pocket, he decided. What did Dennis mean about Hepzibah? And why should any one want to hurt Dennis? Had one of the mutineers found out that Dennis had helped to spoil their plans? Did this mean more mutiny? The Captain-Major had got rid of Machado and Rodriguez. Was there a new leader of revolt?

'He may,' Shane thought, listening for any sound that was not the comfortable talk of the ship going forward before the steady wind, 'be outside in the passage waiting for me to call or run out. Here I stand like a sheep waiting for the butcher to hit me!'

He moved over to the rack on the cabin wall that had Nicolau Coelho's swords and battle-axes stuck in it. Shane was pulling an axe out of the rack when the ship lurched and sent something rolling against his foot. He stooped down and picked it up. It was a pottery jar of marmalade. Beside it was a pewter plate.

The jar was cracked and the marmalade was oozing out of it. The plate had a dark stain on its sharp edge. Sticky. But not marmalade, as he had thought at first. Blood. Dennis's blood.

Shane, with his fingers cramped on the battle-axe, was scowling at the plate, when he heard footsteps. He stiffened his arm and raised the heavy axe.

Nicolau Coelho's voice called cheerfully: 'What's for dinner, my long-tailed astronomer with the thousand eyes?'

The Captain swung into the cabin and he stopped short at what he saw. Shane, with every freckle standing out on his pale face. The green light of the lamp flashing on the blade of the axe. Dennis's quiet figure in the bunk with the purring, green-eyed cat beside him. The table with the scattered papers, the dark spots, the stained pewter plate, the red pottery jar with the crack in its side.

The Captain stood silent while Shane gasped out what he knew. Little enough it was, as Nicolau Coelho said.

'Is it mutiny again, Señor Captain?' Shane asked.

'Why should they mutiny now with the seas calm and our bow at last pointed straight for India? And with Machado gone? And why begin on Dennis, who is liked by everyone, who quarrels with no one, but sits writing and adding figures and drawing pictures all day?'

'I don't know—unless they think it was he who helped get word to Vasco da Gama about the mutiny. I thought they never guessed about the harp and Joãn's guitar, but they may have. And they may think Dennis put us up to it.'

Nicolau Coelho was silent, pulling at his black beard. Then he said: 'How's your courage, boy?'

'I—it's nothing much. But for Dennis—and for you—I can do what needs doing—I think.'

'Good lad. Walk to the bow first. Then go to the galley for my dinner as usual. Whistle as you go—or sing, if you can't whistle. You always do one or the other. That will make them think you have not found Dennis yet. Notice if there is anything unusual on deck, or anywhere in the ship. Bring the food. And tell these men I want them; Martinez, Pero Escolar...' Coelho named over half a dozen names of men he knew to be loyal, and added: 'Stick this knife in your belt. And give me the axe. Go along now, and whistle.'

Shane started. He puckered his lips to whistle, but they stiffened and no tune came through them. He began to sing. His voice stuck in his throat, and what little noise he made sounded queer and rough in his own ears.

> *'Sing, for a road that's long*
> *Shortens with singing,'*

Shane croaked, thinking: 'It's a long road to the galley. Shall I get there?'

He reached the sailors' quarters. They were throwing dice and carving little ships and making bracelets of coconut fibre rope and chewing sugar cane just as usual.

> *'Sing when night turns the day*
> *Darker and colder,'*

Shane sang, and then called: 'The Captain wants to see you, Señor Escolar, and you, Fernan, and you Sancho Mexia.' He called the other sailors the Captain had named.

Sancho Mexia, a little brown-faced man with a mop of crinkly hair, got up yawning, shoved his sugar cane into his mouth, and trotted off chewing, and trying to keep up with Fernan's long strides. The other men followed him more slowly.

On deck the voice of the helmsman and the cries of the sailors sounded as they always did.

'*Song to each toiler brings*
Peace for his sorrow,'

Shane sang, and reached the galley.

'You're late,' grumbled the cook. 'I fried the last of those chickens we got in Melindi. Fried them all brown in olive oil. Now they're all dried up. Am I to stand over this hot stove all night with no one to help but that black savage that can't speak a Christian word? He may be a grand pilot, but he's no more use in the galley than a penguin with the toothache.'

'What's he doing here?' Shane asked, looking at the Mozambique pilot, who was washing some pewter cups. He had his back turned towards the cook.

At Shane's question the man looked around, but turned his head quickly away again. There was a raw scratch on his dark cheek.

'Do? Nothing!' the cook said crossly. 'My helper died of scurvy. The Captain ordered the irons struck off this fellow—he's the pilot those traitors at Mozambique lent us—and gave him to me for a cook's helper. Well, curses on all presents that eat, I say. He eats more than he cooks! Here, take the tray and tell the Captain it's no fault of mine if the chicken tastes like a patch on the mainsail. He's lucky to get anything with savages in the galley eating sugar cane and oranges, and licking out the jar that the preserved pears came in, which I happen to be fond of myself, and it is proper that I should have it and any marmalade left over also. Not waste it on heathens. Don't stand there letting the chicken get cold. Hop!'

Shane hurried back with the heavy tray.

'Escolar and the others say there is nothing wrong on the ship,' Captain Coelho said, as Shane set the tray down. 'What do you think?'

'I think the same. But why should anyone hurt Dennis?'

'When he wakes, he may tell us,' said the Captain. 'We'll guard the cabin. Stay here now, Fernan and Sancho. Replace them at midnight, Escolar, with two of the others.'

All night the guards watched in the cabin. All night Dennis slept heavily in the Captain's bunk. The Captain dozed in his velvet chair. Shane lay on his mattress on the floor, watching the lamp swing and the shadows shift on his brother's pale face.

Fernan and Sancho Mexia paced up and down. Sometimes the light was on Fernan's dark face under his red sailor's cap: sometimes it showed Sancho's wrinkled brown face and wide grin. Sancho had had the scurvy. All but two of his teeth had fallen out, but the little man always looked cheerful.

The other sailors came on guard at midnight. Shane slept for a while. When he woke, Fernan and Sancho were on guard again. Shane opened one of the shutters. The fresh breeze blew through the cabin with its smell of burning oil and stale food and wine.

Dennis stirred and opened his eyes.

'Hello, my young cock of the morning!' he said in his own gay voice.

Then he sat up staring around him, and put his hand to his bandaged head.

'What am I doing here in the Captain's bunk? The Captain asleep in his chair! Fernan—Sancho—armed—axes—swords! What's all this, Shane? Mutiny? I must get up.'

'Lie down, Dennis! Don't start your head bleeding again! Leave the bandage alone! Captain—wake up, Señor!'

Captain Coelho jumped up. He saw Shane holding his brother's hands and Dennis laughing weakly.

'I've no more strength than a kitten, Captain,' Dennis said. 'See how this little runt that I used to carry on my back can hold me down! Yes, a cat is strong compared to me. Let me go, Shane. I'm glad enough to lie quiet. What was it he hit me with, the thieving rascal?'

'What who hit you with?' Captain Coelho asked quietly. 'Shane found you with a gash on your head and that's all we know. You muttered some nonsense. He couldn't understand it. So all night we've been on guard against mutiny.'

Dennis laughed.

'Not mutiny. Marmalade!'

'That's what you said last night, Dennis! Tell us what you mean,' Shane said eagerly.

'It grew too dark to draw. I put my pen down and lighted the lamp. The flame was slow coming up. It was only a speck of light and where I sat it was dark. The cat was on my shoulder— the way she often is while I write—and we sat there waiting for the flame to grow...

'Just then someone sneaked in on bare feet. It was that Mozambique fellow. The one you let loose from his irons, Captain, and sent to help the cook. He never looked my way, but went straight to the cupboard and grabbed a jar of marmalade. He was just putting his black paw into it when I jumped for him. I grabbed for the jar, and somehow managed to come down on his foot. He dropped the jar and spoke some few curses at me.

'I'd have let him go with nothing worse than a few hard words of my own, but he'd snatched up a pewter plate and he tried to strike me with it. Hepzibah was still on my shoulder, the claws of her pricking into me and her tail switching against my neck. She lets go of a sudden and flings herself spitting and scratching in the pilot's face. I suppose he clipped me with the edge of the plate—it's as sharp as some razors I've seen. I don't seem to remember much more.'

'I'll throw him overboard with a marmalade jar full of lead on each foot,' Nicolau Coelho roared.

'Don't now, Captain! If it hadn't been for the cat clawing at him, I doubt if he would have touched me. I think he'll not have seen who it was—the light being so dim and me between him and what there was of it. He and I are friends in a way. Hassan's his name. I've been to see him often in his cell. He was teaching me his talk. Anyway it was my fault, for it was I that asked you to take the irons off him.'

'Fernan! Sancho! Bring that Moorish thief in here,' Captain Coelho said sharply.

The pilot was a fat little man, no taller than Sancho Mexia. He was a strange gray color under his dark skin. The tracks of Hepzibah's claws were purple on his cheek. He stood shaking between his guards, with one foot pulled up from the floor and the toes of it curled tightly.

Nicolau Coelho glared at the trembling man.

'Ask him what he means by trying to kill Señor Dennis, Fernan,' he said.

Fernan spoke to the Moor, who burst out in rapid talk. He shook his head so hard that the silk that covered it slipped and fell to the floor.

'He says Señor Dennis is his father and his mother and all his most favorite relations. He says he wouldn't hurt hair of Señor Dennis's honorable head. Says pull out his own hairs with red-hot tweezers if he ever meant to hurt Señor Dennis.'

'Since he's mostly bald that wouldn't trouble him much,' Nicolau Coelho observed.

'He says,' went on Fernan, 'that he is Señor Dennis's slave. It was a devil told him to take the marmalade and then hit him in the face. Otherwise he would never have hit the Señor. It was all a mistake.'

Nicolau Coelho said: 'It seems he's your slave, Dennis. What will you do with him? I give him to you. You can heave him overboard, or put him in irons again, or send him back to the galley.'

'Oh, let him go, Señor Captain,' Dennis said. 'I believe he'll make no more trouble.'

'Very well. Say this, Fernan: "You, Hassan, are the slave of Señor Dennis. Whatever he tells you, you must do it. But if I ever catch you near my cupboard again, I'll throw you into the sea and you can swim back to Mozambique. Now march back to the galley and cook your master some breakfast. Jump, you Mozambique marmalade hound!"'

The Mozambique marmalade hound hastily withdrew.

Nicolau Coelho chuckled.

'There's nothing like a little mutiny to stir up an appetite,' he remarked. 'Shane, get us some of those rice cakes the King of Melindi gave us. And don't forget the marmalade!'

LAND OF INDIA

THE wound on Dennis's head healed quickly, but the days went by slowly. For twenty-three days they saw no land. Scurvy broke out again among the crew and there were many who groaned that this ocean where the wind always blew now from the southwest went on forever.

Yet one day when the sun rose there was a hazy line below it. Hazy, but thicker than a cloud.

On the San Gabriel the pilot from Melindi said to Vasco da Gama: 'There, Señor Captain, lies the land of India.'

Vasco da Gama stood looking quietly at the misty line for a moment. He saw nothing at first except the sea and a cloud a little darker than the sky. Then, as he looked, the sky cleared and against its faint blue was the dim blue shape of a mountain.

'There is India!' Vasco da Gama said. 'Let us thank God, who has guided us there.'

He knelt down and the crew knelt around him. There was silence except for the creaking of ropes and the singing of the waves. Some of the sailors were wiping their eyes, but no one spoke.

Vasco da Gama got up from his knees.

'Call to the other ships, Joãn,' he said. 'They don't know yet.'

Joãn climbed high up the mainmast.

'India!' he called, waving his red cap. 'The land of India!'

The Berrio was only a little behind. Shane heard Joãn's voice. Joãn could see Shane dancing on the deck and hugging Dennis. Hassan, the Moor from Mozambique, came running out of the galley with his dark arms covered with flour and an egg in each hand. Fernan Martinez slapped Hassan on the shoulder and Hassan dropped both eggs on the deck. The cook came out and began scolding Hassan. Shane shinned up the mast and called back to the San Raphael.

Just then there was a low rumble of thunder. A black cloud above them opened and drenched the decks of the three ships. The blue shadow of India slipped behind the curtain of rain, but it was there behind that curtain. They had seen it.

Late that day they anchored near the city of Calicut. It lay

on flat land with the mountains they had seen rising sharply behind it. The city was a strange mixture of straw-thatched huts, temples, pagodas, and palaces, and of tall Moorish buildings roofed with tiles rising here and there.

'The Captain-Major,' wrote Dennis after sketching the city with the hot mist steaming away from it, 'sent me ashore with Davane the next morning. Our ships did not enter the harbor, for there were many ships there, and if they had attacked us, we could not have escaped with that southwest wind always blowing against us. We dropped anchor outside the city in a place where we were a little sheltered by a rocky point of land, but still the waves kept the boats bobbing about.

'Davane and I were walking through a narrow street with many dark people crowding close around us when a voice said behind me in Spanish: "May the Devil take thee! What brought you here? For what are you looking so far from home?"

'"For spices," I said, looking around.

'The man who had spoken was dressed like a Moor, but he was a Spaniard. He said his name was Monsayde. We went with him to his house and he gave us bread made of wheat with honey on it.

'These Hindus of Calicut are a brown-skinned people. They clip their hair short or shave their heads, leaving only a tuft on the crown, but they wear moustaches. Gold rings swing from their ears. They are bare to the waist with skirts of fine cotton stuff. The women are small and ugly. They wear many jewels hung around their necks, bracelets on their arms, and rings set with precious stones on their toes.

'There are many Moorish men on the streets with long beards and hair. I thought some of them did not look at us very lovingly, but no one did us any harm. We found that their ruler—the Zamorin they call him—was away from the city at another palace. We sent a message by the man they called his Gozil—that is what they call the Zamorin's chief minister—to say that an ambassador from the King of Portugal had arrived in Calicut and asked for an audience.

'Monsayde went back to the San Gabriel with us. As soon as he was on board he said to the Captain-Major: "A lucky venture! Plenty of rubies! Plenty of emeralds! You owe great thanks to God for having brought you to a country holding such riches!"

'The crew were all astonished to hear him speak Spanish in this distant place. It seems that many years ago he went to Tunis in Africa with some Moors. They took him to Mecca with them and from there he came to Calicut and has stayed here ever since. He works in the King's warehouse. The King's factor, who has charge of all goods that enter and leave the port, is a Moor.

'The next day came a message that the Zamorin had come back to the city and would receive the Captain-Major. The Spaniard Monsayde and our good friend Davane told the Captain-Major to ask for hostages before he went ashore. The Zamorin sent them—three young soldiers called Nairs. Men of good birth they were, and fine-looking besides. They stayed on the San Raphael with Paulo da Gama.

'The Captain-Major set out—it was the twenty-eighth of May—and took with him thirteen men, of whom I was one. They were all splendidly dressed, except me, in fine liveries of red and white. The Captain was in blue, with a cloak that had a lining the color of a red water jar. Palha and Pirez were there—fine-looking big men in their gay clothes with their bushy brown beards. With my old black suit and my bare thin face, I looked like a starling among peacocks. Even Fernan

Martinez, who was in prison with me in Setubal, looked more fit to be received by a king.

'Shane and Joãn Coelho were left behind, and angry enough they were. Neither did the other two captains like the Captain-Major to risk his life on shore while they were safe on the ships, but they had to obey his orders. He told his brother that if any treachery took place on shore Captain Paulo must sail back to Portugal with the news, for none of their lives were of any importance compared to letting King Manuel know that the sea route to India had been found.

'The Gozil came to meet the Captain-Major. They brought a litter—they call it a palanquin—for him to ride in. Six men carried it. The road was crowded with people watching us. Even women with children in their arms came out of their houses and ran after us.

'Men beat drums and blew on pipes and trumpets. Armed men escorted us. Crowds of people from the roofs looked down on us. It was almost sunset when we reached the palace. We had to push our way through the courtyard and then through four doors. There were men with knives all around us. Some of our men were cut as we forced our way through the crowd.

'The Zamorin was in a small court, lying on a couch covered with green velvet. He was a very dark man, half naked. He had on his arm a bracelet of three bands, each shining with jewels. A diamond as thick as my thumb hung down from it. It seemed a precious thing. Round his neck was a string of pearls the size of hazel nuts. The string took two turns around his neck and reached his waist. He also wore a pendant made of emeralds and rubies. His page had a red shield with a border of gold and diamonds. The rings inside for the arms were of gold. His sword had a gold hilt with jewels in it.

'In his left hand the Zamorin had a gold cup. He was chewing a nut called betel nut that has a red juice. At his right was a basin of gold so big that a little man like Sancho Mexia could just stretch his arms around it. This held betel nuts wrapped up in leaves. When the Zamorin had finished chewing the nut, he threw the husk into the gold cup. There were many silver jugs near him, and the canopy above the couch was all gilt.

'The Zamorin told our men to sit down on a stone bench. We did, and they gave us some bananas to eat and some melons. We sat there eating them and the Zamorin sat chewing the betel nut.

'At last he told Vasco da Gama to follow him to another room. Of course he spoke to a Moor and the Moor spoke to Fernan and Fernan told Vasco da Gama what the Moor said. The Zamorin said that the Captain-Major's interpreter and secretary could go with our master, so Fernan and I followed. This happened a little after sunset.

'The Zamorin threw himself on a couch with a cover of gold embroidered silk and asked through the interpreters what the Captain-Major wanted.

'The Captain-Major told him that he had been sent by a great king far across the sea, that this king, Dom Manuel, wished to be the Zamorin's friend and brother. The Zamorin said that Vasco da Gama was welcome, and after he had asked many questions, he said that the King of Portugal was now his brother.

'It was now getting very dark, too late to go back to the ships, so the Zamorin said we must stay in the city for the night. He told the Moorish interpreter to find us a lodging. We went back to the court. Our men were still sitting on the stone bench. There was a roof over them, but rain was pouring down in the middle of the court. There was a huge candlestick, lighted, beside the bench. Even Pirez and Palha, strong, brave men though they are, looked pale in the fluttering light of it.

'We followed the Moor. A great crowd pushed after us in spite of the rain that was making rivers of the streets. The Captain-Major was carried in the palanquin, but the rest of us splashed along through the mud and the rain. The Moor took us to his own house. It seems he was the King's factor that Monsayde had told us about, the one in charge of all the trade of the port.

'We slept on carpets on the floor. There were great candle-sticks like the one at the palace. At the tops were lamps, each with four wicks. They burn oil, or butter, and give much light.

'On Tuesday, the twenty-ninth of May, the Captain-Major got ready a present for the King. A party from our ships came to bring the things. The Zamorin had told Vasco da Gama that he could buy and sell whatever he liked. So the Captain-Major had sent word to his brother to send some goods ashore. Shane and João Coelho came to help carry the goods. Very pleased with themselves they were for having got ashore.

'The present was made up of the following things: twelve pieces of striped cotton cloth, four scarlet robes, six hats, four strings of coral, some Flemish mirrors with doors all finely gilded, six wash-hand basins in a case, a case of two casks of olive oil, and two of honey.

'When Vasco da Gama tried to put these things into the hands of the Gozil and of our Moorish host, the Zamorin's factor, they laughed at the goods.

'The Gozil said: "Is this a present from one king to another? Why, the poorest merchant from Mecca or India would give more! The Zamorin would not accept such things. Your present should be in gold." The factor called in some Moorish merchants and they all laughed at the present too, and said that no one should send such trash to the palace.

'Vasco da Gama said: "If you will not send my present to the Zamorin, I will go and speak to him myself and then go back to my ship."

'"Wait a short while," the Moorish factor said, "and we will escort you to the palace. First we must go on some other business, but we will be back soon."

'The Captain-Major waited all day, but they never came back. The Captain-Major was angry and would have gone to the palace alone, but we persuaded him that there was much danger. He walked up and down angrily, biting at his moustache. I sat down under some palm trees to write this, and I listened to the seven bells on the temple near-by tinkling. As for the others, they enjoyed themselves singing and dancing on the beach. Shane had his harp with him and Joãn his guitar. There is a tune Shane has made up that the men seem to like to sing. There was also some blowing of trumpets. Altogether they had a fine time, and Joãn beat them all by jumping the farthest in the sand. This was on a beach near the warehouse. Shane threw a heavy stone farther than anyone else. The boy has muscles like copper under his freckles.'

Dennis stopped writing and went to sleep in the shade of the palms. When he awoke it was growing dark. The Spaniard Monsayde and Vasco da Gama were sitting beside him. Vasco da Gama looked angrier than ever, and he jerked at his beard with his sunburned hand as he listened to the Spaniard.

'You must be patient, Señor,' the Spaniard was saying. 'The Moors here are afraid that you will take their trade away from them. They will do everything they can to make you angry so that you will go away and never come back. If you lose your temper and use force, you will never see Portugal again, Señor. And I must not be seen talking to you or I shall find myself hung up by my thumbs.'

Monsayde hurried away into the darkness.

What he had said proved to be true. The Moorish factor and the Gozil continued to make trouble for the Portuguese. The next day Vasco da Gama was escorted to the palace. He was kept waiting outside in the blazing sun for four hours. When he saw the Zamorin, the Captain-Major was told that he had better go back to his ship and take all his people with him. The Zamorin refused to look at the Captain-Major's present, but said that the Portuguese had better move his ships closer to the docks at Padarani—a place outside Calicut near where the ships lay—and send his goods ashore and sell them for what they would bring.

Vasco da Gama then sent word to his brother to tell him to send the goods ashore, but he told him not to move the ships, but to leave them where they were.

Paulo da Gama, by Davane's advice, sent on shore to a warehouse near Calicut a chest of a hundred pounds of red coral in branches, a barrel of quicksilver, a hundred pounds of vermilion, fifty pigs of copper, twenty strings of large cut coral, and the same of amber. He also sent Portuguese coins of gold and silver, a table with a green cloth, and a wooden balance with four weights. The Portuguese sold these goods and bought instead pepper and ginger and other spices.

After Vasco da Gama saw that his goods were being sold and that everything was going well, he went back to Padarani, where he had left Shane and Joãn and some of the other men on the beach. He asked the Gozil, whose house was near the beach, for a boat to take him out to the San Gabriel. The Gozil

refused with many smiles and polite excuses. It was too late in the evening, he said. The Portuguese must spend the night in his house. He would get a boat for the Captain-Major in the morning.

The Portuguese slept in the Gozil's house that night. The next morning the Moorish factor came. He and the Gozil told Vasco da Gama that they would get a boat for him, but that first he must send one of his men with a message to tell the ships to come inside the harbor and anchor close to the shore.

Vasco da Gama said: 'When I left my ships, I told my brother, who is in charge of them, not to move from where he now is. I told him, too, that if he thought I was in trouble, he had better sail back to Portugal without me. If I send my brother the order you suggest, he will think you are holding me prisoner, and forcing me to send the order. He will hoist his sails and leave this place. And when King Manuel sends another fleet, you will see that you have made a mistake. I will not order my ships to come nearer.'

'Then you can have no boats,' said the Gozil.

'Very well,' Vasco da Gama said quietly. 'The Zamorin

ordered me to return to my ships. If you will not let me obey his orders, I will go back to the palace and speak to him again. Do not forget that I am the ambassador of a great king.'

'Give us your sails and your rudders,' said the factor. 'Then we shall know you mean peace.'

'We mean peace,' said the Captain-Major, 'but we will leave our ships where they are and our sails and our rudders with them.'

Shane heard one of the Moors behind them say: 'Shut the doors! Shut the doors! That captain of theirs has a dark look.'

Shane slipped through the crowd to a small door in the wall of the courtyard. He was wearing a white Moorish robe that he had bought in Melindi and he had a striped piece of silk bound over his red hair. No one noticed him go. The main gates shut with a clang. He was only just in time. The small door was open, but he had barely reached the corner of the house when he heard the door slammed shut and the iron bar inside it fall into place with a crash.

He got to the back of the building without being seen, twisted his way through a hot, steaming bit of jungle and reached a slow-moving river with swamps along it. Every old log in it looked like a crocodile. Some of them were crocodiles. Shane followed the river, keeping a good distance between him and any logs that might possibly be alive. At last he found himself on the rocky point near which the ships were anchored. The ships were north of it. South of it lay some tall warehouses with docks in front of them.

Shane crawled between two rocks that tilted against each other, sat down in the small patch of shade between them, and tried to think what to do next. When he slipped out of the Gozil's house, he had thought it would be an easy matter to get a message to Paulo da Gama. He had thought that he could hail one of their own boats on their way back and forth with goods, but no boats either left the Portuguese ships or went out to them. The docks were crowded with people, many of whom seemed to be watching the strange ships.

'If I wave and they send a boat out for me,' Shane thought, 'there'll be a hundred Moors to grab me before the boat lands. They can see me from the Gozil's house and the dock too. If they think I've warned Captain Paulo, I don't like to think what they might do to the Captain-Major. And Joãn's there too. And Dennis. No, I'll just have to stay here till dark and swim for it. I wonder if crocodiles ever swim out of the river in the evening...'

He sat there watching the ships. They were close enough so that the wind brought the sound of the sailors singing as they scrubbed the decks. Some of the men were stitching at the sails and mending them. That red spot on the Berrio must be Veloso fishing. Shane could hear him roar with delight as a fish flapped its silvery way out of the water and was yanked over the edge.

The breeze set the flags fluttering at the mastheads. The Berrio was the nearest.

'She can't be more than a quarter of a mile out—less, perhaps,' Shane thought. 'I can swim it easy enough.'

The shadow hardly covered him. The sun beat down on the rocks until they were as hot as a stove. Only a few yards away was the cool, green water, but it was no use looking at it. Shane heard the Berrio's bell call the men to dinner. The white figure moving along the deck carrying something must be Hassan with the tray for the Captain's dinner. Once, when the breeze blew hard, Shane thought he smelt fish frying. He had eaten nothing since the night before. He was hungry, but his hunger was nothing to his thirst.

When he thought his cracked lips and swollen tongue could stand it no longer, there came one of the sudden showers of that time of year. Shane rolled out of his shelter and let the rain beat down on him. He opened his mouth and water dripped into it, but his lips still burned. When the rain stopped, a little cup-shaped place in the rock was full. He bent over and lapped every drop out of it.

The afternoon was better as the sun was behind him and he had more shade, but it seemed endless. At last the sun went down behind the ships into a bed of red clouds that licked up out of the water like tongues of flame. They faded quickly to bronze and then to an inky purple. Someone lit the Berrio's port lantern. It glowed like one of the Zamorin's rubies against the blue-black velvet of the sky.

Shane slipped out of his Moorish clothes and threw himself into the water. He swam fast, driving his arms hard. The thought of possible crocodiles made him keep up a brisk pace, but the Berrio's lantern seemed to come no nearer. He looked back and saw the dark line of shore still close to him. There were lights on the docks. Above the noise of his own splashing, he thought he heard a boat slide into the water. He hoped it was! Yes, there were paddles chunking, but which would be worse—crocodiles or angry Moors?

He decided that Moors would do him at least as much harm as a stray crocodile. He turned on his back and floated, hardly moving a finger. The boat went south along the shore, he thought, but he stayed floating for a moment listening to make sure about the boat and looking up at the stars. The North Star was there, and the Great Bear.

He thought: 'Zacuto may be looking at them now. And

Rachel. Perhaps Joãn's sister can see them too. I wish Rachel knew her. Rachel must be lonely and Luisa must be bored. I hope that Governess isn't making her do doves' toenails. Why not embroider something sensible? A nice crocodile, now!'

He turned over in water that seemed full of stars and swam through them. Still that port-colored lantern drifted on and on. There was a red path led right to it, but it always seemed to be the same length no matter how hard he swam. He swept through the starry mirror with long strokes, but there was always more water, more stars, and still that red light, dancing, dipping, drifting.

The water had seemed warm at first, but the tide had turned against him and now it was cold. The wind had died at sunset. Now it came up again; turned ripples to waves that broke against his chin. Suddenly the rain poured down again. The stars were hidden and the Berrio's lantern was only a faint pink spot miles away. Water ran down into his eyes, stung the top of his head, splashed little fountains under his nose. Then the rain stopped as suddenly as it had begun. The red lantern swung at the top of a dark wall high above him.

The links of the anchor chain bruised his knees as he climbed it, but he was too cold to feel its hardness. His teeth rattled together as he shivered and dripped along the deck.

He thought: 'Every thief in Calicut—including the Gozil and the factor, who are the biggest ones—could climb on board the Berrio and not get caught!'

Then Captain Nicolau's voice roared: 'Stand where you are!'

Shane said through chattering teeth: 'It's only me, C-Captain.'

'Shane! What are you doing here like this? Where's the Captain-Major?'

'In p-prison, S-Señor. And it's you that's got to help him out.'

'Get some clothes on, you stammering jellyfish!'

'S-send for S-Señor P-Paulo, won't you, Captain?'

'All right—all right! Escolar! Row over to the San Raphael and ask the Captain for the favor of his presence here. Veloso! Tell the cook to heat some wine and spice it well with some of our new cinnamon. Get some clothes on, I say, you red-headed iceberg!'

CHAPTER 17

SING IN A PRISON GRIM—

VASCO DA GAMA and his men passed all that hot day most anxiously. At night they were no longer allowed to walk about in the big courtyard, but were shoved into a smaller court. The jailers wore threatening scowls on their dark faces. A hundred men, armed with swords, shields, battle-axes, and bows and arrows, guarded them all night, some watching while others slept.

In the morning—it was the second of June, Dennis said, though the others felt as if weeks had passed—the Gozil and the factor came and told the Captain-Major that he must have all the merchandise in his ships sent on shore. They said that it was the custom of the port that all ships should land all their goods at once. Besides, they said, it was the Zamorin's order.

It was not really the Zamorin's order. The Gozil and the Moorish factor wanted the goods for themselves. They had planned to seize the ships and kill the men on them, but when Vasco da Gama refused to have the ships move close in shore, the fight seemed too dangerous. The factor said it would do almost as well to make him send all the goods on shore, and then kill the Captain-Major and his men...

It was Paulo da Gama who saved his brother's life.

When Shane brought the news that the Captain-Major was a prisoner, Nicolau Coelho was so angry that he would have turned his cannon on the town of Calicut and on the Moorish ships anchored near them. Paulo da Gama, however, refused to allow any violence.

'It will only cost my brother his life,' he said.

Nicolau Coelho growled: 'We'll go on shore in a party and get him out of that house. Shane will show us the way.'

'My answer is the same,' Paulo da Gama said firmly. 'The first thing they would do would be to kill the prisoners. Even if we could rescue them—which I doubt—we should be on bad terms with these people with whom we've come across the world to be friends. No, I see only one thing—or rather two things—to do. And one not to do.'

'What are they?' Coelho rumbled.

'I promised Vasco that if he were seized I would sail back to Portugal. That I won't do—not so long as I know he is alive. What we will do is this: first get a message to Vasco to tell him to be patient a little longer; then—release the hostages.'

'Release the hostages! Are you losing your mind?' Nicolau Coelho thumped his big hand down on the table and stared at Paulo da Gama. 'Why, they are the only reason those rascals haven't killed our men already!'

Paulo da Gama sat quietly and let his friend roar. He looked white and tired in the dim light of the lamp. Perhaps it was only the lamplight, but Shane thought that Señor Paulo's hair and beard had turned, not white exactly, but a paler gold in the last few months. His hands looked thinner than ever. He rested his head on one of them, and with the other gently tickled Hepzibah behind the ears.

In spite of his weary look, his blue eyes still had their old brightness, and there was a smile in them as he watched Nicolau's thumping red fist. After a while Captain Coelho stopped for breath, and there was no sound in the cabin but Hepzibah purring under the touch of Señor Paulo's long fingers.

'We will release the hostages,' Paulo da Gama repeated mildly, 'because they are men of honor. One of them is a kinsman of the Zamorin himself. From what Shane tells us, it is not the Zamorin who is holding our men prisoners, but that Moorish rascal, the factor, and that delightful old gentleman with a face like a hungry tiger who is called the Gozil. They were the ones who were laughing in their sleeves—no, the Gozil didn't have any sleeves—behind their hands on the dock when they sold us that last year's cinnamon. When the Zamorin finds out that his minister and his factor have been trying to cheat him, I think he will not be pleased. I feel quite sure that the Gozil intends to get most of our goods and all of our money for himself. Probably the factor has much the same plan. I am going to send the young Nairs ashore in the morning and ask them to remind the Zamorin that they came as hostages for my brother's safety. As the Zamorin probably thinks Vasco is safe on his ship, he is not going to like it. Force will get us nothing, Nicolau. Let's try generosity and fair dealing.'

'He is a gentleman—and strong. And wise,' Shane thought, as Señor Paulo put the purring cat down and stood up.

'You did well, Shane!' he said. 'We'll have them back safely, I know—our three brothers: yours, Nicolau's, and—mine. They'll all stand sometime in the chapel at Batalha before Prince Enrique's tomb and tell him that his dream has come true...

the sea route to India. You'll be there too, Shane.' He was silent for a moment, and then said, half to himself: 'I'd like to smell the pines above Batalha again. And the rosemary and thyme when you crush them under your feet. Down in Lisbon the girls will be burning blue thistles in their windows some long June night. And the larks will be singing in the morning. I'd hear them when I was riding...That was a good horse of mine, Shane. Do you remember? I rode him from Batalha to Lisbon. Swift he was, and with a mouth like velvet.'

'You'll be riding him again before long, Paulo,' Nicolau Coelho said. 'We've done what we promised the King. It's time we sailed home and told him so. As for me, I'm sick of palm trees and boiled mutton and treacherous Moors.'

'We have all three in Portugal,' Paulo da Gama said, laughing.

'But not so many to the square foot,' said Nicolau Coelho. 'Well, let your hostages go if you like, Paulo. I might as well agree. Any plan that will save Vasco and start us home finds favor with me.'

The next morning Paulo da Gama set free the three young Nairs, who were the hostages. Shane and the Mozambique pilot, Hassan, were the interpreters. The three Nairs were dark young men with gold embroidered cloth wrapped around them below the waist, gold bracelets on their arms above their elbows, and gold rings in their ears. The sun blazed on their splendid shields of vermilion and gold and on their sword-hilts of gold and jewels.

Paulo da Gama told them that the Gozil and the Moorish factor had taken the Captain-Major prisoner.

'My brother was an ambassador to the Zamorin, and the Zamorin promised peace and friendship to our master, who is the King of Portugal. The Zamorin sent you here to be pledges for my brother's safety. Is it not so?'

'It is so,' said the Nairs.

'And I have a right to cut off your heads if he is harmed. Is that not true?'

'It is true.'

Paulo da Gama said: 'We Portuguese scorn to do such things. Instead I set you free. You are men of honor and can take care of your own honor. I ask you only to tell the Zamorin that his servants have taken my brother prisoner. I am sure the Zamorin means no treachery to our great King and that he knows nothing of this injury to my brother. The next Portuguese fleet that comes will not forget what has happened here. We came in friendship. We wish to go away in friendship.'

He gave to each of the Nairs a red cap, a fine Flemish knife and sheath, three yards of red satin, and some gold coins of Portugal. Then he sent them away in a boat. With them went the Moorish pilot, Hassan. Both he and Shane had asked to be allowed to carry the message, but Hassan was chosen to go.

What happened to Vasco da Gama seemed of little interest to Hassan. He said over and over again: 'I am a slave; I must save my master. My master, Señor Dennis, saved my life. I must save him.'

'It's a trick to escape from us,' Nicolau Coelho said.

'Do you think so, Shane?' Captain Paulo said.

'No, I think he's honest—when it isn't a question of marmalade. But I wish you'd let me go. I got out of the place. I could get in again.'

'You were lucky to escape,' Captain Paulo said. 'It was a miracle. Don't expect another. Hassan can easily make his way through the crowds. One more Moor in the mob you describe won't be noticed. But a Moor with green eyes and freckles won't get past the guard. Let us try Hassan. We will give him no message in words—only this letter, which I have written to Vasco. Even if the Moors get it, they can't read it. Hassan can't tell them our plans, because he doesn't know them. Make him understand that all he has to do is to get into the Gozil's house and give the letter to one of our men. If he can't get in, tell him to come back to the point where you were yesterday and wave. Then we'll try something else—not before.'

Shane made Hassan understand what he was to do. Shane and Veloso rowed Hassan and the Nairs to the shore. Shane landed long enough to pick up the Moorish clothes he had left there the night before. The three tall Nairs, with Hassan trotting at their heels, disappeared among the palms.

'If it hadn't been for Captain Paulo,' said Veloso, 'I'd have choked every one of those black robbers with my bare hands.'

'And eaten their swords, I suppose,' Shane said. 'I didn't know you were a sword-swallower, Veloso. I saw a man swallow one in Calicut the other day. Snakes, too. Have you been taking lessons? That will be a fine way to amuse your customers when you get back to Portugal and open that little inn you are always talking about.'

'I have not been taking lessons,' Veloso said; 'and I am not sure, but I think those are fighting words you used to me. You had better be careful, young O'Connor, for I am a terrible fellow when roused.'

'I wouldn't rouse you for anything,' Shane said. 'If you choked me with your bare hands, I'd be in no shape to eat dinner, and I heard the noon bell ring on the Berrio just now. What do you say, Veloso, to putting our backs in to it and getting there before it's all eaten?'

In the Gozil's house Vasco da Gama paced up and down
a small tiled court. It was the hottest part of the day and the
place was quiet. The Portuguese soldiers and sailors lay asleep
on stone benches along the walls or on straw mats on the floor.
The guards with their two-edged swords dozed in the courtyard
outside. Beside a small iron-barred window Dennis O'Connor
sat playing with his pen.

He had grown tired of writing. He leaned his head against
the iron bars and breathed in the air that blew in from the
southwest. It was hot, but it struck his damp hair and on his
forehead with a little freshness.

The Gozil's house stood on a piece of rocky ground higher
than the land around it. Dennis could look down on roofs and
courtyards back of the docks, on jungles and swamps on the
other side, and straight ahead on the silvery green bay with
the strange ships in it. Moorish zambuks lay there; Hindu
ships, too, with their sails of matting and planks stitched with
coconut fibre and smeared with fish oil; stranger still, ships
called junks from Cathay.

'From China where Marco Polo went,' Dennis thought. 'He came back in a ship like that. He may have been in this very harbor.'

He started to say this aloud to the Captain-Major, but Vasco da Gama's face was so stern and fierce that Dennis turned back to the window without speaking.

Out beyond the rocky point that shut in the harbor, he could see their own ships with the red and white flags snapping in the breeze against the glaring blue sky. He saw a boat crossing the water to the Berrio. It went north of her and he saw it no longer.

'Some Moorish boat with fish to sell,' Dennis thought, and picked up his pen again.

Joãn Coelho was asleep on one of the straw mats. Thinking he might go to the Zamorin's palace with his master, he had come ashore in his best red satin suit. His black head was against one red satin sleeve. His suit was wrinkled from having been slept in. His guitar was beside him. The gay clothes that all the Portuguese had worn looked strange in this bare hot room. Vasco da Gama had thrown aside his blue velvet hat with the white feather in it, and his blue cloak with the tawny red lining, but he still wore his suit of blue satin. His white leather shoes were stained with mud, and so were his stockings of blue silk.

His men had been dressed in liveries of red and white. They were a sad sight now, for the red had run into the white and stained it. The trumpeters were asleep with their brass trumpets beside them. There were banners of red and white with gold spheres embroidered on them still hanging from the trumpets, but the banners were creased and spotted. The trumpets had been polished so that they looked like gold, but they were tarnished now. Shane's harp was leaning against the wall. The strings were loose.

Outside in the court there was a stir. The Gozil's servants came in bringing boiled fish and rice wrapped in fig leaves for the prisoners. A little man with a striped cloth hanging down over most of his face carried a dish of figs. He passed it to the Portuguese trumpeters, who were yawning and stretching after their sleep. The court was crowded with the Portuguese waking up and the Moors chattering as they set the dishes down on the floor.

The little man with the figs came close to Dennis and said in a low voice: 'Take a fig, master. Very nice. Nice as marmalade.'

Dennis found himself looking into the face of Hassan, the pilot from Mozambique.

'Say nothing,' Hassan muttered and added louder: 'Take a fig, master. Take two. There are plenty, for our lord the Gozil is a generous man.'

He slipped a paper from under his robe. Dennis took a fig and the paper too. He slid the paper under a picture he had drawn of the Captain-Major standing fiercely among the sleeping men.

Hassan let the cloth fall over his face again and moved on with his dish of figs.

Dennis thought the meal would never end, but the Moors finally gathered up the empty bowls and left the prisoners alone. When the last Moor had gone, Dennis gave the letter to Vasco da Gama.

The Captain-Major had hardly spoken that day. Now he stared at the paper and muttered: 'Paulo! Paulo wrote this! How did it come?'

'The little Moor Hassan brought it, Señor Captain. He slipped in here with the servants who brought our dinner.'

Vasco da Gama held the letter without opening it.

'It is to say good-bye, I suppose. Are the ships still there, Dennis? They should be raising the sails if they are to sail with this tide.'

'The sails are still furled, Captain-Major.'

Vasco da Gama broke the seal and read what Paulo had written:

> My brother, be patient. There is hope. Nicolau will be at the mouth of the river north of the harbor with the boats. Come straight there when they release you. Tell Dennis his brother is safe on the Berrio. I will not sail without you, Vasco.
>
> PAULO

The Captain-Major frowned.

'He is wrong to wait. He promised to go. My life is nothing compared to the news of this voyage. I tell you the truth, Dennis, that even now if I were in the Tagus, I would not sail up to Lisbon, but would take my life with my own hands rather than appear before the King and tell him I turned back from my task. I settled this in my soul. I do not value my life at anything.'

'Your brother values it, Señor,' said Dennis quietly.

Vasco da Gama looked through the iron bars at the Portuguese ships. The southwest wind still kept the King's standard flying.

He said more calmly: 'I will be patient a little longer since Paulo wishes it. But if in three days the Zamorin has not released us, I will send Hassan to tell my brother that if he does not sail, it will be only my dead body that he will leave behind. This news that we have found India must reach the King. I am sorry, Dennis, that I have led you and the others into this prison. For myself I care not at all.'

'One prison is much like another, Señor,' Dennis said quietly. 'This one has a pleasanter view than the one you and Señor Paulo took me out of.'

He picked up Shane's harp, tightened the strings, and began to strum on them.

'What shall I sing you, Señor? Some song of brave knights and fair ladies? Of brave deeds by land and sea?'

'I heard you sing once a song of Portugal. There were no brave deeds in it, but—today I should rather hear that.'

The talk around them stopped as Dennis's voice rose above the purring sweetness of the harp.

> 'The meadow is a carpet red and white,
> A lizard flickers green along the wall,
>   A bee goes humming on her busy flight,
> The cuckoo wanders, singing, over all.'

'Sing with me, Joãn,' Dennis said.
Joãn Coelho sat up on his straw mat and sang:

> 'The church bells echo in the cooling air,
> A little wind no stronger than a sigh
>   Brings home the fishing boats to anchor where
> Above the cliffs the swallows wheel and fly.'

Vasco da Gama stood looking out through the barred window at the ships. He had asked for the song, but he scarcely seemed to be listening to it.

> 'Climb up! Climb up, oh, sailor, to the height
> Of our topgallant mast! What's that you call?'

sang Dennis, and Joãn's voice rang out in answer:

'Good news, my Captain! Coming into sight
Are Spain and our bright land of Portugal!'

The harp strings were quiet. Palha coughed. Pirez cleared his throat.

Vasco da Gama, without turning from the window said: 'Something gayer, Dennis. What's that tune the men danced to on the beach the other day? The one where they stamp on the sand and swing around. Let's have it. Dance if you like, men. Let the Moors know we're not afraid of them.'

'You know it too, Joãn. The one Shane made up,' Dennis said.

Joãn picked up his guitar and tightened the strings. The jigging, cheerful little tune seemed to bring courage and coolness into the bare, stuffy court.

The Moorish guards crowded in the doorway looking on.

'These Christians have no fear of anything,' one of them muttered.

'Or they are mad, perhaps,' observed another. 'See how they hop and spin!'

The court was a strange sight. Men in stained red and white liveries stamping and singing. Joãn in his crumpled red satin pacing about thumping his guitar. Dennis pale, but with his green eyes glowing above the dull gold of the harp. Vasco da Gama at the window with his face still turned towards the harbor.

'When we get—home again,
We will have—gold enough,
Rings for our—fingers and—
    Rings for our toes'

sang the sailors.

'Mad indeed,' said another Moor. 'See! They slap each other, but they still smile!'

'Pepper and—cinnamon,
Ginger and—satin stuff,
Jewels and—perfumes that—
   Smell like a rose.'

There was a noise in the courtyard outside, but no one noticed it.

'Ladies will—smile at us,
We'll look 'em—over and
Pick out the—prettiest,
   Little or tall;
Ask 'em to marry us,
To live in—clover and
This is the—song that we'll
   Sing to 'em all.'

'Make way, there!' someone shouted in the court, but the men in the red and white liveries went on singing and stamping.

'Some girls like—India
Others like—Africa
Coconuts, spices, and
   Ivory too.
'We have in—Portugal
Wine, olives—páprika
So we like—Portugal.
   What about you?'

Cries of 'The Zamorin!—Messengers from the Zamorin!' came from the outer court as the last notes of the harp and guitar died away.

The crowd at the door divided and three young Nairs—the hostages Paulo da Gama had released—came quickly into the court. Their scarlet and gold shields were on their arms. Their sword-hilts and bracelets flashed in the light of the setting sun that shone through the barred window.

The Spaniard, Monsayde, was with them.

'Say to the Portuguese Captain that he is free to go,' the oldest of the Nairs said to Monsayde. 'Tell him that our lord the Zamorin knew nothing of this treachery. When the Captain's brother sent us ashore we went to the Zamorin. We said to him: "Sir, if you are going to kill this Portuguese ambassador, say so at once, for then we will kill ourselves. We owe our heads since they were pledged in good faith, and we will pay them, for we are men of honor." The Zamorin was angry with the men who have done this thing. He sends you this present of silk and gold and pearls, and begs your pardon for this trouble.'

When Monsayde had told Vasco da Gama what the Nairs had said, the Moors who had been guarding the prisoners hurried away.

Vasco da Gama thanked the Nairs for their help and said that he was proud to have friends of such honor and courage.

The Nairs said that the Zamorin hoped that the Portuguese would come on shore freely and buy and sell what they liked, and that they would allow some of his people to visit the Portuguese ships. After many speeches and compliments they went away, and the Portuguese left the Gozil's house.

The guards with the sharp swords had vanished and the Gozil was nowhere to be seen. The present that the Captain-Major had meant to give the Zamorin had vanished too, but the Portuguese spent no time looking for it. They were glad to get away from that place and to reach the river where Nicolau Coelho was waiting for them with the Berrio's boat, and to see a red-headed, freckle-faced boy in Moorish clothes sitting at the bow oar.

CHAPTER 18

WHEN WE GET HOME AGAIN

DENNIS wrote in his diary: 'The noise in this cabin makes it hard to write. My brother bought a parrot in the town of Calicut and has taught it to talk. It's an educated bird indeed, being able to say "Good morning" in Irish, Portuguese, Arabic, and the Hindu tongue, as well as cursing in the two last, and singing in Portuguese. Shane has taught him to sing that song he made. So we pitch along through thunder and rain with him cackling out:

> *"Some girls like India,*
> *Others like Africa."*

'When I sit here writing, he'll call: "Portugal, Portugal. Calicut"—that's his name—"Calicut like Portugal! How about you?"

'Little he knows about Portugal, poor bird, and we have been through such storms that it has seemed many times that he would never see it—nor we either.

'We did not stay long in Calicut after we got out of the Gozil's house, only long enough to buy some more spices and other goods. Many men came on board our ships to see them. Some brought small children with them. Our Captain ordered that they should be fed, and indeed they were very hungry. It even happened that when some of our men were mending a sail and had taken biscuits with them to eat, old and young took the biscuits out of the sailors' hands and left them nothing to eat. Our men went ashore and traded their shirts for goods of Calicut. And indeed the people there could do with a few shirts! We bought cinnamon and cloves and ginger—those of us who had any money. Some bought a pearl or two.

'After we left Calicut we visited Cananor, a place farther north. There the Captain-Major made terms of friendship and peace between the King of Cananor and Dom Manuel. The King of Cananor sent to our King a splendid gold collar with jewels and pearls broad enough to go on the shoulders, and ten pieces of silk with gold thread—a very handsome present. He gave to each of the captains a thick round gold chain with a gold ornament set with emeralds and rubies, six gold rings with valuable gems, and pieces of fine white stuff.

Our present to this King was much branch coral and vermilion, and quicksilver; also scarlet cloth and basins of copper, brass, and silver.

'At Cananor the Moor Davane, who had helped us so well, left us; for he had friends there who would take him to Cambay, where he lived. The Captain-Major gave him a hundred cruzados besides the money he had promised him, and pieces of silk and damask, and a letter telling of all the help Davane had given us. Davane said that if the Portuguese came again he would gladly serve them. He went ashore sitting very straight in the boat. We were sorry to see him go.

'Because of calms and bad winds, it took us three months

to cross the sea between India and Africa. All our people suf-fered again from scurvy. Our gums grew over our teeth and we could not eat. Thirty of our men died of it. There were only seven or eight of us left able to sail the ship, and we were not so well as we ought to have been.

'At last it pleased God in his mercy to send us a wind which carried us within sight of Africa, and on Monday, January 7, we cast anchor off Melindi. We were as glad to see it as if it had been Portugal. We hoped to get well there as we had before.

'The good King, our friend, sent us a present of sheep and kind messages. The Captain-Major sent me ashore to buy oranges, which were much longed for by our sick. In spite of the good food, more of our men died. We stayed five days resting from the hardships of a passage in which we have all been face to face with death.

'We left Melindi on January 11 and passed Mombaza. On Sunday, January 13, we anchored and burned the San Raphael, for we no longer have enough men to sail three ships. The goods from the San Raphael and her figurehead we put in the other ships. On February 1 we anchored near Mozambique. I would have put Hassan ashore, but he would not leave us.

'As if that parrot of Shane's—that green and scarlet chatter-box—did not make enough noise, Joãn Coelho has bought one too. It is a gray-and-rose-colored bird and he calls it Melindi. So now we have one parrot from India and one from Africa, and a fine row they make between them. Joãn's bird knows the African tongue as well as Arabic, and he is quickly learning all that the other bird knows.

'Before we left Melindi, the King gave the Captain-Major a letter for King Manuel. It was written on a palm leaf covered with gold. The King sent also to our King a neck chain of gold with precious stones and pearls; also a chest with ornaments of silver and ivory full of white stuffs and silks embroidered with gold thread.

'Besides there were twenty rings of great value and a piece of ambergris as thick as a man's waist and half a yard long set in silver. Such a piece none of us had ever seen. When the Captain-Major saw it, he told the crews to shout, and ordered the trumpets to be sounded so that the King of Melindi could hear them on shore.

'Then Vasco da Gama put into a boat ten chests of different colors of coral, and much amber and vermilion; also brocade and scarlet cloth and mirrors and knives and red caps, and drinking glasses with gilt on them. He sent the King a dagger of his own hanging from a belt richly fringed, and asked the King to wear it for his sake.

'When the King saw these things, he said: "I am a poor man! Can I pay for all this?"

'He sent the Captain-Major many pieces of satin of gay colors and other kinds of cloth and said: "These are poor things—not good enough for you, just what I would wear myself. Give them to your sailors to dress in when they reach Portugal."

'The King sent also two great jars of preserved ginger for the Captain-Major and for Captain Paulo, which they were to eat at sea when they were cold.

'The pilots who had guided our ships to India sailed with us to Portugal, for they knew the winds and currents along the African coast. Vasco da Gama promised to send them back to Melindi. They were glad to go with us, for they wished to see our country.'

Dennis stopped writing and drew pictures of the two parrots with their wings spread screaming at each other. Then he went on: 'Our birds have just had another argument. It is funny to hear them. The boys are making cages for them.

'I call them boys, although they seem like men now, and have done the work of men on this voyage. Joãn came to the Berrio after we burned the San Raphael. He and Shane have been ill only a little, and they have taken the places of sailors who have died.

'On March 3 we reached San Braz, where we caught anchovies, seals, and penguins—those solemn birds without wings dressed in black coats and white jerkins. We salted them for our voyage home. Fresh penguin is no treat. Salt penguin is just a little worse, but we are lucky to have food at all.

'The Lord gave us such a good wind that on the twentieth of March we were able to double the Cape of Good Hope. Those who have come so far were in good health and strong, although at times we nearly died of the cold winds. I think it is not so much the cold as that we have been used to hot weather too long. I like cold winds better than the hot air in the Gozil's tiled courtyard.

'After we had rounded the Cape and we knew that we were sailing for Portugal, the men of the crews shouted with great joy and fell on their knees, praying and giving thanks.

'I was on the San Gabriel at the time, helping the Captain Major to reckon up the expenses of the voyage.

'Vasco da Gama said to the pilot and to the seamen whom he had put in chains at the time of the mutiny: "What do you men now say of the great shame with which you covered yourselves, when from fear of storm you wished to lose this great thing that we have done?"

'The pilot said nothing. One of the sailors, Joãn D'Ameixoeira answered. He said: "Sir, we acted according to what we are.

You acted according to what you are. Now, sir, on a day of so much joy, ought we not to be pardoned?"

'Vasco da Gama replied: "I forgive you. There is no anger in my heart to you. But because of the vow that I made, I will take you in irons to the King. I will beg favors of him for you and your children, but the chains shall be in memory of this perilous voyage, the honor of which shall last you as long as you live."

'Then he ordered them to bring on deck the things that the King of Melindi had sent, and he divided them among the crews of both ships. He gave to the Moorish pilots dresses of scarlet cloth and robes of yellow satin such as they desired.

'These pilots were useful on this west coast of Africa even though they had never been here before, because they knew the stars. Shane helped them with his astrolabe and compass, and he wrote down much that they told him and drew many pictures of the sky at night on his charts, so that he could show them to Zacuto, his old master.

'For twenty-seven days we had wind astern. Then there were many calms. We found a place where there was a weed called sargasso. It grew high above the water and gave us much trouble. I think this has been the worst part of the voyage—the vessels moving slowly through the weed, the glare of the sun on the water, the sound of the pumps always going, the men working at them with the sweat running into their eyes and pouring down their backs.

'We are a strange-looking crew—those of us who are still alive.

'There are thunderstorms here that spit fire out of an arch of clouds. In one of these storms we lost sight of the San Gabriel. We are sailing for Portugal without waiting for Captain Vasco. That was his order.'

One day—it was while the ships lay becalmed in that hot steaming sea off the coast of Guinea—a boat came from the Captain-Major to ask Captain Coelho to come on board the San Gabriel.

'Your brother is to come too, Señor,' said the sailor who brought the message, 'and the two O'Connors. Captain Paulo da Gama wishes to see you all.'

The man's face was sad as he added: 'He might get well—if only we could get out of this burning sea.'

'Is it scurvy?' asked Nicolau Coelho.

'I think not, Señor Captain, but I am no doctor. He lies there on his bed all day. He has hardly left it since the wind failed us. He lies there and smiles—you know how he does, Señor—and laughs with his brother about things they used to do when they were boys in Portugal. He wants to see the parrots and hear them talk. And the harp and the guitar—you are to bring those too. He seems gay enough, Señor. Only weak and tired with the voyage.'

The San Gabriel lay rolling a little on a sea of hot, green

glass. Every sail was set, but not even the faintest puff of air filled them. The streamers at the mastheads were only limp red streaks that ran down over the dingy sails. The red cross on the mainsail had faded to a dull reddish brown not much different now from the color of the canvas itself.

Below the San Gabriel in the green water lay a shadowy picture of the ship—a thing of crooked masts and wavering sails and curving hull all washed over by a sultry green light. As she rolled with the swell of the glassy waves, a fringe of seaweed showed along her side. There were little shells growing among the brown and green slime. The beating, gasping sound that they heard was the pumps sucking at the water that seeped in slowly where pitch and oakum no longer kept the seams tight.

It was cooler in the cabin than on the blistering deck. Shane could hardly see anything at first. His eyes were dazzled from the glare outside. After a second he saw that Señor Paulo was lying on the Captain-Major's bed. There was a pillow covered with fine white linen under his head. His face was so pale that it hardly showed against the pillow. The gold of his hair and beard had almost all changed to silver now. His brilliant blue eyes had dark shadows under them, but they still looked gay as he saw his visitors.

'Nicolau!' he said. 'They'll think those boys are Moorish pirates in Lisbon! And you look little better yourself. Dennis is the color of any Moor, but somehow he doesn't look like a pirate—more like a young scholar captured by pirates. But you, Nico, in those Moorish clothes, are a perfect captain for a pirate zambuk.'

'They are cool and comfortable,' Nicolau Coelho said, laughing. 'No more stuffing myself into tight jerkins and velvet coats in this weather. It would be a pity if we could travel under and over and around so much of the world and come home to Portugal having learned nothing at all.'

'Portugal! Portugal!' squawked the parrot Calicut, and Joãn's bird answered with a cry of 'Africa! Some girls like Africa!'

Shane's red and green bird was chained to his wrist by a long silver chain. He sat on Shane's shoulder, squawking, moving his soft leathery feet up and down, cocking his head sidewise, rolling his eyes, nipping with his curved beak at Shane's red hair. Melindi, the gray-and-rose-colored parrot, was chained to a perch that Joãn had carved. Melindi swung on it, whistling once in a while, but after his first speech refusing to say anything, and ruffling his pink and gray feathers sulkily.

Calicut flew to the end of his chain in a great whirl of emerald and scarlet, made some rude remarks in Arabic, and settled down on his master's shoulder. The cause of his displeasure was the San Gabriel's dignified and gentlemanly cat, Señor Patapito. He had been lying on the table asleep. On seeing the birds he had arched his back, spat hissingly, and made small cat-growls in his white throat. At the flapping of feathers close to his head, Señor Patapito decided he had business somewhere else. He left the cabin suddenly with his black tail following him like an angry snake.

Paulo da Gama lay quietly looking at the two boys and the bright-feathered birds; at Joãn's steady gray eyes under the black brows and the line of silky black moustache curving around his mouth; at Shane's broad shoulders and strong arms and at the faint red and gold shadow on cheek and chin.

'How long is it since we left Lisbon?' he said at last. 'You were boys when we left. Men now. Two years nearly? Well, we have all changed, except Vasco. He is the same always, an old brown bear.'

Vasco da Gama smiled down at the sick man, but he did not speak. He was sitting beside his brother, moving a fan made of peacock's feathers back and forth with a steady swing of his hard brown hand.

The breeze from the beat of the fan helped to make the cabin seem cool. The sailors had hung up awnings of striped cotton stuff over the windows, so that the only light that came in was the green light from the water below. In that shifting, rippling light, Paulo da Gama with his pale face and folded hands looked like a figure carved out of stone.

Shane thought suddenly of that afternoon in the monastery of Batalha when he had prayed by Prince Enrique's tomb and Señor Paulo had found him there. The stone figure of the navigator prince on his high tomb in the cool chapel and Paulo da Gama lying in the dim hot cabin of the San Gabriel, with the peacock feathers flicking back and forth above his head, had the same peace and calm.

The parrots were quiet for a minute, and there was no sound in the cabin but the beat of the fan. Below in the ship the pumps

still throbbed. From the deck came faint creaks from ropes and yards as the ship lifted and sank on the lazy green rollers. Outside in the passage someone whistled Shane's tune.

'Can you play with that bird on your shoulder?' Paulo da Gama asked.

'He likes it,' Shane said, picking up his harp. 'What shall I play, Señor?'

'What the man was whistling,' Señor Paulo said, and Shane began to play the gay little tune.

Joãn hung up Melindi's perch near a window and picked up his guitar.

'When we get—home again,
We shall have—gold enough,'

Shane sang, and the parrot on his shoulder looked down at the harp and chuckled: 'Gold enough! Gold enough!'

Paulo da Gama smiled as he listened to the strange combination of sounds—Joãn's deep voice, Shane's gay tenor, the liquid notes of the harp, the sweet ringing of the guitar, Melindi fluttering gray and rose wings and whistling, Calicut echoing the words with squawks and chuckles,—

Dennis was not singing. He stood staring through the window at the glassy green water. Nicolau Coelho leaned against the wall looking gravely down at his friend. He hardly seemed to hear the noise around him.

It ended at last in a fine crash of sound, leaving Calicut still chuckling: 'How about you? How about you?'

Paulo da Gama laughed.

'I wouldn't have missed that,' he said; 'not for all the pearls in India. And that reminds me...'

He picked up a gold-embroidered bag from the bed and

tipped it with one thin hand so that the things in it began to run into the other palm.

'They look like green peas in this light, don't they?' he asked, putting down the empty bag and pouring the pearls from one hand to the other. 'Pretty, aren't they? And they feel cool. As if they were still under the sea. Hold out your hands, you pirates, and hold fast all I give you.'

Into Shane's square pink palm with the marks of the oar below the fingers slid cool, smooth globes of light. Joãn's brown fingers closed over faintly gleaming spheres.

'For you, Dennis,' Señor Paulo said, 'and the rest for you, Nicolau.'

Pearls in Dennis's hand with the ink marks on the first two fingers. A little heap shut in Nicolau Coelho's big red fist.

They all tried to speak, but Paulo da Gama stopped their murmurs of thanks.

'I feel like a king today—or at least like a zamorin! I lie here and my faithful slave fans me. I wave my hand and there is music—remarkable music such as was never heard on land or sea! When I am pleased with my servants, I pour jewels in their hands. If I were displeased, I could, of course, have their heads chopped off. Luckily I am pleased. Why shouldn't I be?'

He was quiet for a moment and then went on: 'We have done what no man ever did before. I have had my share in it, though it was only a small one. And now I am going home.'

Vasco da Gama said gently: 'You have talked enough, Paulo. You are getting tired. Our visitors had better go.'

'Not quite yet,' Señor Paulo said. 'Sing for me once more. My song, Dennis. You know.'

So Dennis began the song that he had last sung in the prison in Calicut. Into the cabin, where the green light from the hot sea outside wavered on the ceiling, seemed to come a cool breath from some Portuguese meadow—or perhaps it was 'the little wind no stronger than a sigh' that brings the fishing boats home.

Dennis finished the second verse, but he stopped, coughing a little, and the boys went on without him. It was Joãn who sang:

'Climb up, climb up, oh sailor!'

and Shane who answered:

'Good news, my captain! Coming into sight
Are Spain—and our bright land of Portugal!'

'Do you remember, Vasco,' Paulo da Gama said, 'how at Sines when we were boys we ran away with the fishing boats and came home one night at sunset?'

'Yes, I remember,' Vasco da Gama said. 'You must sleep now.'

Paulo da Gama's blue eyes were already half closed.

'I liked the music,' he said softly. 'Thank you. And goodbye.'

CHAPTER 19

YOUNG MOORS AT BELEM

LUISA COELHO stood in the cool, high dining-room of her uncles' house looking down at the two old men, who were still sitting at the table.

Señor Martinho Coelho sat twisting a silver cup with red wine in it between his fingers. Señor Affonso leaned back in his chair with his head against the faded crimson velvet. His beard had turned white since that day two years before when Luisa had been dragged off the San Raphael. His face was pale against the red velvet, and his hand trembled as he took a scrap of meat from his plate and threw it to the red dog standing beside Luisa.

Connemara snapped the meat neatly out of the air, swallowed it, and lay down with his head on his paws. He lay as if he were half asleep, but his golden-brown eyes missed nothing.

Luisa Coelho said: 'But, my uncles, we *must* do something. For more than a year now the Zacutos have lived every day thinking it might be their last, but still hoping that the next day the ships would come. They have held out because of that hope. But now they are going to be turned out of their house. They've had that at least—the place where they have always lived—even if they've had barely enough to eat. They have sold things one by one—their chairs, their rugs, their tapestries and mirrors. They have fed themselves and their poorer friends that way. Some of their cousins, a poor little tailor whose hands were burned because he was a Jew, and some old women live there. They go in and out as carefully as rabbits do. They will all be without shelter if the Zacutos lose the house. It will kill the old man, I think.'

Luisa looked cool and tall in a dress of pale gray, the color of the shady side of a pearl, but her cheeks flushed pink as she went on:

'Yesterday a man who says he is one of the King's household came and told Zacuto that unless he and Rachel left the house before tomorrow, they would be accused of being still Jews and be tortured. Uncle Martinho, this is a cruel thing. Can you not go to the King and tell him that it is being done—and by one of his own men?'

She stopped and took a red rose from the bowl on the table and began pulling it to pieces. The petals made a little crimson pool on a napkin of white damask.

Martinho Coelho said sadly: 'The name Coelho has little power with Dom Manuel now, Luisa. Affonso and I are known now only as uncles of a man who has lost one of the King's ships for him and failed in the thing the King has set his heart on. Suppose I ride to Cintra through the hot sun—'

Señor Affonso broke in with his shaking voice: 'Yes, the King is up there on the mountain where it is cool enough. Suppose we get sunstroke and shake our old bones to pieces to ask him to help this Zacuto—what will he say? Something like this:

"Why, Señor Coelho, I am surprised, grieved, shocked that you and your brother would help a man who is our enemy. It was he who told me to send the ships to India. They have been sucked into a sea of pitch-just as wise men said they would be. And it's this Jew who sent them there. Do you help and shelter Jews, you and your brother, Señor Coelho? And especially a Jew who sent your own nephews and those brave men, Vasco and Paulo da Gama, to their deaths?" Then he'll look around the torture chamber and see if he has a nice pair of thumbscrews to fit us. That's what your precious King will do if we try to help this unlucky Jew.'

'He is not a Jew any longer,' Luisa Coelho said. 'The King's favorite Bishop baptized Zacuto and Rachel. They are better Christians than many who were born so: kind, gentle, going without food to feed others hungrier than they are, forgiving to their enemies. Zacuto says: "King Manuel spoke kindly to me and gave me a purse of gold. For I was Astronomer Royal once."'

Martinho Coelho set down the empty wine cup.

'We will give him and his daughter shelter here—though it is a danger to all of us to do so. But we cannot go to the King, Luisa. What my brother says is true. It will do Zacuto no good and may do us all great harm. Has he himself asked you to go to the King? When you spoke to us about him last year, I remember you said Zacuto thought it would not help him.'

'No,' Luisa admitted. 'He says it is better for the King to forget him. So he must lose his house tomorrow?'

'Tomorrow or some other day,' Señor Affonso said. 'If they have made up their mind to take it from him, they will. Send Damian to tell them they can come here. You can find work for the daughter, I suppose. The old man can copy some papers for me at the warehouse, for my hand shakes so that no one can read what I write. As for you, my dear, you had better go to church and pray. It is better for women than so much thinking.'

Luisa kissed Señor Affonso on top of his bald head.

'You are good, both of you. It is generous of you to help those poor people. I am sure no harm will come to us because of it—only good. I will ride down to Belem and pray there. It is growing cool and the horses are waiting. Come, Con!'

Connemara got up stretching himself and trotted after the pearl-gray dress.

The Tagus had been like a sheet of steel all day under the hot July sun, but now that the sun was sinking, a breeze from the southwest sprang up and ruffled the river into a pink cloth embroidered with gold. A pink and gold haze hung over it.

The bells were sounding from the old church at Belem as Luisa got off her horse at the churchyard gate. She stopped as she had done so many times before, to look down the Tagus. The sardine boats were beginning to come home with the tide. Their crescent-shaped bows cut through the ripples. Silver fish shone in them. The men sang as they pulled the heavy oars. A small boat with new red sails swooped out of the sunset mist like a butterfly. Far behind it was a larger boat, but it was only a dark blur in the bright haze.

Luisa went into the church. The chanting of the monks took away some of her anger for the Zacutos' sufferings.

'My uncles are right,' she thought. 'They are kindness itself as they always are. I will go to Rachel on my way home and tell her that she will be safe with us.'

Luisa had grown very fond of Rachel since they had first met that cold winter afternoon more than a year before. Since Catarina de Ataide had become one of the new Queen's ladies-in-waiting, Luisa saw little of her. Rachel was the friend she liked best. It would be pleasant to have Rachel always in the house. Sewing wouldn't be so bad with Rachel to help her.

Something touched Luisa's skirt. She looked down. Connemara had been ordered to stay with Damian, but as usual he had sneaked in and taken his place beside her. He seemed more restless than usual. His tail brushed along the stones. Once he gave a low whine and walked towards the door, but came back and lay down again.

At last the service was over, but Luisa stayed on her knees. The Latin prayers were beautiful, but none of them was the prayer she had come to say: 'Please, God, bring them safe home. Bring them soon. Amen.'

A monk was putting out the candles on the altar. It was growing dark in the church, though the sky was still rose and pale yellow outside.

As Luisa got to her feet, Con got up too. For a moment he stood as still as a dog carved out of copper, not a hair on his tail moving, one paw raised. Then he bounded towards the door, barking so loud that the whole church rang.

Luisa turned toward the door. She saw a strange figure against the pink sky—a young Moor with a bird on his shoulder. He bent down, bird and all, over Con. His voice sounded as if he were laughing—or crying—but she could not see his face; only the striped silk thing on his head and the white robe over his broad shoulders.

The vermilion and green bird, as big as a sparrow hawk, shrieked something that sounded like 'Pick out the prettiest little or tall! Little or tall!' and the red dog whimpered and sobbed and licked the young Moor's face.

Luisa moved forward thinking: 'Con has gone mad, and I have too. I thought I heard that bird talking Portuguese.'

Then another figure in a white robe came through the twilight. This one had a gray and pink bird swinging from a perch in his hand, but he dropped it, perch and all, and ran forward shouting: 'Luisa! Luisa!'

It was Joãn's voice, she knew, even before he picked her up in his strong arms and swung her off the ground: Joãn, burned brown and with a silky black moustache, but still her brother. She found herself looking over Joãn's shoulder into Shane's green eyes. There were tears in them, but he was smiling too.

'See what I brought you from India,' he said, and the parrot cocked his wise eye at her and chuckled: 'Some girls like India!'

'He talks,' Luisa said. 'He talks Portuguese!'

'Indeed he does, though with a slight Irish accent,' Shane said smiling. 'For it was myself that taught him. As for that pink and gray thing of Joãn's, he says what isn't fit to listen to.' And indeed poor Melindi, flung down on the cold stones of the churchyard and held there by the heavy perch, was saying some very rude things in purest African.

There were voices coming up the path. The churchyard began to fill with people—thin, brown-faced men strangely dressed, with ragged beards and hollow eyes and smiles that showed toothless gums. Many of them shivered in the evening coolness, and all walked with a curious sway and swing, as if the ground were tipping under their feet. The monks hurried from the cloister. One of them began to pull at the bell-rope. The noise of the bell rang out above the voices of the monks and the sailors. Louder still came the booming sound of the Berrio's cannon.

The roar of the guns ceased, but the church bell kept ringing. Candles shone on the altar again. The Berrio's lanterns were lighted. The port-colored one made a bright streak on

the rippling water. A boat cut across it and more men began to climb the path.

Someone held a lighted torch near the top of the path. They came marching through the orange light, keeping step, yet always with that dipping swing: Nicolau Coelho in blue velvet, with a jewelled clasp on his shoulder that flashed in the torchlight; Dennis O'Connor's slim black figure, with the pencase and inkhorn at his belt and a gold-handled dagger shining beside them; Fernan Martinez towering over everyone else, splendid in yellow satin, gold rings swinging from his ears; Veloso swaggering in a new cloak of crimson and gold.

'We should have waited and dressed ourselves in style, Joãn,' said Shane, 'not let everyone see us in our usual appearance, which is that of pirates.'

'Never mind,' Joãn said. 'Nicolau is upholding the honor of the ship. And Veloso. Anyone to see him would know he had found India all himself!'

Nicolau Coelho and his guard of honor could not keep their dignity long, for in a minute Luisa's arms were around the

Captain's neck, and the sailors stood looking on and smiling as she asked him a dozen questions, too fast for him to answer.

'Where is Vasco da Gama? Did you really find India? What a wonderful jewel! Did some pretty girl give it to you? Or did you steal it? Have you brought home a beautiful Indian princess for your bride? Did you know I thought Shane was a Moor? Are you glad to see me? Is that really the Berrio? She doesn't look like the same ship. Where are all the banners? And where is Vasco da Gama?'

Everyone was asking that question, and Nicolau Coelho said loud enough for everyone to hear him: 'Our Captain is somewhere behind us. The Berrio sails faster than his ship. His orders were to make sail for Portugal with all speed. We have done so. Now let us go into the church and thank God for bringing us safely through all our dangers, and pray for Vasco da Gama's safe return.'

The bell had stopped ringing. Soon the church echoed with men chanting: Te Deum, laudamus—we praise thee, O Lord!

The wild ringing of the church bell and the Berrio's guns had aroused the city. When the sailors came out of the church there were people streaming towards it. They had come on boats, on horses, on mules, on donkeys. Many had come running along the dark road. There were women looking for their husbands, sons for their fathers, sisters for their brothers, girls for their lovers.

Many, of course, had come purely out of curiosity, and these talked the loudest. The words 'Vasco da Gama—India—riches—jewels—spices' buzzed through the courtyard, but many people were silent either from grief or joy.

An old woman with a wild face under tangled white hair seized Shane's arm sobbing: 'My son, Pero Escolar. Where is he?'

'He's over there, Señora, by the Captain,' Shane said.

The woman turned without thanking him and went clawing her way through the crowd.

A brown-faced little man came up to Joãn and said quietly: 'Can you tell me anything, young Señor, about a sailor called Sancho Mexia?' And Joãn answered sadly: 'I can, Señor. I am sorry. He was a brave man. He died crossing the Gulf of Guinea two months ago.'

The little man whispered: 'Only two months ago,' and leaned against the wall for a moment. Then he said: 'He was my brother. Did he see India and the streets all paved with gold? Did Sancho see India, Señor?'

'He saw India,' Joãn said.

'Thank you, Señor,' the man said, and limped away into the darkness. Joãn heard him repeat as he went: 'Only two months ago.'

Joãn said to Shane: 'This is worse than the prison in Calicut. Nicolau gave us leave to sleep on shore tonight. Let's find Luisa and take her home.'

A voice close to him growled: 'And time enough too! Are my horses to wear their legs off standing on these stones all night?'

Joãn turned.

'Damian, is that you?' he said, looking up into the groom's face. 'I'm glad to see you.'

'Thank you, Señor. It is I and no one else. I don't know anyone else who would be good enough to be standing here since sunset catching cold and rheumatism and fever and very likely smallpox for all I know. I'm glad to see you back, Señor, but there's reason in all things, and I'm a groom, not a night owl, as I have often remarked to your sister. Would you and your friend like my horse, Señor? He is old and blind in one eye, which makes him stumble, especially at night, but you are welcome to him, I am sure.'

'Not I,' Joãn said hastily. 'I'd rather run, thank you, Damian, and feel the good earth under my feet. How about you, Shane?'

'Running for me,' Shane said; 'and for Con, too,' he added, putting his hand on the dog's head.

It was always at his knee. Con moved with Shane as if he were chained to him like the sleepy parrot on Shane's shoulder.

They found Luisa and helped her on her white horse.

'Take hold of her mane,' the girl said to Shane, and they trotted forward together, moving like one piece—the white horse, the girl in her pale dress, the young man in the Moor's robe with the bird on his shoulder, and the dog.

There was so much to say that no one tried to say it. Once Shane, remembering the day he had tried to lead that very white mare out of the fight with Nuno Calves's grooms, panted: 'I hope you have your whip—in case we meet any robbers,' and Luisa bent forward and tickled his cheek with the lash of that very whip.

Once Calicut woke up and chuckled: 'Ladies will smile at us.' Damian grumbled from time to time that Luisa's uncles would pull every hair out of his head, to which Luisa replied that at least Señor Martinho would do no hair-pulling, since he was in the churchyard when they left, dancing with his arm around a fat monk's shoulder.

Joãn whistled once. It was only a bar or two, but Shane knew the tune and smiled in the darkness. It was the one Joãn used to play on the deck of the San Gabriel to tell Shane that mutiny had not come yet.

'High on that thorny rose-tree...'

'We'll go home by the Street of the Rat,' Luisa said to the old groom, who said crossly: 'Another hour won't matter.'

'It won't take ten minutes,' Luisa said. 'It's on the next hill.'

The old house was dark against the star-sprinkled sky. There were roses growing over the garden wall. Red roses, though, Joãn thought, breathing in the scent. He remembered the first time he had knocked at that heavy oak door: Shane tumbling through it with Con at his heels, and Rachel with the lantern turning her pearls and her dress and her cheeks pink.

He lifted the iron knocker and let it fall with a clang. Silence inside: a long silence while the horses panted and the wind sent the rose branches scratching against the wall. Then footsteps inside.

Luisa called: 'Rachel! Rachel! See what I've brought you!'

The iron bars clattered and the door opened.

Rachel had no lantern this time, no pearls in her hair, no dress of white brocade. The light in her hand was the end of a smoking tallow candle. Her dress was black. Above it and under her cloud of dark hair her face was thin and white. Her dark eyes looked too big for it.

Yet Joãn thought: 'Why, she's prettier than ever!'

'Is it the house? Can we keep it?' Rachel asked, lifting her candle and looking up at Luisa.

'Yes, Rachel,' Luisa said. 'You can keep it. The Berrio's home.'

JOÁN

CHAPTER 20

FORTUNATE KING

UP IN the laboratory Zacuto sat watching the stars.

At the noise downstairs, he started up. He had eaten nothing all day and his head was dizzy.

'They have come,' he muttered. 'They will take my house. But it was tomorrow they said. Surely it was tomorrow.'

He stumbled down the long flights of stairs. Strange noises echoed through the empty house—a dog barking, people sobbing, or was it laughter? And a strange squawking noise.

There were people in the bare hall. The Señorita, who had often brought them food—and courage with it—when things seemed worst. Two men dressed like Moors. Birds that flapped their wings in the candlelight. Birds that cursed in Arabic. Shane's red dog running around and barking.

He stood there only a moment. Then Rachel saw him and ran to him saying: 'The Berrio's home, Father. The Berrio's home! It's Joãn! And Shane! They're back from India!'

Then the shorter of the two Moors turned, and it was Shane with his sunburned nose and his freckles and his green eyes and his old friendly smile.

He put his hard arms around Zacuto and said: 'You just watch them try to take this house away from you! It's the greatest pleasure in the world I'll take to choke them one at a time.'

Zacuto stammered: 'Sirius, the dog star! And Procyon at your heels! You have come again!'

'Yes, we've come again, Señor. I have much to tell you about the stars of the south and charts to show you of strange lands. That will keep till tomorrow. Tonight I should like to sleep on the old straw mattress in the laboratory and be here to meet your visitors in the morning.'

Zacuto's visitors the next morning were met by a young man with red hair showing under his Moorish headdress, with a jewelled-hilted curved sword stuck in his green and gold sash: a young man who spoke excellent Portuguese, though in a soft way that made it sound strange, and who made in it some very unpleasant remarks.

The result of this conversation, during which the young man kept his hand on the hilt of his sword and kept his green eyes half closed, was that the visitors ran down the Street of the Rat so fast that they nearly fell into the Tagus.

The one who claimed to be a member of King Manuel's household—although he was not—said that the redheaded Moor had a devil on his shoulder that spat fire at him and talked good Portuguese. The other said that there was a big red dog, larger than a cow, that was also a devil and would doubtless have bitten their legs off if they had not run off so fast.

Their neighbors agreed that they were lucky to escape.

It was many weeks before the San Gabriel sailed into the Tagus and anchored at Belem. In the meantime Nicolau Coelho did what King Manuel ordered about the cargo of the Berrio. The King even came down from Cintra and looked at the dingy little Berrio. He did not go on board her, but he took a good deal of interest in adding up the value of the spices on board.

About that time he began to write letters in which he called himself 'I, Dom Manuel, by the grace of God, King of Portugal and of the Algarvaes on this side and beyond the sea; in Africa, Lord of Guinea and of the Conquest, the Navigation, and Commerce of Ethiopia, Arabia, Persia, and India.'

King Manuel had a new wife. Perhaps she believed that her husband had conquered Ethiopia and India. At least she never told anyone that he had not. After a while people began calling him King Manuel the Fortunate, just as Zacuto had said.

To this fortunate King in his cool garden at Cintra came a message, brought by a swift caravel, to say that Vasco da Gama's ship had reached the Azores and was within four days' sail of Lisbon. There was a great welcome prepared for the explorer—cannon ready to be fired, flags hung from all the houses, flowers to throw for him to walk on, a great feast spread in the palace.

King Manuel watched the dark blue sea from high on Mount Cintra. He had looked many times in the last two years for sails that might be ships from India. Now at last he saw one—a square-rigged ship with a whole fleet of smaller vessels around it, sailing for the mouth of the Tagus. With his pale-faced Spanish Queen and a troop of nobles dressed in their most splendid clothes, King Manuel rode to Lisbon.

He waited there in his cabinet, biting his fingernails and scribbling on a paper figures about the profits of this voyage. The ships cost so much. Pay of the crew—so much... If he brings so many quintals of cinnamon... the price is good now... cloves... ivory. Coelho's cargo sold well, but would the price fall with so much merchandise in the market at once...

King Manuel threw down his pen impatiently.

'Why doesn't he come?' he asked one of his counsellors fretfully. 'The wind was behind him. He should be able to sail here as fast as I'd ride to Cintra.' He turned his head, hearing his secretary at the door, and snapped: 'Well, what is it? What is it?'

'Vasco da Gama has anchored at Belem, Your Majesty. He has sent a messenger to bring you the news. The Captain-Major himself is praying at the monastery.'

The messenger was Dennis O'Connor.

King Manuel said to him crossly: 'At Belem? Praying? Was he not told that we would receive him here?'

'Yes, Your Majesty, but he is praying for the soul of his brother, Captain Paulo da Gama, who is—dead.'

'I am sorry his brother is dead,' King Manuel said coldly. 'He died in India, I suppose.'

'No, Your Most Worshipful Majesty. He died at Terceira in the Azores, the day after the San Gabriel reached there—less than two months ago.'

'Oh, two months ago,' the King said. 'Vasco da Gama has had time to recover from his grief, then. Why were you sent me? I remember you. I never forget a face, though your name I don't happen to think of. You were one of those convicts we turned loose from that jail in Setubal... Well, old Judge Calves will not clap any more men into prison. He died last year... Why were you sent?'

'I kept the records of the voyage, Sire. I have them here, if Your Majesty cares to read them.'

The King waved away Dennis's book with its drawings that he spent so much time on, its careful black writing, its borders of leaves and colored flowers and strange beasts.

The Lord of the Conquest of Ethiopia, Arabia, Persia, and

India said: 'I've no time for reading. I have all the books I need. I wish to hear from da Gama himself. Tell him that for my sake he must console himself for his brother's death. I am sorry that he does not come before me with his happiness complete so as not to take away any of that which I now enjoy. Tell him to come to me tomorrow.'

Dennis bowed, and went away with his book under his arm.

Vasco da Gama would have gone to the King in the black mourning-clothes that he was wearing, but Nicolau Coelho persuaded him to leave his mourning aside and put on a tight-fitting tunic of thin red silk. The Captain-Major's beard fell far down over it, for he had never cut it since he left Lisbon.

His sailors were more gaily dressed than he, for while they were in the Azores they had had clothes made of the stuffs that the King of Melindi had given them. They marched up from the river with the people shouting and staring. Behind them went the pilot and the master d'Alenquer and Alvarez—stumbling along with the heavy chains about their feet. The sailors in chains were further behind.

Nicolau Coelho, grandly dressed, had Shane and Joãn behind him. They carried the chest full of jewels for the King. Fernan Martinez was there in his yellow satin, with what teeth he had left shining as he grinned. He carried a great bale of silks and satins, and white muslin embroidered with gold.

Veloso walked proudly with his red cloak swinging in the sun. He carried a shield of red and gold that he had stolen from a Nair who was visiting the Berrio. The Nair had put it down for a minute, and Veloso had slipped the shield under his cloak and told the Nair that it had fallen overboard.

All the girls said: 'There goes a brave man! No wonder they got home safely with a soldier like that to fight for them!'

When they reached the Palace, Dom Manuel the Fortunate was there in his great hall. Vasco da Gama walked through it with the prisoners behind him. The clanking of the chains was the only sound.

Vasco da Gama knelt down before the King and said: 'Sire, all my hardships have come to an end at this moment. I bring these men to you to show you that besides storm and treachery on land, and sickness, we had other dangers to face on sea. These men led a mutiny against me. Later they served me well, so I ask your mercy for them.'

'They are yours,' King Manuel said. 'Do with them what you wish. Execute them, imprison them, or set them free.'

Vasco da Gama turned to the prisoners: 'I have kept my word in bringing you here in irons. Since the punishment is left to me, I pardon you freely because of your hardships. Go in peace, and be happy with your wives and children. You will live with them with more ease and pleasure than you would have if you had returned flying from storms and bringing me back a prisoner, as you meant to do.'

The prisoners fell on their knees and said: 'Sir, may you have your reward from God.'

Vasco da Gama sent them away and ordered their chains taken off. Then he told Nicolau to step forward and said: 'Sire, Nicolau Coelho has been of no small account in all our hardships, and I know Your Majesty will show him favors according to his great merits.'

The King smiled and said: 'Dom Vasco da Gama, it shall be as you desire.'

He then told the Captain-Major that he gave him the title of Dom not only for himself, but for all his descendants forever. Then Dom Vasco kissed the King's hand, which Nicolau did also. They opened the chest and showed the necklaces and rings and the gilded palm leaves from the Kings of Melindi and Cananor. The Queen sat looking on with her eyes staring out of her white face. She smiled a little when she saw the ambergris and the musk for making perfumes, but she scarcely seemed to notice the beautiful silks and the porcelain bowls and cups from Cathay. The King hung one of the great jewelled collars around her neck. She looked paler than ever with the blazing jewels close to her face.

The King asked the Captain-Major so many questions that Dom Vasco stayed there till the evening came, answering them. Among the Queen's ladies, Dom Vasco saw only one face he knew. It was Catarina de Ataide, the daughter of his old friend, a little girl he remembered playing on the beach at Sines when he and Paulo were young men. She looked very pretty, and she was the only one among those chattering women who dared speak to him that day about his brother. She did it so kindly and sweetly that Dom Vasco made up his mind that very day that of all those splendidly dressed ladies Catarina was the only one he liked. A few months later they were married, so Catarina became the Countess de Vidiguera, for that was Dom Vasco's title. They had six sons.

They lived in a house that was painted outside with figures of Hindus and Indian animals and plants. There was gilding on it made from gold that Dom Vasco had brought from India. The street where it stood in the town of Evora is still called the Rua das Casas Pintadas—Street of the Painted Houses. Vasco da Gama made two more voyages to India. On the third voyage he went out as Governor of the Portuguese colony at Goa, a place north of Calicut.

King Manuel paid the crews of the San Gabriel and the Berrio well for their services. He could afford to do so. When the cargos of spices were sold and the money spent on the voyages and for fitting up the ships was reckoned up, he found that for every cruzado he had spent he had received sixty in return.

He gave to Vasco da Gama and Nicolau Coelho the right to bring a generous amount of spices into Portugal free of duty. To Coelho he gave the rank of captain in any fleet with which he might choose to sail. Zacuto's services were suddenly remembered. People began to think his prophecy was very extraordinary. Many of them wanted him to read the stars for them. He and Rachel no longer had to starve and live in fear of their neighbors.

Veloso got enough money to buy a little inn at Setubal. The stories he told were so wonderful that people hardly noticed what they were eating. This was lucky because his wife, who did all the work, was not a very good cook. She was better at sewing, and Veloso always had a fine red cloak and embroidered jerkins, so he looked very grand while he told his customers all about how he had discovered India.

Machado and Rodriguez never came back from Africa. They liked it better than Portugal. Machado became very successful in business there.

The pilots from Melindi had a fine trip through Portugal. They saw the grand ladies of the King's court, and the palaces, and churches, and men fighting bulls with canes. They had plenty of stories to tell when they got back to Melindi. In fact, one of them always said that he had discovered Portugal.

Joãn Coelho and Shane were well paid too. Vasco da Gama had paid them their wages in Calicut, and with the money they had bought spices. They sold them to Joãn's uncles, Señor Martinho and Señor Affonso. After that business was finished,

Señor Martinho put down his pen and said with a sigh: 'I suppose you young traders will be going back to India with the next fleet.'

'Not I!' Joãn said, and Shane added: 'No more voyaging for me.'

Señor Martinho looked surprised.

'I thought "once a sailor, always a sailor,"' he said. 'Nicolau only laughed at me when I said that he had better stay at home and help us with our business instead of sticking his head into hornets' nests in strange countries. We need help here, Affonso and I, for we are not getting younger very fast. Nicolau is bound for India with the next fleet. I was sure you two would be at least as foolish!'

Joãn and Shane started talking both at once. 'We hate the sea!

'We hate being seasick, hot, frozen.

'We hate salt fish and salt beef.

'And salt penguin!

'We hate scurvy, though we weren't very sick and still have our teeth left.

'We've seen all of the world we want to. Portugal's the best place in it—unless indeed it might be Ireland.

'We're going to stay at home.'

'So that's it,' Señor Martinho said. 'And what might you be planning to do at home? Loaf about the docks till you've wasted this money you've squeezed out of me? And tell tales about India to the fishermen?'

'No, Señor,' Shane said. 'We thought—'

He stopped, and Joãn said: 'We thought, Uncle—' and then stopped too.

'You thought, I suppose, that Affonso and I would take you into our business,' Señor Martinho said. 'You come and squeeze a hundred and eighty cruzados for a quintal of cinnamon, and a hundred and twenty for ginger, and a hundred for nutmegs! Piracy, such prices are—just piracy. And then you expect to be taken into our business! Well, I don't know what Affonso thinks, but as for me—I'll do it!'

He chuckled, looking at the boys' surprised faces.

'I can use two sturdy young fellows who know something of the spice trade and have the sense to hate the sea.' Señor Martinho added, 'You might,' he said to Shane, 'go up through the garden and tell Luisa that you will dine with us this evening. I think she may be interested to hear about this dislike you have taken to the sea.'

Shane turned pink under his freckles, and went.

Chapter 21

MUSIC IN A GARDEN

At BELEM King Manuel built a new church for the monks; and—because Vasco da Gama had landed there at the end of his voyage—the King also built on the shore below the monastery a high square tower for all sailors to see.

The church is a very beautiful one. It is all carved with chains and ropes and spheres and plants of India and Africa. Inside, carved columns spring up like palm trees to the roof.

It was like walking through a forest of palms, Shane thought. Only this forest was full of a clear, cool light instead of steaming heat. If there were any crocodiles peeping out of the wreathed foliage, they were stone ones.

Shane and Luisa were married there one blue June morning when the flower-sellers had their baskets full of big blue thistles. Joãn and Rachel were married there that same day. Afterwards they all rode north to Batalha. They took a present of spices to the monks there. Shane played his harp for Brother Pedro, and set the novices dancing while they baked the bread for supper.

They stayed at the little inn above the monastery and saw

RACHEL

the map that Prince Enrique had drawn on the wall, and ate the famous chicken cooked with cream and paprika.

'A mild red pepper it is. My grandfather brought the seeds from Turkey and my cousins still grow it. Much better for you than this hot stuff from foreign lands. I don't know what the world's coming to with people not content with anything. Have some more chicken, Señor. There was another gentleman besides the Prince that liked that chicken too.' The old woman set a great dish of olives and a jug of red wine on the table. 'He always said he would come back and eat it, but he never did. I forget the last of his name, but the first name was Paulo.'

No one spoke for a minute, and then Shane said: 'He would change that map of yours for you if he were here, I think.'

'No! No one shall ever touch Prince Enrique's map. It is never touched except to brush the cobwebs away.'

'I'll draw you another then, Señora, on the other wall,' Shane said.

He picked up a piece of charcoal and began to draw rapidly. The great curved shoulder of Africa. Little ships cutting across the Atlantic to the Cape of Good Hope. Seals and whales around the Bay of San Braz. Winds, waves, and zambuks near Mombaza and Melindi. Black men with spears and shields. Ships again, blown north to India.

'Why, you draw as if you had been there, Señor!' the old woman exclaimed delightedly as Shane threw the charcoal aside, brushed off his fingers, and went back to his dinner. 'Your husband is a great artist, Señora. You must be very happy!'

'My husband is a merchant,' Luisa said, 'and at home he is not allowed to draw pictures on the walls. But we are very happy—so far.'

'And is that other gentleman your brother? He looks like you, Señora. He is handsome as a prince. And what beautiful horses you have, but none too fine for such beautiful ladies.'

'Happier than the only king I know,' Joãn said.

'You will find those compliments on the bill,' Rachel said, as the old woman returned to her cooking. 'I don't think they ought to be paid for too highly. After all, she only said you and I were as beautiful as horses, Luisa!'

Joãn laughed. 'See what a wife I have. Sensible, as well as beautiful. Her father always told me she was a remarkable girl.'

Dennis was a wanderer all his life. To Shane's five children— Paulo and young Dennis, and especially a red-headed little girl named Angela Luisa, who did not look at all like her mother Luisa and who certainly was not an angel—a visit from their Uncle Dennis was the most exciting thing in the world. So it was to the young Coelhos who lived on another floor in the same big house—tall young Joãn Abraham Zacuto Coelho, and little round Vasco da Gama Coelho—and to the little girls whose names Dennis never could be quite sure of because they looked like Coelhos with straight black eyebrows, but then their names might be O'Connor. They all kept growing so fast he couldn't tell.

Sometimes their Uncle Nicolau would come at the same time—an enormous man who always smelled of spice and liked to swing small boys around his head with one hand. They would sit talking about Africa and America and far Cathay, Uncle Nicolau pulling at his black and silver beard with his big red fist, and Uncle Dennis resting his black head on his thin white hand and watching everything with his shining green eyes.

They both said the world was a round ball spinning among the stars. They had sailed around most of it, so they ought to know. Although some people, including the kind nuns at the school where Angela made life exciting, thought it whizzed around like a dinner plate.

Uncle Dennis had a dignified cat, black with white jerkin and gloves. Señor Patapito was his name. The Coelhos' cat, Hepzibah, had been as far as India, but she seemed to like a domestic life now. She was the grandmother and great-grandmother of many kittens.

A little dark-faced man named Hassan was Uncle Dennis's servant. He always spoke very politely to Hepzibah. Even when she purred at him. Especially when she jumped on his shoulder and sat switching her tail.

There were always wonderful presents when the uncles came: Blue and white porcelain bowls with little slant-eyed people painted on them. White stuff for the girls' dresses—Uncle Dennis said the fairies embroidered it. A jewelled dagger for young Dennis O'Connor that his mother never let him take out of the sheath. (But Angela did, and cut all the buttons off Great-Uncle Martinho's coat and after that—well, never mind!)

A trumpet of ivory that made small Vasco da Gama Coelho puff his cheeks out like red apples when he tried to blow it.

There was always music in the garden after supper when Dennis came. Joãn Coelho would tune his guitar and Shane would take his harp out of its old leather case. They would sing over the old songs and Shane would make up new verses. There was one that had a verse for each letter of the alphabet. That was how the Coelhos and O'Connors learned their letters, dancing through the garden after Shane's harp, singing rhymes about animals who might possibly have eaten Shane's harp string. Bats, cats, koodoos, and lions were all accused, but still the song went on:

> 'If it wasn't the tiger
> It must be the snake.
> The way that he wriggles
> Just gives me an ache!
> But—sing, sing, what shall we sing?
> That snake hasn't eaten my little harp string!

And so on, naturally, down to the zebra, who hadn't eaten it either!

One tune would follow another as the children went dancing around the fountain under the white rose tree. Luisa would put down the piece of tapestry that she had been making ever since Shane came home from India, and follow them. She would drag Rachel after her, saying: 'You know Rachel, you always sit there embroidering so beautifully that I have to pretend to, and here I am still doing the left hind leg of that awful crocodile. Well it's better than doves' toenails, anyway.' And Rachel would laugh and follow her.

Fernan Martinez—he was steward at the Coelhos'—came out from his office one evening and looked on smiling.

Fat little Grandfather Zacuto, who wore a black robe with stars on it and lived in a tall house a little way off with four cousins and two of the cousins' aunts, and one of the aunt's daughters and her two babies all keeping house for him, jigged up and down happily.

He said: 'I don't know when I've enjoyed an evening so much. I was Astronomer Royal once, but it was never as pleasant as this. Look at my granddaughter, Fernan! Look at my grand-daughter dance! And the boys too. Remarkable children, all of them, don't you think so?'

'Yes, Señor. They certainly are extraordinarily fine children,' Fernan said. Then he spoke to Dennis, who was sitting with Patapito on his shoulder and Hepzibah on his knee. They were growl-gurgle-purr-spitting at each other, but they didn't mean anything by it.

'What you doing in those old foreign places, Señor Dennis?' Fernan asked. 'What you do all the time in that black old India?'

'Last time I helped a man named Correa paint a portrait of Vasco da Gama. Full-size it was, and with his very weapons that he wore, all dressed in dark embroidered silk, with the cross the King gave him around his neck, and his shield at his feet. I made him look fierce enough—the way he looked in the prison at Calicut. Even the Nairs knew who it was. They looked the other way—as if Dom Vasco had his eye on them.

'That's right,' chuckled Fernan. 'Everybody look the other way when our Captain-Major put that bright black eye on him. Seen crocodiles and tigers jump, I have, when Captain Vasco looked cross at him. You not ever afraid of snakes and tigers biting you or getting that scurvy sickness, Señor Dennis? What would you do for medicine out in that black old India?'

'I'm never sick,' Dennis said. 'Once a doctor brought me some medicine—I had a little sword-cut, not three inches long, on my arm. I smelled the medicine and then I poured it on a rose bush. I got well, but the rose bush died. That was in Persia.'

'Did you ever paint a picture of Captain Paulo, Señor?'

'No, Fernan. He wasn't—easy to paint.'

'I wish Captain Paulo could see these children dancing in his garden.'

'I think everyone wishes that,' Dennis said.

'This is the last tune, children,' Luisa called. 'What shall it be?'

'When we get home again,' called Paulo da Gama O'Connor.

'Home again! Home again!' said Vasco da Gama Coelho.

Shane and Joãn began to play the skipping little tune.

'Follow the leader,' Luisa Coelho called, and the line went winding through the gardens, past the white roses and the red ones and the pots of heliotrope and the lilies and spicy carnations.

Luisa pulled her husband's hair as she passed him and dropped a carnation in his lap. She wore crimson brocade, and the pearls that Paulo da Gama had once held in his hand swung around her neck on a gold chain. Behind her was little Rachel Joanna Coelho tripping and stumbling and laughing. More girls in white dresses. Solemn little boys in black silk. There went Angela Luisa skipping and bumping. She had a tear in her dress and one of Hepzibah's great-grandchildren squeezed under her arm. An old dog walked stiffiy beside her and put his gray muzzle close to her red curls. Last of all came Rachel Coelho—there were pearls around her neck too—with young Vasco da Gama Coelho tugging at her pale dove-colored skirt.

'Some girls like—India,
Others like—Africa,'

went the guitar and the harp.

Under the white rose tree whose flowers were too high to reach, the wind blew its white petals on Rachel's soft dark hair. Soon the last of the dancers had gone. The music stopped. The garden was empty.

But—not quite empty. There were still voices in it. The green and red parrot stirred in his cage. 'Portugal, Portugal,' he chuckled sleepily.

In the other cage Melindi flapped his pink and gray feathers.

'I like Portugal. How about you?' he asked. But no one answered him.

THE END